Praise for *A*

"Cora's best book yet!"

—Jennifer L. Armentrout,
#1 *New York Times* bestselling author

"Football and falling in love are two of the greatest things ever. It would take Cora Carmack to make them even better. . . . *All Lined Up* is a touchdown!"

—Jay Crownover, *New York Times*
and *USA Today* bestselling author

"Feisty, sparkly, and sexy, feel the rush of falling in love all over again with Carson and Dallas! Confession: Cora Carmack's new series is my brand-new addiction!"

—Katy Evans, *New York Times*
and *USA Today* bestselling author

"Cora Carmack's done it again! *All Lined Up* is a fantastically sweet and sexy new adult love story."

—Monica Murphy, *New York Times*
and *USA Today* bestselling author

Also by Cora Carmack

Seeking Her (Novella)
Finding It
Keeping Her (Novella)
Faking It
Losing It

ALL LINED UP

A RUSK UNIVERSITY NOVEL

Cora Carmack

wm

WILLIAM MORROW

An Imprint of HarperCollins*Publishers*

ALL LINED UP. Copyright © 2014 by Cora Carmack. All rights reserved. Printed in the United States of America. No part of this book may be used or reproduced in any manner whatsoever without written permission except in the case of brief quotations embodied in critical articles and reviews. For information address HarperCollins Publishers, 10 East 53rd Street, New York, NY 10022.

HarperCollins books may be purchased for educational, business, or sales promotional use. For information please e-mail the Special Markets Department at SPsales@harpercollins.com.

FIRST EDITION

Designed by Kevin Estrada

Library of Congress Cataloging-in-Publication Data

Carmack, Cora.
    All lined up : a Rusk University novel / Cora Carmack. — First edition.
        pages ; cm
    ISBN 978-0-06-232620-1
    1. Young women—Fiction. 2. Football players—Fiction. 3. Texas—Fiction. 4. Love stories. 5. College stories. I. Title.
    PS3603.A75374A78 2014
    813'.6—dc23   2014006365

14 15 16 17 18   OV/RRD   10 9 8 7 6 5 4 3 2 1

To my dad—
Thank you for enduring my endless questions and ideas. I couldn't have written this book without you. Moreover, without you I wouldn't be where I am today. Unending stubbornness, insane competitiveness, and unwavering heart—they're all things I inherited from you. Like Dallas and her dad, we've had our share of arguments, but I have never doubted the fierceness with which you loved, protected, and championed me. There aren't words to describe how glad I am to be your daughter. (I'm still a wee bit bitter about that time you made me do push-ups in class, but I figure that's probably an indicator that I inherited my dark sense of humor from you, too.)

And now that you've read the dedication, you should hand this book to Mom and let her tell you which pages are safe to read.

All Lined Up

Chapter 1

Dallas

In Texas, two things are cherished above all else—football and gossip. My life has always been ruled by both.

"This is a bad idea, Stella."

Stella straightens her shirt. And by *straighten*, I mean she pulls it down to reveal what little cleavage she has (which is about twice as much as me).

"We're in college now," she says. "Bad ideas are the goal."

"Maybe it's *your* goal. You don't have a parent on the faculty. If this gets back to him—"

It's Friday night, our first on campus, and she stops just before the walkway of a frat house that hums with pent-up music. More than a head shorter than me, Stella reaches up and forces me to look at her. "Okay, sister. Let's nip this in the bud right now. No one is telling anyone anything. There are like ten thousand people on this campus. You, my dear, are *finally* a small fish in a motherfucking ocean. Loosen up and enjoy it. This isn't high school any-more."

Could it really be that simple?

Loosening up has always been easy for Stella. Her mom is a bigger party animal than she is. She'll probably get a high five if we get caught. Me . . . well, I'm a little scared to think of how my dad would react. What little freedom I have would disappear faster than the hot water in my dorm on days that end in a *y*.

For one glorious month, I had entertained visions and fanta-sies of what college would be like. Rusk wasn't my ideal school, far from it, but it was *something*. I could finally make my own decisions and not have to worry about them migrating to the coach's office before lunchtime. I had ached for high school graduation day like there was a knife in my gut, and I couldn't pull it out until May. Then my dad was offered the open po-sition here at Rusk, and I feel like I'm still gasping for breath around that knife.

Maybe we aren't in high school anymore. But it's the same damn misery with a different name.

Unless I do something about it.

But it's easier to be miserable, so I shake off Stella's grasp. "All it takes is one person to say something to someone, who tells someone else, who mentions it at church or practice or anywhere, and I'm dead. Stick a fork in me and dip me in hot lava. Dead."

"God, you're so overdramatic. Sooner or later, you've got to stop being scared of your dad. If you don't, you're going to gradu-ate college a virgin with half a dozen cats, some dumb-ass degree he wants that you couldn't care less about, and only professors and academic journals for friends."

I wince, because she's right about *almost* all of it. She would be furious if she knew I wasn't a virgin and didn't tell her. I'd always meant to, but it isn't exactly my proudest memory, and the longer I'd put it off, the easier it had become to pretend that it wasn't a thing. I refuse to let it be a thing. Instead, I roll my eyes and say, "Thanks for the vote of confidence."

"Hey, I'm just being the voice of reason here."

"More like the devil on my shoulder."

"I accept that role." Stella cackles and nudges her elbow in my side like she's just said the funniest joke ever. And in spite of myself, I crack a smile.

I stare up at the Delta Sigma house. All the frat houses on campus are old colonial-style mansions with creeping ivy and pearly white columns. They look so presentable . . . probably in an effort to hide the absolute debauchery that happens inside.

God, I just thought the word *debauchery*. Stella's right. I *am* going to end up a lame cat lady, probably yelling at people from my front porch and waving my cane around like a madwoman.

It just isn't fair.

College is supposed to be a time to break free, to start fresh. You would think being the football coach's daughter would be a benefit. I know more about the sport than half the guys at our school, knowledge that should make it easy to land a date.

If they weren't all petrified of my father.

Or even worse . . . panting after him like he's bacon dipped in

Nutella wrapped in more bacon. I could probably walk into this party wearing only my bra and underwear (slathered in some of that Nutella), and some idiot would bumble over, completely unaware, to ask me about my dad, what his plans were for the season, or how many high school state trophies we have lying around the house.

Stella's slim fingers snap in front of my face.

"Earth to Dallas. Are you actually frozen in fear right now?"

I roll my eyes, a habit of mine, especially around Stella. "I'm not afraid. I'm just . . . not optimistic."

"Don't tell me . . . you were brainstorming all the ways you could be a killjoy tonight."

I give her a playful shove. "I was contemplating covering myself in Nutella, actually."

"Now, *that* is what I like to hear! Ten points for creativity."

"Yeah, yeah. Let's just get this over with."

Stella skips off ahead of me, and I have to mentally remind myself not to drag my heels. I love the girl, and she is my best friend in the entire world, but I honestly don't have any clue how. She is outgoing, and I (frequently) prefer the company of books to people. Or movies to people. Anything over people, really. I'm easily self-conscious, even more easily irritated, and she blows through the front door of that frat house like we're seniors instead of lowly freshmen.

And perhaps our biggest divide . . .

Stella loves football.

I'm talking majorly fanatic groupie. She goes to games and

watches it on TV and reads the blogs and follows a bazillion players on Twitter. I'm convinced that if she weren't a five-foot-tall little Asian pixie that she would be out there playing herself. Hell, maybe one day she will be. She's a force to be reckoned with.

I go to games and watch it on TV, too. I know the players names and can rattle off the different plays and positions and whatever else you want to know.

But that's not because I love it. I've just lived it. Every day of my life for as long as I can remember. Through every new town and new school and new friends, football was the one thing that never changed. And when you spend that much time with something, you either love it or loathe it.

One guess which category I fall into.

I step inside the house behind Stella, and the manic grin she shoots me over her shoulder lets me know she's just stepped into her own personal heaven. A dozen or so people near the entrance glance up, and their eyes slide right over us. My shoulders relax their stone posture just a smidge.

A roar rises up from the kitchen, and I glance over in time to see two lines of people, one held at gunpoint. Water-gunpoint, anyway. Though from the cheers that ring out when one side starts shooting, aiming for the open mouths of their partners, I'm guessing they're spraying beer instead of water.

"We are so doing that!" Stella cries out over the thumping music.

Note to self: stay far, far away from the beer guns.

Knowing my luck, I'd take a shot to the eye.

A guy runs past us in a tutu and a deep red wig, hollering something unintelligible at the top of his lungs. Stella grins at me, her eyes shooting to my own red hair. "I found your long-lost twin. Tutu and all."

"What a coincidence! I found your twin, too." I cast my eyes in the direction of two girls carrying a third friend between them toward the door. "Messy drunk and all."

"You take that back! I am *not* a messy drunk."

"And I'm not a giant dude with probable back hair and an identity crisis."

She throws up her hands. "You're right. *Sorry.*" Cue her mischievous smile. "He had *way* bigger boobs."

I thump her hard, but we're both laughing. And it feels as easy as the parties we attended in high school, easier really, because Stella was right. No one here gives a damn about me.

"Big D! Heard you were on campus. I'm surprised to see you here, though."

And . . . I spoke too soon.

There's only one thing in the world I despise more than football, and he's making his way down the stairs toward me.

My eyes flit around me like I'm scanning a battlefield instead of a blowout: fraternity banners, litter of red Solo cups, and a freshman pledge dragging around a trash bag playing reluctant maid. Part of me wants to keep doing that, to pretend like I didn't hear him.

But I can't. If I ignore him, it will only prove to him that he still bothers me.

I face him as he steps off the last stair, crossing his arms over his broad chest and grinning at me. Levi. My ex.

He leans his hip against the banister of the grand staircase, and I spy not one but two girls sitting halfway up the stairs, obviously upset that they've lost his attention.

Behind me I hear someone shout, "Ready. Aim. Fire!" and I know the beer guns are back in play.

"Alcohol and bad decisions, Levi? Can't say I'm surprised to find you smack-dab in the middle of that."

He kicks off from the banister, swaggering a few steps closer. His dark hair and eyes are as striking as always. I'd fallen for him so hard my freshman year of high school: doodling our names together in my spiral, watching him play from the bleachers, wearing that monstrous mum he gave me for homecoming, beaming on his elbow at his junior prom.

The memory of all that just makes me nauseated now. But as Stella always says, hindsight is a pretentious, know-it-all bitch.

"You come here to make some bad decisions?" He moves closer, his voice pitching lower. Intimate. His gaze drifts down my body with an arrogant familiarity. "Because you *know* I can help you with that."

Levi Abrams has been the cause of enough bad decisions for a lifetime.

Stella steps in, her voice colder than I've ever heard it. "I'm fairly certain she'd rather sandpaper her own skin off."

I nod and plaster on the fakest smile in my arsenal. "And then take a bath in lemon juice."

Levi smiles back, and I'm pretty sure the bastard is enjoying this.

He's bigger than when I last saw him. Bulked up. I guess that's the difference between high school and college ball. But it's not just muscles . . . he reaches out a hand like he's going to touch my hair, and as I jerk back, even his hands seem bigger than I remember. A man's hands, rather than those of the boy I knew. Or maybe his head got so big that his inflated ego overflowed to other parts of his body. Also a possibility.

I knew Levi was here when I chose Rusk University—hard not to when he's the starting quarterback—but I didn't think I'd ever have to see him. Since Dad wouldn't let me leave Texas, and only a handful of universities here actually have a true dance major, Rusk was the best option out of the schools to which I was *allowed* to apply.

Levi lets his hand fall away and turns to leave, but then stops to say over his shoulder, "You don't have to pretend to hate me so much, you know. I'm here. You're here. We could start fresh, D."

Why does no one get that it's *impossible* to have a fresh start when nothing has really changed? God, I knew that better than anybody because no matter how many new coaching jobs Dad took, every school ended up the same.

Levi is still a douche-bag who only cares about himself.

Dad still approaches parenting like I'm a member of his team.

And I . . . I'm still stuck. In my father's shadow. In Texas. In this lame state school with a joke of a dance program.

And now I'm stuck at my first frat party with the ex who broke my heart.

Yay college.

As soon as Levi is out of sight, I bolt for the door. Stella wraps her arms around my waist to stop me, but she's a foot shorter than me, and her idea of a workout is marathoning *Project Runway*. She clings to me, her feet slipping and sliding as I drag her forward like she weighs barely anything.

In an exasperated voice she yells, "Stamp of approval!" I hesitate, slowing, but not stopping my attempt at escape. "I said stamp. Of. Approval. Skank."

I sigh. *Crap.*

We have this rule, something that's helped us stay friends despite how completely polar opposite our personalities are. It's a system of give and take, wherein I temper her crazy side and she forces me to live a little.

When Stella showed up to take the SATs drunk, she got the Dallas Cole Don't-Be-A-Douche Stamp of Disapproval. It was my non-nagging way of telling her that she'd gone too far. And though there wasn't much to do about it that Saturday, Stella signed up to take the test again, and when the next testing day rolled around, she was sober and serious and pulled off a decent score.

Alternately, there is the Stella Santos Suck-It-Up-You-Prude Stamp of Approval. That stamp has gotten me into more trouble than I care to list, including Stella's *brilliant* idea to wrap a house with toilet paper and stick maxi pads to the glass front door. What her plan didn't include was the knowledge that said house belonged to a policeman, who was *not* keen on being an advertisement for Kotex.

There is one and only one rule when it comes to the stamps. You have to listen.

I spin, and Stella narrowly misses getting laid out by my flailing elbow. Her exotic eyes narrow on me, and I know she's not backing down.

"*Fine.* I'll stay. But remember those stamps work both ways, sister."

She moves closer so that she can speak quietly, pushing her short dark hair out of her eyes. "Listen, I'm sorry. I didn't think douche-badger would be here. I heard that athletes don't usually come to the frat stuff, so I thought we'd be in the clear. But this place is huge." A stream of people exit out of a nearby door that I guess leads to a basement, as if to illustrate her point. "There's nothing that says you can't stay and have fun."

We have different ideas of *nothing*. My brain has already pinpointed *at least* seventeen reasons to leave.

Some idiot with a backward hat lurches toward a trash can just outside the kitchen, and a jet of *disgusting* pours out of his mouth.

Make that eighteen reasons.

"Right. Well, I'm officially sucking it up." And trying not to copy backward-hat's display of stomach pyrotechnics. "What's up, first?"

"I want you to actually enjoy this. Try to look like you're not dying inside." I attempt a smile. "A little less Freddy Krueger, a little more person who actually has a soul." I flash her more teeth, more menace than mirth, but I'm mostly teasing.

I *want* to enjoy myself. I want so badly for college to be different that I can taste the desperation on my tongue.

Stella starts to open her mouth, but I beat her to it. "Drinks?" Maybe that will help me loosen up.

"You learn fast, grasshopper."

On her tiptoes, she manages to loop an arm over my shoulders. She looks around and sighs happily, a *this is the life* kind of sigh, and I wonder what she's seeing that I'm not. "Our first college party. Puts those high school pasture parties to shame, doesn't it?"

I wasn't a particularly big fan of the parties she used to drag me to out on the Beane Ranch or the abandoned church turned party grounds out on Oakcliff Road. But I don't see how this is any better.

Finally, I manage to find a pro. "No mosquitoes. That's a plus." And all I've got.

She directs me to face the group of guys hanging out by the kegs in the kitchen and says, "I see several pluses in our future."

As long as those pluses aren't in conjunction with an STD test . . . I can deal.

Chapter 2

Dallas

A new song starts, one that's been blowing up the radio, and the dancers crowded in the living room let out a cheer. Stella does, too. And as we head for the archway that opens up into the kitchen, she throws out a hand and belts the words. I bump her hip and open my mouth to sing along, but no sound comes out.

The catchy tune shrivels in my throat as I make eye contact with one of the most gorgeous guys I've ever seen. He's sitting on top of the island counter in the kitchen, and even sitting I can tell he's tall. He has messy dark blond hair, artfully sculpted in that way that makes him look like he's jumped right off the pages of a magazine. Add to that a strong jaw and eyes that smile more than his lips, and no matter how hard I pull my gaze away, it keeps wandering back to him.

And I get caught.

Not just once.

Like four times! I should have learned my lesson after the first, maybe the second, but now I have officially crossed over into creepy territory.

It takes talent to be a gawking hot mess, and I am a gawking hot mess to the third power. I jerk my eyes away again, a billion years too late to retain my dignity. He's sitting right next to the keg, though, so I have to look back his way a few seconds later or risk adding *frat-boy face-plant* to my list of special skills.

This time his lips join the smile in his eyes, and my heart picks up its tempo.

He *did* have to keep looking at me in order to catch me. So maybe he doesn't mind that I'm staring.

And maybe Stella was right about this particular stamp.

While she fills up a cup, I try to look casual. I never know exactly how to hold my arms or how far to cock my hip. The dancer in me doesn't feel comfortable unless my posture is perfect, but that makes me stick out like a sore thumb in a sea of slouchy college kids.

My hands are floppy, dead fish. Or that's what they feel like anyway as I try to arrange them in a way that doesn't make me look like a mental patient. While I'm still trying to figure it out, a red cup enters my vision.

I follow a muscular arm up to that pair of smiling eyes.

"Pretty girls shouldn't have to wait in line."

I eye the half-full cup, then manage a casual shrug.

"I'll wait. Thanks."

Nothing about Stella's stamp says I have to do something as

stupid as take a drink from a stranger, no matter how good looking he is.

Stella moves aside, but not before waggling her perfectly sculpted eyebrows at me. Gawk-worthy guy slides down off the counter as I step up to the keg.

"You don't trust me?" he asks.

This time I catch him staring at my legs, and how *not* covered they are by the outrageously short skirt Stella picked out for me.

"I don't *know* you," I reply, trying to sound at least a little stern and failing.

He smiles unabashedly and glances one more time at my legs. I only agreed to the stupid skirt because it has pockets, and I *cannot* resist a skirt with pockets.

Now I wish I had tried a little harder.

"So get to know me," he replies.

God, do they make WD-40 for flirting? Because I am *rusty*. Not enough practice thanks to four years of high school with an overbearing dad as the football coach. Then again, this guy is scary gorgeous, so he would make me nervous no matter how much practice I had.

I hold out my hand and say, "I'm Dallas."

He eyes my proffered hand, and I know I've made a mistake. Laughing, he takes my hand and bends to kiss it in a princely bow, and I can't tell if he's making fun of me or not.

"Dallas and Silas," he murmurs, his lips still close enough to my hand that I feel his breath skate across my skin. "Sounds like fate to me."

No one has ever been so audaciously flirtatious with me in my entire life, and it muddles my brain.

"Nice to meet you, Silas."

I am thinking about how it will be impossible for us to have a couple nickname if we get together because every combination ends up just being one of our names when he laughs.

He moves closer to me, and instinctively I take a tiny step back.

"You're never going to get to know me like that. Come on."

He lays an arm across my shoulder, hooking me closer to his side, and starts leading me out of the kitchen.

"Wait. My friend."

"She'll be fine."

I'm not worried about *her*.

"He's right!" Stella calls behind me. "I *am* fine," she announces to a group of three guys that she's already managed to ensnare. Good God, it's like she's found her natural habitat. I envy her confidence.

I envy a lot of things about Stella.

He pulls me toward the living room, and I automatically fall into step with the rhythm of the music. But when I see the room packed full of grinding bodies and decorated with wandering hands, I panic. It's not that I'm incapable of dancing like that. My tastes run more toward ballet, lyrical, and jazz, but I've taken a few years of hip-hop.

It's not the movement that intimidates me. I can roll my hips with the best of them. It's the intimacy I can't handle. There are no secrets when your body is that close to another. Hell, it took me close to a year before I could comfortably press up against Levi that way.

Fat lot of good all that caution did me.

As much as I get annoyed with the way my father affects my love life, a really small part of me is glad to have him as an excuse to not get too close. As an excuse not to get hurt again.

"Bathroom," I blurt out, grasping for another excuse. "I, uh, need to use the ladies' room." I thought *ladies' room* might sound less embarrassing.

Wrong on all counts.

He gives me that look again like I'm behaving like the grandma who I apparently stole my personality from.

I cough and add, "Bathroom," once more, like that somehow might clear the air of all the terrible, but yeah . . . this place is officially polluted. He raises an eyebrow, and I wait for him to ditch me because I am *clearly* the least cool person in this house, counting the dude asleep underneath the table in the foyer currently sucking his thumb.

But my weird doesn't phase him. It's a miracle. "Sure, there's one upstairs, I think. Maybe we can find a quiet place up there to talk, too."

Oh my Jesus. Make that miraculously scary.

His finger draws little circles on my shoulder, and I concentrate on swallowing down all the irrational excuses that I want to make to run away.

Claiming flesh-eating bacteria to get out of a private conversation *might* be overkill. Malaria might work, though.

As we climb the stairs together, my heart climbs higher and higher into my throat until it throbs on the back of my tongue. The two girls who'd been all over Levi earlier are still on the stairs, and when they see us coming, they sit up straighter. One fluffs her hair, her gaze darting between Silas and me, and I can see her confusion in her glossy-lipped frown. She stands as we near, petite to the point that she would look twelve years old were it not for the giant rack that *has* to completely throw off her balance.

"Hey, Silas," she breathes.

He only nods back, but he smiles while he does it, and she looks grateful for even that little bit of attention.

Dear God, please tell me I don't look that pathetic. Because I will not be that girl, begging for scraps, no matter how gorgeous the guy is.

Upstairs is surprisingly deserted. Or at least it appears to be. The long hallway of closed doors is probably hiding plenty of things I don't want to be party to. Discomfort sweeps through me, and I'm grateful when he stops outside a closed door that I hope (oh please, please) is the bathroom.

He gives me another mock bow and says, "All yours, pretty girl."

I cannot escape into that bathroom fast enough. And maybe (okay, definitely) it's overkill, but I lock the door as soon as it's closed.

Get a grip, Dallas.

I suck at the whole meeting new people thing. I've had plenty of practice, what with Dad's propensity to up and move us every few years, but it never gets any easier.

All in all, I just really blow at being a normal human being.

But I am going to start now, damn it.

Note to self: do not use the world blow in front of Silas . . . in any context. It won't turn out well.

No matter what I have to do, I will not let my dad limit my life here, too.

I don't look in the mirror as I work to gather my composure. If I do, I know I'll obsess over my hair—how the deep red color clashes horribly against my no doubt pink cheeks. I can feel the light perspiration above my brow, so my bangs are probably a clumpy, oily mess, too.

Nope. Better to avoid the mirror altogether. Silas didn't seem to take issue with whatever he saw, so neither should I. Instead, I take a few seconds just to lean against the door and breathe.

By-product of having a coach for a father? A natural gift for mental pep talks.

But now . . . I wasn't sure which pep talk to give. The familiar *be cautious and careful* routine? Or take a cue from Stella and treat myself to a *live it up* talk to get my ass in gear? In the end, I decide on something carefully in the middle. I'll see what happens with Silas, but I am not staying upstairs with him, and I am not leaving the party with him either.

There. That seems reasonable.

Fun. I need to have some. Stat.

Decided, I open the door quietly, smile situated on my lips, expecting to find Silas waiting, but he's nowhere to be seen.

Walking back toward the stairs, I see him, hands braced on the railing and talking with someone a few steps down.

"Come on. Give me one hint," Silas says.

The answering voice is familiar, and immediately I feel sick.

"Dude, it took me *years* to get in her pants." Levi. *Freaking* Levi. "No way I'm giving you an easy in. And *no way* you're managing it in one night. She's an icebox, man."

I shiver. Like I really have been coated in ice.

Silas chuckles before replying, "Oh ye of little faith."

"Oh ye of little *chance*."

"Whatever," Silas says. "If she gave it up to high school you, all farm fresh with zero game, she can't be that tough."

They talk about me like I am some play to master, a team to beat. I probably matter less to them than their helmets and pads. And, oh yes, I have no doubt now that Silas is on the football team. Levi wouldn't be hanging out with him if he weren't.

My heart drums in my ears, and my mouth waters in that way that usually means I'm about to be sick. I don't scream, even though it would be satisfying. Nor do I pick up the vase on the hallway table and test out how my Angry Birds skills translate to real-life target practice.

Instead, I calmly walk the length of the hallway and escape into an empty bedroom. I breeze past a few twin beds and head straight for the French doors that open up to a balcony on the far side of the room.

Emerging into the surprisingly cool evening air, I close the door behind me, sucking in a lungful of refreshing air.

Then I scream.

Not the shrieky, ear-shattering kind. Lower, more guttural. Like a battle cry.

Gripping the balcony railing, I stand up straighter, like I would if I were standing at the barre in my dance studio, and I let it all out.

Already I feel better.

A few seconds of precious silence passes, filled only by the faint echo of my scream. Then below me a voice calls out, "I'm going to go out on a limb and guess that you've decided against going Greek."

Down in the yard, highlighted by one of the floodlights affixed to the outside of the house, is another gorgeous guy wearing dark, worn jeans, scuffed boots, and a smirk that oscillates between infuriating and adorable. He's got dark hair and a delectable touch of scruff along his jaw, and he looks entirely entertained by my mental breakdown.

And all I can think is . . . *Dear God, not another one.*

Chapter 3

Carson

I t's like she took the scream right out of my throat. I've been out here alone, alternating between convincing myself to leave and convincing myself to stay. And here comes this gorgeous girl with a lion's roar.

She leans over the ledge, her eyes searching until she finds me sprawled at the base of one of the wide oak trees in the yard. I sit up a little straighter under her gaze.

Her pale skin shines a creamy white in the moonlight, and dark red hair frames a heart-shaped face with full, pouty lips. Her eyes narrow on me, or maybe she just squints. After a few seconds of studying me, she offers an unenthusiastic, "Sorry."

"Don't be. That was the best thing I've seen all night."

"You can't have had a very exciting night, then."

No. No, I hadn't. I'd tagged along with some other teammates, thinking I needed to make an effort to get to know them off the field. I'd gotten to know them all right. And I was already tired of them. I knew it wouldn't be easy to walk on to a team like this, it never was. People were nice enough, but none of them took me seriously.

Just a walk-on.

Most people see us as just players for the real athletes to practice against with no real chance of getting any substantial playing time for ourselves. A few are more accepting.

But fitting in isn't worth spending an hour with those assholes. They aren't even drunk yet, so I can only imagine how much worse it will get.

I shrug off that frustration and tell the girl, "At least things are looking up now."

She stiffens, shaking out her hair like a mane. The deep red shines, catching glints from the lights as she moves.

"Listen," she says, "tonight is not the night to flirt with me."

I should probably be annoyed by her brusque tone, but I find myself smiling instead.

"Who said I was flirting?"

She scoffs, her fingers curling tighter around the balcony banister.

"You were."

I grin because, yeah . . . I was. She's not cocky when she says it either, just matter-of-fact. I find it . . . fascinating.

"It's not like I stood below the balcony reciting *Romeo and Juliet*." Not like I could either. I never managed to finish that when we read it in high school English, and the movie version

I watched with guns and gangs got me a big fat F on the exam. She makes a noise, and I can't tell whether she's scoffing at me again or laughing.

"Romeo was a tool."

"Really?" I thought girls lived for that shit.

She crosses her arms over her chest and huffs, "He's head-over-heels, mopey in love with Rosaline, and then in one night, he flip-flops and decides now he's in love with Juliet. If he would have just thrown his whiny tool self at another girl, Juliet wouldn't have died."

"Well, I can promise I'm not going to suddenly declare my love for you. Satisfied?"

She shrugs, and I assume that's the only answer I'll get.

"So was it a Romeo who inspired that scream?"

"Nope. Just the regular kind of asshole."

She stumbles over the last word, her cheeks pinking prettily, and I get the feeling her blunt honesty doesn't usually include swear words.

"Well, fuck that guy." My suspicions are confirmed when her blush deepens, and she pulls that full bottom lip between her teeth. I try to connect this shy piece of her puzzle with the brazen girl who called me on my flirting without blinking.

"Uh . . . yeah," she replies hesitantly.

I make a mental note to cuss as much as possible to keep that sweet flush on her face. "Don't let that dick ruin your night."

I should probably learn to take my own advice. I'm the one hiding in the backyard of a frat house.

"They will *not* ruin my night."

They? There's more than one? Damn.

I start to ask her name, but then someone inside the house shouts out, "Dallas?" and her head whips around in response.

"That him?" I ask.

She rolls her eyes and nods.

"Well then, Dallas. As I see it, you have two options. You can turn around and unleash another of those screams on him, which *would* be entertaining. Or . . ."

I trail off, debating whether or not to try again considering my crappy flirting record with this girl so far.

"Or what?"

"Or forget about the prick, and hang out with me. I'll make my best effort not to be an asshole." She hesitates and I add, "Or a Romeo. Or a tool. Or whatever it is you're sick of."

There's a third option that I don't add, as appealing as it is. She could introduce me to the dick, and I could introduce him to my fist and work off some frustration. But that could get me in trouble with Coach, so while effective, it's off the table.

I am fully prepared for her to say no and lump me in with whatever other guys have pissed her off tonight. Instead, she considers me. Her lips twist, somewhere between pursed and pouty.

"I'm not sleeping with you," she says.

Surprised, I bark out a laugh and feel the last of the night's frustration ebb away. She says exactly what she's thinking, and I love it. I'm shocked by how much I want to keep prodding until I've unraveled every little thought that crosses her mind.

"*Again* with the assumptions," I say.

"Like you weren't thinking about it."

I hadn't actually gotten that far, but *now* I'm thinking about it, about how it would be an even better way to work off my frustration than fighting. I bet that flush is just as pretty across her chest as it is across her cheeks. It's hard to tell from down below her, but she's tall, maybe just a few inches shorter than me, and her legs go on and on. I imagine them going around and around my hips.

I clear my throat before I can wander too long down that trail of thought. "Thinking about and expecting it are two different things. One makes me a douche-bag, the other just makes me a dude."

Tempting or not, I don't have time for that kind of thinking. It was one thing to hook up with girls at Westfield. It didn't take nearly as much effort to secure my spot on the team or keep up my grades there, but I am on an entirely different playing field here. Literally.

"Dallas!" The guy calls out again, and a light a few rooms down switches on. There's a shrill scream before the light switches off and a door slams shut, the guy clearly having interrupted something.

Dallas's face screws up in a laugh, but no sound comes out.

When another room lights up down the hall, she sobers quickly.

"Why would you want to hang out with me? I'm likely to be a roaring bitch for the rest of the night."

So honest. And gorgeous. It's a rare combination. I have to remind myself again that I don't have the time to really appreciate this particular rarity.

"What can I say? I have a thing for screamers."

Her blush had calmed, but now it detonates across her cheeks again, and I'm laughing before I manage to hold it back.

"I'm kidding, little lioness. I'm not looking to hook up with you. I just find your honesty refreshing. That makes you better company than every person I've run across tonight."

She watches another light switch on, just two rooms away, and lifts her chin. She seems to come to a decision. Then she braces her hands on the railing, hefts herself up, and throws a long leg over the balcony's edge.

"Holy shit!" I jump to my feet, sprinting to stand beneath her. She has both legs over by the time I'm standing under her, her toes tucked carefully along the ledge on the outside of the railing.

"Dallas, be careful."

Her legs look even longer now that they aren't blocked by the balcony, and her pale skin almost glows in the moonlight.

"You better not be looking up my skirt right now," she says.

"I'm not!"

Anymore.

She twists her head around, and her eyes meet mine, and I am so caught. Even at night, the bright green of her gaze stands out like emeralds against her porcelain skin. I note, with a wry grin, that her underwear is the same color.

"Does this make me a coward?" she asks, glancing in the direction of the seeking voice.

"You're currently dangling off a balcony. *Coward* was not the word I was thinking of."

She grins, a vibrant gleam in her eye, and before I can smile back in response, she lets go and starts dropping toward the ground.

"Oh shit!"

I throw my arms up while simultaneously jerking my head away so I can't be accused of looking up her skirt again. Her knee makes contact with my shoulder, and when I try to catch her I end up catching her skirt instead, and then I'm tipping backward with her somewhat in my arms. My ass hits first, then the top of her head cracks against my chin a second before her weight slams into my midsection.

"Fuck," I groan at the same time she declares, "You are an *idiot*."

With one hand pressed to the top of her head, she uses the other to push herself up enough to look at me, her elbow planted firmly below the socket of my shoulder.

"I could have landed that on my own. It was *one* floor."

My ribs feel on the verge of caving in, and I force a shaky breath with her weight still on top of me.

"I didn't know. You could have broken an ankle or something." She shifts, and I groan. "Instead I broke my ass."

She laughs again, the same silent one I saw her give on the balcony, and I catch sight of one lone dimple on her right cheek. She lets go of her head to shift herself higher, and before she can climb off me, I reach out to touch her forehead. She stills, and those large green eyes peer down at me. I trace my fingers across her skin, brushing through the bangs swept across her forehead.

"You okay? You hit my chin pretty hard."

In response, she just reaches out and traces my chin in the same manner. In the silent night, I can hear the short stubble along my jaw rasp against her skin. She shivers.

Her eyes are open, and I swear I can see every thought in them. She runs her finger one way across my jaw, and then back, and I can tell she's trying to decide if she likes the facial hair. Then her eyes touch on my lips briefly before flicking away, and then back again, like she knows she shouldn't be looking, but then doesn't really care.

And for all the promises I made her (and myself), I think about kissing her. I think about it, and I fist my hands against her back to keep from following through. Her tongue darts out to wet her lips, and they glisten, calling to me. I'm breathing heavy, and I hope she just chalks it up to having the air knocked out of me, not to the reemergence of the mental image of her legs wrapped around my waist that's the true culprit.

"Dallas?" The voice is in the room directly above us, and we hear heavy footsteps stomp toward the balcony door.

I reach for her hips to shift her off of me, and I touch bare skin. We realize at the same time that when I'd grabbed her skirt as she fell, I'd tugged it up somewhere around her waist, leaving her bottom half mostly bare against me.

Panic flits through her eyes. In her haste to cover herself, she sits up, rushing to pull down her skirt, which leaves one knee on either side of my hips. My hands are still frozen against her warm skin, now hidden beneath her skirt. I stiffen and swallow a groan because I like her draped across me. Entirely too much. And if she doesn't move off me quickly, she's going to know it.

Her name comes again, from outside on the balcony this time. I let my hands fall away from her hips, and I don't mean for my fingertips to brush against her thighs, but I'm certainly not sorry. Not when she lets out a breathy noise that I might have called a moan if she didn't fix me with a glare half a second later. She pulls herself up, more gracefully than I would have thought possible. Her face drawn tight in anger, she steps over me, and I cover my eyes with a groan too late not to catch another brief forbidden glance of emerald green.

This girl is going to be the death of me.

As I pull myself up to a sitting position just below the balcony and out of sight, she turns around to square off against the guy above.

"Pretty girl, what are you doing down there?"

She doesn't answer. Instead she crosses her arms over her chest and gives him a cold look. "Did your *buddy* ever give you that hint you were wanting? Because if not, I have one. Not in a *million* years, asshole."

She doesn't hesitate over the curse word, and I barely resist the urge to applaud her improvement.

"Don't be mad, pretty girl." The guy actually sounds a little worried. Hell, *I'm* a little worried, and her anger isn't even directed at me. "That was just guy talk. We were being stupid. Nothing serious."

Her expression morphs from cold to fiery, and I have a feeling that if she could get back up on that balcony, she would make that guy use his own small intestine as a straw.

"Stay away from me. I'll keep my mouth shut about tonight, but bother me again, and I might just feel the need to unburden my worries. Got it?"

The dick doesn't reply, and the balcony door opens and slams shut once more.

She'd more than held her own, but I can't help being unsettled by what I heard. What had that dude done to her? And who was she threatening to tell that had him bailing without even a reply?

I climb to my feet slowly, my back complaining and my ass bitching like nobody's business. Trying not to grimace, I ask, "You okay?"

She pulls her gaze away from the now-empty balcony and focuses on me.

"Better."

Her eyes turn wary, and I'm pretty sure she's thinking about the skirt mishap. Her hands confirm it when they slip into two hidden pockets at her hips and casually push down to make sure her skirt is as long as she can make it. Fortunately for me, that's still not that long.

I mimic her, placing my own hands into my pockets. A cold front is just creeping into town, the first hint of fall, so it's cold enough to keep everyone inside, but not so cold that it's unbearable. Hell, I hadn't been cold since the minute I'd laid eyes on Dallas.

For a few seconds, we just stare at each other, unsure how to proceed. She reaches up and gathers her thick red hair into her hands like she's going to pull it up into a ponytail. Then she seems to think better of it, releasing it until it settles in crimson drifts across her shoulders. I fist my hands in my pockets, nearly overwhelmed with the urge to wrap that long hair around my fingers. She links her hands behind her back, and it draws my attention to her slim, tall frame.

And damn, I really need to get a handle on this.

When we do speak, it's in a rush and at the same time.

"What were you doing out here alone?"

"So, you jump off balconies often?"

We apologize in sync, and then laugh together, too.

I leave the shadows of the balcony and cross to her. "I needed some space to think. I just transferred to Rusk from a junior college, and it's not as easy to settle in as I thought it would be."

"What junior college?"

I shove my hands deeper into my pockets. I hadn't meant to tell her about that. Most people are weird when I mention junior college, like I am somehow lesser than because I went there first. But she is so open and honest, I didn't even think about filtering myself before I spoke.

"Westfield."

She smiles. "I have a few friends who went to Westfield and are planning to transfer here after a year or two. It's pretty smart, really. So much cheaper to get the basics out of the way there first."

Her smile is genuine, and I've not felt this at ease since I set foot on this campus a few weeks ago to officially try out for the team. "So what about you? Balcony jumping a habit? Favorite pastime?"

She tilts her head to the side and scrunches her nose up cutely before shaking her head. "Not so much. Probably not the smartest thing I've ever done either."

I raise an eyebrow. *"Oh really?* What happened to your whole *Carson, you're an idiot. It was* only *one floor* bit?"

She bites back a smile before asking, "Carson?"

I hadn't told her my name before? Oh, right. I was too busy getting my tailbone broken and accidentally undressing her.

"Well, Carson. Normally, I'm much more graceful than . . ." She laughs before adding, "All of *that.*" She circles her hand, gesturing toward the general vicinity where we'd ended up after my botched attempt at catching her.

I step up beside her, and I'm close enough to her now that I can see the way her eyelashes brush against her cheeks when she blinks. And I must be insane because just the simple act of her blinking has me staring, dumbstruck.

I can deny myself all I want, but one thing I cannot deny is just how fucking gorgeous this girl is. And exactly the kind of distraction I'm *supposed* to be staying away from.

I'm sure there are plenty of people who go to junior college because it's cheaper or the smart thing to do. And yeah, the cheaper thing definitely helped. A lot.

But mostly I went because I didn't get accepted into any state schools, and my high school team hadn't been good enough to get the kind of exposure I needed to land a football scholarship.

So Dad and I had made a plan. One year at Westfield—get my grades up, play football there, train every spare second, reach out to the coach at Rusk, and nab a walk-on spot. Eventually, the goal is to leverage that spot into something more permanent, something with a scholarship.

So far the plan is working perfectly. Right on track.

But the hardest part is standing right in front of me.

Don't get distracted by a girl.

That's Dad's number one rule, and he's probably right.

It's going to take everything I have to keep my grades up here. And I don't exactly have it easy on the field, considering I'm playing second string to Levi Abrams. The guy won two high school state championships, and still holds the high school state record for all-time leading passer. He was redshirted the year before last, his freshman year, and though he had decent numbers in his first season last year, the team as a whole had a disappointing year.

Normally that might have given me a little hope.

But considering the university's new coach was the one to coach Levi to those two state championships in high school, I figure I'm shit out of luck.

I'm sure one of the reasons he was hired was to get Levi back on his game.

Which is why I give myself a break and let myself step a little closer to Dallas. I can afford to get distracted for *one night*. How much could it hurt?

"So what did that guy do to piss you off? You know . . . just so I don't make the same mistake."

"Unless you're lying to me and trying to trick me into sleeping with you . . . you should be good."

"So what if I'm up-front about trying to get you to sleep with me . . . Does that still get me yelled at?"

I expected a blush, but I don't get one. Her face is carefully blank.

"I thought you weren't trying to hook up with me."

"Just keeping my options open. I like to be prepared for all possibilities."

She rolls her eyes. "You can be as up-front as you want. I can promise I will be, too."

There's a devilish glint in her eye, and I wonder how many hearts this girl has broken with her honesty. Not that I'm worried about my heart. I'm more concerned with the hard-on I can't get to subside with her so close to me.

"Then in the interests of honesty, I should say I'm trying really hard not to kiss you."

She straightens, and the strand of hair she was lazily twirling drops from her grasp.

"Why would you tell me that?"

"So that when I slip up and break my promise, you'll at least know I tried."

Chapter 4

Dallas

I roll my eyes, not because I'm annoyed, but because it gives me time to think.

And I *desperately* need time to think.

I wouldn't say I'd been entirely sheltered growing up. I did have Stella, after all. But being the coach's daughter affected the way people treated me. Sure, guys made sexual jokes, but never to my face, and never with a devastatingly handsome grin to back it up.

I stare down at our feet—mine have fallen into third position of their own accord and his boots are scuffed and muddy. I wouldn't have pegged him for country, not with his university sweatshirt and stylishly ripped jeans, but the boots don't lie.

"Stop thinking so hard," he says. "You're giving *me* a headache."

"I can't just turn it off."

"I could distract you." He lifts one side of his mouth in a lazy smirk, and I want to say that I am already distracted by him. No, *distracted* is not the word. *Bulldozed* seems more appropriate.

When he takes my wrist and pulls me down to sit at the base of the oak tree beside him, I'm pretty much putty in his hands. Which is annoying as all get out.

His thumb teases at my pulse point for a few seconds, and I wonder if he feels it pick up under his touch. His shoulder brushes against mine, and the shiver that runs down my spine speeds through my limbs, drawing my toes to a point.

I keep my eyes on my feet as he asks, "So, Daredevil, besides jumping off balconies, what other crazy things do you spend your time doing?"

"Hanging out in backyards with complete strangers, obviously."

His blue eyes are practically twinkling when he nudges my shoulder and says, "I've had my hands up your skirt, Daredevil. I think that qualifies me as an acquaintance at least."

I shove him away, and when he comes back laughing, his shoulder doesn't just brush mine, but presses against me to stay.

I pull on a scowl, but it's getting harder and harder not to smile at him. Not to mention my heart is beating so hard, it might be leaving dents in my rib cage. "Feel free to ease back on the honesty any time now."

He leans his head back against the tree, and swivels his face toward me. "Too late. I'm addicted. It's your fault, really."

I turn my head toward him, and he's closer than I expect him to be. His eyes are this incredible electric blue, and a shock wave ripples through me like his gaze carries a voltage.

It's my eyes that drop to his lips first, just for half a second, but when I look back up his sight is trained on my mouth. There's a drum line in my ears, and my skin feels too tight for me to properly breathe. It's been so very long since I've felt like this that I'd forgotten how consuming it is. How physical attraction really is. All my relationships began in my head first, or at least after Levi they did. I dated guys because it made sense, because they ticked all the boxes, and the attraction came later. Sometimes.

This is different. I don't know anything about this guy except that his eyes make my mind fuzzy, and his muscled arms make my mouth water, and the things he keeps saying . . . they burn—beginning in my flushed cheeks, blazing through my blood, and curling between my legs until I feel like I have to squeeze them together just to keep from combusting on the spot.

I lean into him before I can change my mind, my whole arm lined up against his. Then our knees bump, followed by our pinkies.

His head dips down, the scruff on his chin grazing my shoulder, setting off a shiver that should be measured on the Richter scale.

I tilt my chin up, and his breath skims over my lips in a ghost of a kiss.

And that's all I get, a phantom touch, because he pulls back with a wry grin. I try to school my expression into something detached or annoyed or bored or anything—anything other than the disappointment churning in my gut.

He's just playing with me. Clearly. And the humiliation drowns out everything else.

I turn away, pulling up my knees in preparation to stand. I open my mouth to make an excuse, that I need to find Stella, that I need a drink, that I need electroshock therapy to jolt the stupid out of me. *God, when will I learn?*

I don't even get out a word before he grips my elbow, pulling me toward him, and slams his lips against mine.

I am *not* the kiss-a-stranger type. I'm not even the kiss-an-*acquaintance* type. But I keep hearing Levi calling me an icebox. And I keep remembering the one and only time we had sex, and the horrible day after when it hadn't saved our relationship like I'd thought it would. I'd had very little interest in physical contact since then, and I hate that Levi still controls a part of my life even all these years later.

But this . . . Levi doesn't have control of this because I'm not sure even *I* have control of this.

Carson's hand smooths up from my elbow and curls around the back of my neck, pulling me even closer. He tilts my head back, positioning me just how he wants me. And though my body is a big fan of jumping on that bandwagon (and I totally plan to), my brain feels the need to remind him, "I'm still not sleeping with you."

He huffs out a laugh, his head dropping down until I can feel the breath from his laughter singe my collarbone.

"Oh, Daredevil," he murmurs. "I like you."

I like it when he calls me that. My stomach swoops low in my belly in approval and anticipation.

This time, I kiss him, and his lips press back against mine so hard that a jolt of *something* coils down my spine. The hand at the back of my neck tightens, and his other hand rests lightly against my knee. I know he must feel it shaking.

I can't decide if him being a virtual stranger makes this kind of intimacy more or less terrifying.

His lips open against mine, his breath fanning over my skin, and I think *more* terrifying, definitely.

But also so much . . . *hotter.*

He brushes his open mouth against mine, softly, once and then twice, like we have all the time in the world, and I expect myself to be grateful for his slowness, but instead it's killing me. I want to dive into him headfirst, submerge myself in the way he makes me feel, and not come up for air until I have no other choice.

But I don't. I let him hold me like the porcelain doll that I'm terrified of being because I'm even more terrified of how badly I want him.

He threads a hand through my hair, cupping the back of my head, and gently tilts my lips up toward his. After a few more soft kisses, his thumb runs across my bottom lip and electricity sparks from that tiny touch.

His thumb trails down to my chin, and he presses down just enough to pull my lips apart. His tongue darts out, tracing my bottom lip the same way his thumb did, and I grip his shoulders hard because I feel like I might fall even though I'm sitting down. One of his hands grips my hip in response as he teases my lips with his tongue one more time.

Then, like he'd been teasing himself too, he groans and pushes the kiss deeper. And my body is ready to throw him a damn parade in celebration. His tongue slides against mine, firm and demanding, but not overwhelming. Not scary. Yet.

He leans into me, pressing me back, and the crown of my head touches the tree behind me. I've only had a handful of kisses besides Levi, as sad as that is. And maybe it's the bad memories that make me look back on those kisses with indifference, but I don't remember his or anyone's being this . . . good.

And because I have no filter, I whisper those words against his lips.

"This is good."

He laughs. "I love it when you do that."

"Do what?"

He hums against my lips, and it vibrates pleasantly.

"When you say exactly what you're thinking."

I pull away. "You won't love it when I say something stupid."

And the stupid would come. No doubt about it.

"Are you kidding? I can't wait."

I huff and push at his shoulder. My shove sends his back thudding back against the tree, but he laughs and grips my elbow, tugging me forward in response. Hard. I yelp, steadying myself with both hands against his chest, and my bent knee ends up strewn over his lap.

He sucks in a breath, and grips my thigh with one hand. Part of my brain is demanding that I pull away. Kissing a stranger is one thing, but this is something else entirely. But despite my brain's warning, my body leans into him, shivering when the hand on my leg tightens possessively. His fingers trail down toward my knee, and then slowly, so slowly that it feels like a dance, he pulls until I'm straddling him for the second time tonight. This time, though, I'm not distracted by a wardrobe malfunction. And with him sitting upright instead of lying down, he feels so much *closer* in every way. Our stomachs press together, and I can feel the rough fabric of his jeans against the sensitive skin of my inner thighs. And the fact that my underwear is the only thing keeping the rest of my bare skin from touching him makes that pleasure parade from earlier descend into complete pandemonium.

"I should go," I say.

But even as I say it, I curl his shirt in my fists and pull myself a little bit closer.

Chapter 5

Carson

Just her number, I'd told myself.

Just a touch, I'd thought.

Just a kiss, I'd sworn.

And yet, my hands are now on her hips, my shirt bunched in her hands, and my chest warmed by the press of her body against mine.

"I should go," she says for a second time, but neither of us makes a move. She shifts forward, her hips pulling closer to mine, and I hiss at the pressure of her against me. I'm already straining against my jeans, and the tightness goes from unpleasant to torturous as her thighs squeeze against my hips.

Her head tilts to the side, like she's studying me, and she repeats the movement of her hips. I groan and my head falls back against the tree with a hard thump. Not that I feel it. All the nerve endings in my body seem to be concentrated on where she touches me.

This is the opposite of staying focused, but if this is what distraction feels like, she can drive me to it anytime.

She smiles, and I let it wash away my worries about the future. I let the sweet vanilla scent of her hair override the thought of how badly I need to stay focused on football, of how it's the only chance I stand at a decent future. I bury all that bullshit under the weight of her heated gaze.

And for the first time in a long time, I don't feel shackled to a plan or a problem.

I only feel free.

And I only feel *her*.

I slide a hand from her hip to her lower back, slipping my hand beneath her shirt to touch warm skin. Suddenly greedy, I glide that hand up until my entire arm presses against her and my fingers curl over her shoulder, locking her tightly against me.

She gasps, and though her body arches into mine, her eyes are wide and wary. I worry that I've gone too far.

"Tell me, Daredevil."

She licks her lips, and the muscle of her shoulder tightens under my fingers.

"Tell you what?"

"I won't do anything you don't want me to do. But if you don't tell me what that is, my mind is going to keep thinking of all the things *I* want to do to you, and the list is already very, *very* long."

She licks her lips again, and I jerk her closer, just barely grazing her tongue with my own before it disappears back into her mouth.

She closes her eyes, and her fists pull so hard on the front of my shirt that I know it's going to be stretched and warped whenever she eventually lets go.

"I want," she whispers, her eyes scrunched tight.

I can feel my heartbeat at the base of my spine, and one of us is shaking. Whether it's me or her, I'm too far gone to tell. All I know is that I can feel the heat of her even through my jeans.

"What?" I ask, my voice thick.

"I want," she repeats, her whisper almost pained. Her eyes are still closed, and though I don't understand it, don't understand *her*, I know I'm pushing her too far.

"Do you want me to keep holding you like this?"

"Yes." She says the word immediately on a relieved exhale, and then lets her head drop back.

"Do you want me to kiss you?"

Her knees squeeze against my hips as she says, "Yes."

With her head dropped back, I move my mouth closer to her neck, hovering above the place where I know her pulse is beating wildly.

"Where?" I ask. "Where should I kiss you?"

I'm too impatient to wait for her to answer before I drag my lips over her pulse. Her hips buck into mine unexpectedly, and it's so good I see fucking stars.

"Oh my God," she says, and I would agree, if my tongue still knew how to form words.

"*Oh my God* is effing right." A voice interrupts from somewhere above us, too far above us, because looking up will mean leaving the sweet skin of her neck, a feat I just don't think I can handle right now. "Who the hell are you, and what have you done to my best friend?"

I've got zero fucks to give about the girl talking, but Dallas obviously cares, because with my arm against her back, I can feel her spine straighten. My fingers slip off her shoulder, and like I really had been locking her into place, she's off of me and standing five feet away in seconds.

I stand too, very slowly and with extreme discomfort.

Dallas is gaping at me, like she's just as shocked by the situation as her friend. I try for an easygoing smile, but I'm sure it looks as pained as I feel. It's pretty much impossible to feel comfortable while having a hard-on and being the subject of intense study by two pretty girls.

I clear my throat awkwardly, and when Dallas still doesn't say anything, I look to her friend. She's the opposite of Dallas— nearly a foot shorter, pixie haircut, olive skin, and completely unreadable. I add, "I'm Carson."

Dallas's friend doesn't smile. Instead, she turns to Dallas and asks, "Are you okay? I saw that hottie you went off with inside, and you weren't with him. I was worried."

I think of the guy on the balcony, and the surge of bitterness I feel is so powerful I can taste it on my tongue.

"That *hottie*," I begin, "is a tool." God, I'm even talking like her. "Be glad she wasn't with that asshole." There. That was better.

The girl's hair is barely longer than mine, but when she tosses her head, she somehow has the same effect as if she were tossing a mane as long as Dallas's. She fixes her gaze on me and says, "Hey, *Romeo*, I was talking to *Dallas*. Not you."

Emerald eyes meet mine, and we both burst out laughing. Whatever tension had been wracking Dallas disappears with her laugh. I stop before she does, just watching, enjoying the way the Shakespeare mention makes her face light up.

"What? What did I say?" her friend asks.

Dallas takes a step closer, hesitates, and then crosses to stand beside me.

"It's okay, Stella. I'm fine. Promise."

Stella's gaze flicks back and forth between the two of us.

"You sure? How much have you had to drink?"

"None."

Stella's eyebrows raise, and some kind of silent conversation passes between the two of them. When Dallas faces me, her expression, like her friend's, is hard to read. I miss her openness.

"I should probably go," she says. And unlike when we were kissing, this time I can tell she means it.

Part of me is relieved that one of us is able to step away, but I'm both ashamed it wasn't me and disappointed that it was her.

I shove my hands into my pockets. "Okay, Daredevil."

Her friend snorts. "Daredevil?"

Dallas doesn't look away from me, and neither of us bother replying.

"It was nice to meet you, Carson." She holds out her hand, and I take it. A handshake isn't exactly what I want, but I'll take it. She smiles, and I smile, and I can't resist using her hand to tug her a little closer.

I lean down to her ear, wishing I could talk to her without her friend watching us like we're the best new reality show on TV, wishing she would be the Dallas she was ten minutes ago. "You're not going to make me beg, are you?"

She pulls back to look me in the eye, and her lips are distractingly close to mine.

"For what?"

Even though she definitely kissed me back, I still find myself anxious to ask, "Your number?"

"Oh." Her face falls for half a second before she smiles, and that one second of disappointment undoes me. *What does she want? And more important . . . how do I give it to her?* "Right. Give me your phone."

I hand it over and wait while she programs her number in. Her friend Stella is still there watching silently, and this is quickly becoming the strangest night of my life. But when she hands back my phone and our fingers brush, I know I wouldn't have it any other way.

She smiles and turns to go, but I can't resist pulling her back one more time. This time I'm less controlled and when I whisper into her ear, my lips brush against her skin. Her fingers wrap around my forearm and squeeze.

"One more thing I'm willing to beg for, Daredevil."

The goodbye kiss she gives me is short and chaste and only lands on the corner of my lips, but I feel it all the way down to my knees.

I watch her leave, and am disappointed when her friend is the one to look back over her shoulder and not Dallas. They don't head back inside, but instead slip through a gate on the side of the house. I stay outside for a few minutes, but then decide that I have no interest in sticking around now that Dallas is gone.

There's a sliding door at the back of the house, and when I open it and step back into the noisy house, I pull out my phone.

I start scrolling through my contacts while I meander through the crowds looking for a familiar face to say my goodbyes. I reach the Ds, and *Dallas* isn't there.

My stomach falls, and my feet pull to a halt in the middle of the room. I shouldn't be this devastated by a girl not giving me her number, but I also don't know how to block out the feeling that's spinning through me. I go to shove my phone back in my pocket when I see it.

Daredevil.

It's two names down from where I had expected to see Dallas's name, and the spinning sensation in my chest doesn't lessen, but spirals even faster.

"McClain, why are you grinning like an idiot?"

I look up, and there's Levi Abrams on the couch with a petite brunette sitting in his lap. Silas Moore and a few other teammates are with him, and my grin falls.

The world wastes no time in reminding me exactly why I shouldn't be getting distracted by girls or parties or anything like this.

"Wouldn't you like to know, Abrams." I look around at the rest of the team members. The new coach is strict about inappropriate conduct, so I'm surprised there are this many players here and at how wasted they all are. They take shit for granted . . . things

I would kill for. But I'm used to feeling that way. Growing up poor makes you hyperaware of all the other things people take for granted. But in this case . . . it might eventually work to my advantage. Let them rest on their laurels. It makes it that much easier for me to catch up. "I'm heading out. See you guys at practice."

I hear some calls at my back, some asking, some daring me to stay and party with them. I just wave a hand and head for the door.

And maybe I'm borrowing trouble, but as I head for my truck, I type out a quick text.

> *Still thinking of that list.*

Dallas's reply comes a minute later, and I settle in behind the steering wheel, not bothering to turn the key in the ignition.

Who is this? Carson?

> *I hope there are not any other guys out there making a list like this one.*

And if there are?

> *I'll just have to make sure my list is better.*

Maybe I should make a list of my own.

> *Maybe we should make one together.*

Maybe we will.

Chapter 6

Dallas

Stella kept me out late again on Saturday (thankfully not at another party, but at the coffee place just off campus). Even after we turned out the lights for bed, we stayed up a while longer talking across the small space that separated our twin beds. Because of that, I snooze two too many times, making me a few minutes late for church on Sunday morning. When I squeeze past Dad sitting in his usual spot at the end of a pew a few rows from the back, his gaze turns steely.

I knock a hymnal off the shelving on the back of the pew, and it thumps against the carpet, drawing even more attention to my late entrance as the youth minister finishes greeting the congregation. Dad shifts, flexing his fists on his knees, and I rush to pick up the book and plop myself down beside him.

That would normally be the end of it. I would sit incredibly still until all the eyes left me, but somehow in my rush to sit down,

I ended up with a few stray strands of hair in my mouth. I claw at my cheeks, trying to find the offending hairs and pull them away.

Dad makes a low grumbling noise that reminds me of a grizzly bear.

I show him my teeth in a grimace barely passable as a smile. If he wants a proper and polite daughter, he shouldn't have spent my childhood dragging me to places where I was predominantly surrounded by men.

I fix my gaze straight ahead, taming my hair and clothes just in time for the youth minister to say, "We're so glad to have you all this morning. Please take a few moments to greet your neighbors and say a warm hello to any new faces."

The pianist and the organist start an upbeat version of "Joyful, Joyful," and I wish that I had managed to be just a few minutes later. Maybe it makes me heartless, but this is my least favorite part of church. Dad and I are immediately inundated with former players and parents of players and teachers. It used to be that they all wanted to stay on good terms with Dad so that their kids would get more playing time. I had hoped that Dad's new job might make us a little less popular, but no luck there.

Dad's all smiles, shaking hands and laughing, his loud voice carrying and no doubt drawing more people toward us. I stand there awkwardly, smiling (horrendously fake) smiles and nodding along like I know a good daughter should. Mostly the men talk to Dad, and the women talk to me since there's no mom to play that role. I get compliments on my hair (which I know is a hot mess because it's hella windy outside) and my outfit (which is lined with wrinkles and smells of Febreze since I just grabbed it off the floor of my dorm room).

And of course . . . there are the questions.

"How's college?"

"Have you settled on a major?"

"How are your classes?"

"How does it feel to be all grown-up?"

Plus a few questions about Dad and the university team, like I know or give a crap about that.

On the surface I'm all *Oh, haha. I'm great. Loving it. Everything's great. Just great. Hah. Hah.* And underneath I'm like *Dear God, why is this hymn SO LONG?*

It's the college inquisition, and it's enough to make any recent graduate vow never to visit home again. Unfortunately for me . . . I don't have that option.

One year. Two, tops. Then I'm getting out of here. I have to.

I shoot Mrs. Dunlap at the piano a desperate look, not just because I want her to speed up, but also because she's one of the few people in this building that I actually want to talk to. In addition to playing the piano during the service and teaching the second-grade Sunday school class, she's been my dance instructor since Dad and I moved here four and a half years ago.

The youth minister steps up to the pulpit once more, and people begin making their way back to their seats. I let out a sigh of relief when he tells us to bow our heads.

I try to listen, but I zone out not long after "Dear Heavenly Father."

There's too much quiet in prayers, too much time for my mind to wander. I think about how miserable it was to roll out of bed this morning and watch Stell go right on snoozing while I struggled to kick-start my day. Then I feel guilty for thinking I'd rather be sleeping during church . . . *during a prayer*, no less. But that only makes me think about the other things I feel guilty for . . . like the seriously hot stranger-danger make-out session I had two nights ago. Then I chastise myself over feeling guilty about something that in the grand scheme of things isn't really that bad. But then the minister says, "Amen," and I concede that while kissing someone isn't *bad*, thinking about it when I'm supposed to be communing with the big guy upstairs *probably* isn't winning me any bonus points.

We stand to sing a hymn, and even though the words are written up on a big screen hanging above the pulpit, I grab a hymnal so that I've got something to do with my hands. I follow along in the book, but don't sing myself. I sound like a hyena on my good days (a hyena in the jaws of a lion on my bad days), and I'm too self-conscious that other people will hear me.

I hear Carson calling me a daredevil, and God, how wrong he was. If I were a daredevil, I would have said screw Dad and auditioned for real dance programs instead of caving to what he thought was best (and what his money provided). I would have found a way to make it all work—the auditioning and the moving and the money. That's what daredevils do. I also wouldn't have run off like a timid preteen when Stella caught us together. As if that weren't pathetic enough, I'd then lied to Stella and told her that maybe I'd had a few drinks after all.

Because, of course, that was the *only* explanation for me doing something fun and out of character like actually hooking up with a guy.

A guy who didn't answer either of the texts I sent him yesterday. Clearly he'd gotten over the fascination he'd had with me on Friday night. Maybe *he'd* been drunk.

I don't know if I always hate myself this much and I never think about it, or if it's a product of the reflection that's inherent in church and religion and being wildly unsuccessful at growing up. Feeling like everyone around me can see the failure written across my forehead certainly doesn't help either.

I sigh, and when Dad shifts next to me I catch him looking at me from the corner of his eye. I can't tell if he's disappointed or worried or annoyed.

Dad really only has two faces: normal and pissed.

And football. Football kind of gets its own expression, though it overlaps with pissed a lot.

Eventually, we return our hymnals to their holding places and take a seat for the sermon. I've given up the pretense of paying attention, choosing instead to doodle little dancers in the margins of the church bulletin.

The preacher calls all the little kids up to the front, where he does a short little minisermon for the kids before sending them out for children's church. It's usually a parallel for the more complex message he'll give the rest of us. And I find myself thinking that church is like my kid's sermon . . . it parallels my life as a whole. I show up, but I'm not in it. I go through the motions, but my mind wanders elsewhere. I dress and behave in the ways I know won't get me in trouble. I get by. I bide my time waiting for the moment when it all ends.

But life isn't church. It isn't one hour during one day in the week. It's everything, and I'm wasting it.

By the time the service ends half an hour later, I'm awash with emotions, anger and guilt and bitterness swallowing up whatever hope I manage to conjure. As soon as the benediction ends, I slip past Dad before he stands, mutter, "Be right back," and flee before he's inundated. As I walk away I hear Mrs. Simmons, whose daughter I went to school with, say, "You know, our youngest is shaping up to be quite the receiver. He's just in eighth grade, but I'm sure he'll make varsity as a freshman. Maybe you'll be seeing him at Rusk in a few years."

I resist the urge to roll my eyes. In Texas, everyone is a wannabe coach. Levi used to have strangers hand him plays they'd drawn up "just in case he wanted to try something new." I pass Levi's parents gathering their things from the second row, where they've sat for as long as I've known them. I smile politely and nod as I go.

It's not their fault their son is a jerk.

Levi stopped coming to church not long after he started college. I should feel guilty over how glad that made me, but I don't. Church always feels a little bit like I'm putting on a show, but with him here it was ten times worse. If I looked at him too much, *of course* I was still madly in love with him. But if I didn't look at him at all, I was madly in love (and heartbroken). It was like living under a microscope.

Breakups are a careful and exhausting dance.

That's exactly what I need. Dance. It clears my mind better than anything else. I stand by the raised little nook that houses the piano and wait for Mrs. Dunlap to finish the postlude. She must feel me there, because she looks away from her sheet music and gives me an overdramatic smile. She presses the keys with a bit more flourish for my benefit, and I lean against the wall humming beneath my breath.

She holds on to the last chords for a long moment, and they ring out in chorus with the organ before the song ends and only the chattering conversations across the hall are left.

"Let me guess." Mrs. D turns on her bench to look at me. "You want the studio?"

"How'd you know?"

She snorts. "Because it's all you want. Always has been."

I know that. And she knows it. Dad still insists I'll want other things if I give them a try. After living in a house for eighteen years with me, you'd think he would know me better than the lady who teaches my dance class a few times a week.

"You have a key," Mrs. Dunlap says. "No reason to drag yourself all the way up here to see little old me."

She gave me a key when I started teaching classes to the younger kids, but I still felt bad about using it without her permission.

"You're not old."

She is. The woman is nearly seventy, but she doesn't look it. She's lithe and slender, and if she'd dye her gray hair, she could probably pass for fifty, if not younger.

"Oh pish. You don't need to suck up to me, child."

I step up on the platform and place a quick kiss on her cheek. "Learn to take a compliment, Mrs. D."

I turn to go, and she calls out, "Says the girl who never thinks anything is good enough."

I blow her a kiss and call back my thanks instead of saying the thought that pops into my head.

Good is never good enough.

One of Dad's mottos. He would frequently tack on, "Good may win games, but great wins titles."

As I walk back toward him, he manages to peel himself away from the leeches, I mean, *parents* surrounding him.

He joins me in the aisle, and we head for the door together.

"Lunch?" he grunts.

I shake my head. "Mrs. Dunlap is going to let me use the studio for a while. I'll just grab something fast after."

"Sure?"

I nod. "Yep."

"Okay."

"Okay."

We don't say another word until we're outside, and I press the button to unlock my car.

"Drive safe," he says, and then climbs into his own truck.

I turn the key in the ignition and mutter, "Good talking to you, Dad."

It takes me ten minutes to get to the studio, a nondescript storefront in a strip mall. Not exactly the height of culture, but it's about all this town has to offer. And it's been good to me. I'm careful to lock the door behind me and keep the lights off in the front so no one thinks we're open. I choose the larger of the two studios and push open the door.

Breathing deep, I take in that indescribable smell of the studio. Sweat. Feet. Rosin wood from the barre. You'd think the smell would be unpleasant, but it's not. It's home.

Dance had started as a babysitting service while Dad had practice. He enrolled me in everything from piano lessons to Little League softball, so that I was occupied while he did his thing. I'm willing to bet he regrets that first dance class he dumped me in all those years ago.

I switch on the light and drop my bag by the door. Slipping off my street shoes, I dig out my lyrical sandals, which Mrs. Dunlap always calls dance paws. They leave my toes free and wrap just under the pad of my foot, giving me a better surface to spin and slide, but still allowing me the flexibility of being almost barefoot.

I pad over to the stereo system, the floor cold against my toes. I press play on the CD that's already in there, and start skipping through the songs, waiting for something to speak to me. I flip past a few hip-hop and pop songs, followed by classical music (only in Mrs. D's dance class would she have Mozart following up "Lady Marmalade").

I flip through about a dozen songs, each time more and more frustrated with a feeling I can't quite name. It's not that I'm angry, though it's close. Sad doesn't quite fit either, even though I can feel hints of that dripping from the edges of whatever it is that's eating at me.

Finally, a song makes me pause. Slow and simple, it starts with a long, low chord and a soft, frenetic beat building beneath. It reminds me of my morning spent at church. Serene on the outside, roiling in the depths.

A voice, smooth and sweet, rings out.

I'm wasted, losing time. I'm a foolish, fragile spine.

Yeah. That sounded like it had enough self-loathing in it to do the trick.

I start the song over and make my way to the center of the floor.

I let the music move me slowly at first, gentle swaying. Then right before the words begin, I burst into movement. I don't bother dancing a routine I already know. There's no challenge in that. It's a battle already won, a feeling already mapped and conquered. No . . . that's not how I like to dance, not like my father plays football with a book of mastered plays, each carefully designed with no room for mistakes. I dance the way musicians play jazz, with improvisation and soul.

It means I always dance alone. Group and coupled dances don't exactly leave much room to play and change as you go along. I'm fine with that, though. I've gotten quite used to being alone. I thrive that way.

I move how the song tells me, cobbling together a series of steps on the fly. Some of them are familiar, stolen from previous routines, while some leap into existence of their own accord, rustling through my body before my mind even bothers to make sense of what my body is doing.

I make mistakes. I build to a move that doesn't match with the song. Sometimes I stand there for a few seconds, not sure what to do next, but miraculously . . . it works with the hesitation of the song, of the lyrics. Because sometimes in life, you just have to stand there and do nothing. Overwhelmed by all the versions of ourselves that exist in our minds—who we want to be, who we should be, who we're not, and who we are—it's a jungle that can ensnare your feet and confuse your eyes. But sometimes if you stand still, all those things will snap back into place like a rubber band. And if you can get past the sting, you can keep moving, not quite whole, but held together for the moment.

That's what the dance becomes for me. All the versions of myself. I move toward one corner, playing the perfect daughter, dancing with all the moments I've spent in bleachers burning behind my eyelids. Then I drag myself back to center. I take off toward the opposite corner. I throw myself into the highest leap I can manage, drawing on all the most complex combinations I know. That's the me that doesn't hesitate or question. That's the me that dreams. But then mournfully, I pull myself back to center. I keep dancing—the me that placates Stella in order to keep her while simultaneously burning with jealousy, the me that strives to be better than everyone else at dance and school and everything within my control, the me without a mom, that's too afraid to be feminine or emotional, too afraid I won't know how or worse that I will and the emotion will consume me, the me that jumped off a balcony and kissed a boy I barely knew just so he'd call me a dare-devil and I could pretend for a moment that he spoke the truth. I cover every inch of the studio, and when I drag myself back to the center of the room for the final time, it's on my hands and knees, slicked with sweat, my version of tears.

I lie flat on my back as the stereo plays "Meet Virginia." It's one of Mrs. D's favorites to use in warm-ups, and it's already well into the middle of the song.

Pulls her hair back as she screams,

"I don't really wanna live this life."

I didn't notice as I danced when the music switched, but I close my eyes and breathe, enjoying the familiarity of the song as it pulls me home, drags me back to center.

Back to me.

I don't know that dancing fixes anything. I don't feel magically happy because of it. My problems don't disappear when the music ends. But I understand life better when I dance, and understanding is half the fight of surviving.

Chapter 7

Carson

My Monday begins bright and early with a six A.M. workout. I manage to make it through most of the morning without picking up my phone. Almost to lunch. That's better than yesterday.

I'm sitting in my environmental science class, but I gave up taking notes three minutes ago, and instead I'm staring at my old text messages, wishing I could reply to the texts Dallas sent me Saturday.

Getting to know her had seemed harmless on Friday, but when I woke up the next day and skipped my usual morning run to wait around until it was an acceptable hour to text her . . . that's when I realized what a monumentally bad idea contacting her again was.

I'd dragged myself out of the apartment for a run a few hours later than normal, when the sun was already breaking across the sky. As I mourned the cooler morning temperatures I usually had, I vowed that I wouldn't contact her.

It was just a party hookup. I needed to leave it at that.

And yet here I am, ignoring a lecture in favor of looking at her last text.

How's that list coming?

Bad. Very bad. Me, that is. Not the list. My list was still growing despite that vow I made on Saturday. How am I supposed to pay attention to a lecture over sustainability when my mind is full of all the mental images that text conjures?

I'd signed up for this environmental class because it was supposedly one of the easiest science credits, but it wouldn't be a breeze if I didn't pay attention at all. For me, especially. Nothing about school came easily to me.

But *that text*. I bite back a groan at the thought of her somewhere, maybe on her bed in her dorm, making a list of her own, contemplating the things she wants to do with me. It is entirely possible her list consists of things like going to dinner or a movie or for a romantic walk.

But there is also the possibility her list is a little more *focused*. A little more like mine, and if I'm not careful people are going to think I'm *really* passionate about the environment.

As soon as the professor dismisses us, I'm on my feet and heading for the door, and I know I'm gonna have to borrow someone else's notes to catch up on what I missed today. Not a great way to start out the semester.

A run. That should help. I have a two-hour break for lunch on Mondays, Wednesdays, and Fridays, enough to give me time to eat and join at least part of the one-o'clock workout if I want. I don't have to since I do the morning one, but it pays to put in the extra time, especially while the coaches are around to see you. Or that's what I keep telling myself anyway. If I swing by the student center and grab a couple wraps to go, that will give me even more time.

That's the plan, until I walk out of the environmental science and geology building at the same time that Dallas is walking in.

I grind to a halt in the doorway, and my grip is so hard on the doorknob, I'm surprised I don't snap it off.

She speaks first.

"Hey."

I clear my throat. It's a sign of weakness, but I can't help it. Ignoring her text message is one thing . . . Ignoring her in person isn't something I can (or want) to do.

"Hey." It comes out quietly, so low that I don't even know if she heard me.

"Move, douche-bag! You're blocking the door."

I step out of the way, but that brings me closer to Dallas. She moves too, letting the line of people behind me exit first.

I stand there in silence for a few moments, fighting the urge to look at her, and I feel like such a fucking coward.

"Listen, I'm sorry I—"

She cuts me off. " Remember that time you promised not to be a tool? You already screwed that up, but keep that promise in mind while you formulate whatever excuse you're making up right now."

Ouch. "I deserve that."

It occurs to me in that moment that whatever reasons I have for staying away from her aren't as good as the reasons for why I want to be around her. I *like* her. I need people in my life to tell it to me straight. I need a friend. Friends, really, but I've got to start somewhere. Life is a balance, and mine tends to fall heavily toward work with too little play. And of all the people I've met, she's the only one I've met that could actually be that kind of friend.

"I am sorry I didn't answer your text. I wanted to." She'd never let me hear the end of it if she knew how often I'd typed out a reply only to delete it a few seconds later. "I just wasn't sure how to answer it."

"You didn't seem to have any problem texting me Friday night."

"Friday night, I wasn't really thinking straight."

She scoffs and rolls her eyes, bolting for the door even though there's still a steady stream of people exiting.

I grab her elbow and pull her back. Her breasts brush my chest for the barest second, and I fight the urge to suck in a breath. Her glare is ferocious, but I don't drop her arm. I know she'll be gone in two seconds flat if I do.

"I've got a lot of shit on my plate right now, Dallas. And I'm doing a piss-poor job of handling it." Part of me thinks I should just man up and ask her to dinner. I could take a page from her book and tell her up front that I like her, want to date her even, but can't handle a relationship. Maybe she'll appreciate that. Or maybe she'll see me as a massive waste of time. The other part of me knows that's a terrible idea. Friends is all I can afford to be right now, but if I start by throwing out the *I just want to be friends* bomb, she might just slap me. After all, I was the one who pulled us firmly out of the friend zone on Friday night. I sigh and continue. "This isn't the best time to talk about this, but I *do* want to talk about it. Are you free tonight?"

She hesitates and looks toward the doorway, which is now clear.

Before I can think too much about it, I take her jaw and pull her back to look at me again. "No excuses, I promise. I just want to tell you what I'm thinking. Honestly. And then we'll figure out where we go from there."

Damn. I shouldn't have used the word *we*. That probably sends the wrong message, but her lips twist in that distracting way that she does when she's thinking something through, and I don't say anything else.

"Tonight?" She still looks unsure, but her shoulders have relaxed a little.

"I'll come to your dorm. We can go for a walk."

"It will have to be late. I've got plans for dinner. I should be back on campus by nine, though."

My stomach twists, and I tell myself that it's because I'm hungry, not because I'm bothered by the idea of her having dinner plans. I'm the one that's going to drop the friend bomb. Maybe.

"Nine thirty, then. What dorm?"

"Schaefer."

I still haven't let go of her face, and I force my hand down by my side.

"I'll be there."

I take a quick step back and nod before I turn.

"Carson?" she calls after me.

I swallow and then turn back. "Yeah?"

"Think you can manage to text me when you arrive?"

She's smiling, but the bite in her words lets me know she's only half teasing.

I grin back in lieu of an answer, but as I walk away, I pull out my phone. Unlocked, it automatically comes up to her text message, since it was the last thing I looked at.

How's that list coming?

Finally, I reply.

> *I thought about it all weekend. And through most of my last class.*

I shove the thing back in my pocket and am both grateful and disappointed when she doesn't reply. I'm sending mixed messages. I know that. But that's because I'm a little mixed up myself.

Maybe my run will sort me out.

The athletic complex is on the far side of campus, and it takes me a good twenty minutes to walk there. Normally it only takes fifteen, but I stopped in at the student activity center to grab some food to go after all.

I stop by the locker room to change. There's one dude asleep on the couch when I come in, probably waiting on the one-o'clock workout, otherwise it's empty. Most of the room is done in the deep red that the school affectionately calls *Rusk red*. On the far wall is a painting of the school mascot, a wildcat that has to be at least ten feet long. Beside it in big, bold letters it says, "Bleed Rusk Red." The locker room is a huge step up from the one I knew in high school and the one I spent last year in at Westfield, that's for damn sure. It's big and newly remodeled with plenty of space and amenities. Rusk might not have much in the way of a win-loss record, but they aren't hurting for money, not with how much tuition at this damn place costs.

That's another part of the plan. Between what my parents and I have saved up and financial aid, I have enough to go three semesters at Rusk. That gives me this season and the next to make myself an integral enough part of the team to warrant a scholarship if they want me to stay.

It's damn near impossible to play college ball, go to class, and work a job. I busted my ass while I was at Westfield, saving every damn penny I could. My parents are doing the same. We have our ranch, but our area of Texas has been in a drought so long that there is no decent grass left for the livestock, and feed prices are sky-high. We had to sell more of our animals last year than ever before just to pay for everything we needed for upkeep. And considering they were underfed, we didn't get nearly as good a price on them as we needed. Our only other income is from the store where we sell and repair tractors and other agricultural equipment. And the drought means no one else has the money to go around buying new equipment. It's been a lean couple of years, but still my parents have managed to put some away.

I just hope it will be enough.

I should call them soon, but I'm not up to talking to Dad about *the plan*. And with all the money issues and the fact that Granny is in worse shape than she's ever been, I'm swamped with guilt every time we talk. I should be there helping. The only thing worse than not being there to help is the thought that I might fail and all our planning will have been for nothing.

Goddamn. My mind is a mess today.

I change clothes quickly and head into the weight room. I catch sight of Coach Harrison, the defensive coordinator, along with two grad assistants, through the glass window to the coaches' office. I raise a hand in greeting, and then head for a treadmill. There's only a handful of other players in the room, as most of them come in the morning. One's last name is Salter, but I've only spoken to him once, and the rest I don't know. I've been working out with the team for several weeks now, but with over one hundred players on the roster, there are still plenty that I haven't gotten to know.

There's a trainer supervising as we work out, but otherwise we're on our own. The coaches are only allowed to formally train us for a set number of hours a day; anything above that we have to do on our own.

But even if the coaches aren't leading the extra workouts and they're not "mandatory," they're not exactly optional either.

Another part of my plan? Put in more work than anyone else.

I turn the treadmill up to a brisk run and set about doing just that. I set my timer for half an hour and run hard, until the sweat runs off me in rivers.

I like the quiet that comes with running. As the sweat runs

off, so does everything else, and I feel lighter when I'm through. I've always been this way. If I'm working—whether it's out in the fields back home or on green stadium grass or here in the weight room—that's the only time when my head goes silent.

That, and when I've got Dallas sprawled across my lap.

I run an extra ten minutes for that thought because *clearly* my head didn't go quiet enough. If my schedule allowed, I'd run several times a day just to hold on to this feeling for a little longer.

When I'm done, I take a seat on a bench, using a towel to wipe at my face and arms.

"Need a spot?"

I look up. The guy standing next to me is one of the team managers, I think. He's got blond, curly hair, and is tall, but a little too thin to be a player. I vaguely recall seeing someone with a similar build setting up before practice a few days ago. I look behind me and realize I've taken a seat at the bench press rather than just a normal bench.

After a moment, I shrug and say, "Sure."

I did lower body this morning, so I can get away with some time spent on my arms.

"I'm Ryan Blake, one of the student managers," he says, confirming my suspicions.

I lift my chin in lieu of hello and reply, "Carson McClain."

"I know. You're here almost as much as I am." He slides around behind the bar, and I hold back a smile at his statement. At least one person has noticed; hopefully the right people will notice next.

I help him load weights on the sides of the bar, and then lie back against the bench. "You like being manager?" I ask, pulling the bar off the rack and steadying my grip.

He answers as I start in on my reps, keeping his hands poised to catch the bar should I falter.

I won't.

"Sure. It's my first year, so I haven't gotten to travel with the team yet or anything. I imagine that will make up for all the dirty work."

I wrinkle my nose, blowing out a calm breath as I push the bar up. I can only imagine the kind of dirty work he does. And with the way our locker room smells sometimes, I definitely don't envy the dude.

"I'm hoping to do this for a year or two and then jump to student trainer. I'm a kinesiology major."

I've still got the rest of the year to declare my major, but kinesiology is definitely one I'm considering. I'm pretty sure I can't hack the math and science classes it requires, though.

I lift with Ryan for the next half hour, moving through a few other stations. He sticks with me even when I don't need a spot. He's good about knowing when to talk, when my arms are tired and the distraction helps me think past the weight. But he also knows when to shut up, when I need all my focus to finish out that very last rep. And as crazy as it sounds, in the space of thirty minutes, he becomes my closest friend at Rusk.

Besides Dallas.

Sitting at the weight machine, working my lats, I pull down a little too hard on the bar, and then let it go too fast, and a loud bang follows.

Ryan raises an eyebrow at me. "Now, what did that machine ever do to you?"

I grip the narrow bar and pull it down more smoothly this time.

"Wrong place, wrong thought, wrong time." I need to leave all thoughts of Dallas at the door. I'm doing a shit job of that, though.

He nods but doesn't ask questions, and I'm glad for it. I increase the weight so that it takes more of my concentration. I've hit my stride by the time a gruff voice barks, "Blake!" from the direction of the coaches' office.

We both turn to see Coach Cole leaning out of the doorway. I focus on staying steady, but the head coach is only looking at Ryan, not me.

"Yes, sir?"

Coach Cole's looks are as intimidating as his background. He's tall, about the same height as me, but he's as thick around as one of the hundred-year-old oak trees in the campus commons. In twenty-two years of coaching, he holds seven state championships and nearly double that many regional championships. And he has a history of taking failing programs and turning them into powerhouses in astonishingly short time frames. Hence his appointment as the head coach here, where despite having a program with decent financial backing and solid recruiting, the team has had six losing seasons in a row.

"We good to go?" Coach asks Ryan.

"Yes, sir. All set up."

Coach's eyes stray to mine then, and though they stay there for several long seconds, I see nothing in them.

He leaves, and I take that as my cue to wrap up my additional workout. I use my towel to wipe off the machine first, followed by my face.

"Thanks for the spot, man," I tell Ryan. I don't thank him for the company too, even though I am grateful.

"Sure thing."

He disappears to do whatever it is managers spend their time doing, and I head for the locker room. It's half-full when I enter, with more players streaming in by the second. I stand at my cubby, rubbing at my face with my towel. My muscles are fatigued, and I think maybe I should have taken it a little easier today. My shirt is already soaked with sweat as I pull on my shoulder pads.

I've been tuning out the conversation in the room, but raucous laughter draws my attention.

"Dude, she shot you down so hard I felt it out in the hallway."

There's a group of guys gathered around Levi Abrams as he razzes his friend Silas about something. One of them pipes up to add, "Yeah, Moore. I was downstairs, and I felt you crash and burn." Silas slugs the guy in the shoulder, but doesn't seem too bothered by it.

"I would have had her if it weren't for Abrams. She hates you so much, she blew me off just for talking with you."

Abrams shrugs. "What can I say? I'm a heartbreaker."

"Could you get her back?" one of the other guys asks. "Before Moore, that is?"

Silas laughs so hard, he sounds like he's on the verge of choking. He pulls off his shirt, following the rest of the team as they change from street clothes into their workout gear. "No fucking way," he says to Abrams. "That girl is likely to break your dick off if you come within two feet of her."

"You, my friend, underestimate the power of first love."

Silas shakes his head. "You're just asking to get your ass handed to you by Coach, man. You got lucky first time around when she didn't say anything; no way you'll get that lucky a second time."

"It has nothing to do with luck," Abrams says. "Coach loves me, and so does she, even if she doesn't want to admit it."

"When I sleep with her, and trust me, I will, QB, you're stocking my fridge with beer for a month."

Abrams surveys his friend, and then shrugs. "Sure. I'll take that bet." Silas grins and a few of the surrounding guys laugh and cheer, egging him on. Abrams adds, "Because it's never going to happen."

"What if one of us gets to her first?" another guy joins in, blond and heavyset, one of the defensive linemen.

Abrams surveys the bulky guy and says, "Carter, if you somehow manage to work a miracle and sleep with her before either of us, I'll stock your fucking fridge for a year."

The locker room descends into laughter, and the topic falls away, and I wonder which poor coach's daughter they're targeting. We've technically got nine coaches on staff. I don't know any of them well enough to know which ones have kids our age, but I'm fine being left out of that particular piece of information.

In fact, I wish I were in a different part of the locker room.

It would be better for my focus if my cubby weren't so close to Abrams and Moore.

Coach comes in not long after, and I wonder what would have happened if he'd come in a few minutes earlier.

"Listen up!" He doesn't really need to yell. The team has a sort of sixth sense for when Coach enters the room, and everyone was already quiet. But his loud voice echoes around the room, and it makes him that much more intimidating. "As you know, we're cutting practice a little short today."

Some idiot behind me has the nerve to cheer, but from the "Oof!" that follows, I'm guessing someone already shut him up.

"Hot date tonight, Coach?" Abrams asks.

"Shut your mouth, kid," he growls, but I can tell there's no heat behind the words, not like there would be if someone besides his QB had said it.

"I might be giving you all the gift of a shorter practice, but I still expect there to be some blood, sweat, tears, and vomit left on my field today."

Damn. I have a sneaking suspicion that I'm going to regret that extra workout I just squeezed in with Ryan. When he tells us to wear our pads, I know we're in trouble. When we head out onto the field, a groan cycles back through the team as they spill out of the hallway.

Mat drills.

Or as they like to call it at Rusk, *a bleeding day*. I know they have them a lot during spring training, but the only time I experienced it was during my tryout for the team. Split into smaller groups,

the team rotates through a series of stations, each one with a specific drill designed to make us miserable. If any group is too slow
moving to their next station, the entire team starts over.

After my taste of it at tryouts, I didn't stand, sit, walk, or *sleep*
without aching for nearly three days.

Coach's smile is the stuff nightmares are made of.

"Well then, gentlemen. Let's get started."

Chapter 8

Dallas

It's Dad's birthday, and we're going out to dinner to celebrate. I had planned to wait for him in my car, as I had no desire to venture into practice, but here I am heading off to find him anyway.

I skipped lunch to squeeze in some extra time in the studio, and even though Dad said he'd be wrapping up practice early, I don't trust him to actually stick to his word. My grumbling stomach pulls me out of my car, but my stubborn pride is what keeps me walking into the athletic complex.

As Levi said at the party, I'm here; he's here. We definitely won't be starting fresh, but I won't be falling all over myself to avoid him either. College doesn't have to suck because I'm sharing it with my ex and my dad—that frat party taught me that. I just have to take the good in with the bad and hope the good comes out on top.

That's my plan for the meeting tonight with Carson, too.

So he pissed me off. (And made me confused and annoyed and self-conscious and a little bit hurt.) That doesn't mean I have to completely shut down. That's how the old me reacted after everything with Levi. That's how I've always reacted with anything emotional. I can't feel pain if I don't let myself feel anything at all.

But I promised myself that things would be different in college. I'm starting over. And that means I can't keep living the same way, afraid that everything is going to break me. I survived growing up without a mom. I survived a broken heart. I survived my first frat party and a stupid football player's attempt to get me into bed just for kicks.

That's why I'd decided in my little lunchtime dance session after my run-in with Carson that whatever he had to say, I could forgive him. Or understand. Or whatever. I'm not going to run away from the first real connection I've felt in years just because he didn't text me back for a couple days.

I've spent too much time pretending, too much time on the outside, too much time feeling spineless. This time . . . I'm going after what I want.

I hear a whistle blow as I walk down the hallway that leads out onto the field. Tugging my messenger bag higher on my shoulder, I continue out onto the springy grass searching for my dad.

I pause, overwhelmed with the number of guys practicing and just how freaking *big* they are.

Toto, we're not in high school anymore.

The players and coaches are scattered all over the field in small groups, all of them doing something different while a coach stands over them yelling. Normally, I would say that my dad would be easy to find. He's the loudest person I've ever met in my life, but among all the coaches yelling and the players grunting and yelling back, it's a barely controlled chaos. I walk along the perimeter, searching for Dad.

There are guys doing ladder drills, intimidating and tiring, but I like to think I'm quick enough on my feet that I could give most of them a run for their money. Not so with most of the other stuff I see. There's one group of guys facing a set of hurdles, jumping over each one leapfrog style instead of using the form you see at track meets. There's a group with guys crashing into one another whenever the coach says go, growling and trying to take their opponent down. Another set is doing monkey rolls, my favorite drill to watch because it's just so damn impressive (and entertaining). Three guys all start out lying on their stomachs beside one another. In turns, they throw themselves up or roll across the grass, so it looks like they're being juggled by large, invisible hands.

But I catch sight of Dad at the far end of the practice field. He has two lines of guys set up to form a narrow corridor, and while one player runs through carrying the ball, they all attempt to make him fumble.

Apparently Levi did just that, because I can hear Dad tearing him a new one from over here. "I don't give a damn if you're tired or bleeding or about to pass out on my field, Abrams. You don't drop the damn ball. You're the QB. You protect that ball like it's the only one you have, because it just might be if I see it hit the ground one more time."

I wince. Nothing like the threat of castration to brighten up your day.

"Again!"

Levi runs the gauntlet again, and the players are none too gentle as they try to strip the ball away, probably by Dad's order. This time, Levi holds on to the ball. Dad sends him through a few more times, and when he's satisfied, he moves on to the next player.

"McClain, you're up!"

The guy on the end takes the ball from Levi, who fills his post as one of the last members of the gauntlet. The new guy tucks the ball close, keeps his shoulders hunched, and speeds through the middle, holding tight to the ball.

"Again. Faster."

The guy had already appeared faster than Levi to my eyes, but maybe he's a running back. It would make sense for him to be faster.

He turns around, runs back through the gauntlet, his feet even quicker this time.

Dad runs him again and again, pushing him harder each time, and the guy holds up.

Dad sounds angry, but he's not. He wears this thoughtful expression on his face, and I can tell whatever he's thinking . . . it's big. He's pleased.

I may not give a crap about football, but I know my dad well enough to know when he's excited about something, when he's inspired. I like to think it's the same look I get on my face when

I'm choreographing a routine, and my body seems to know instinctively what move should come next. I only wish he could see the correlation, see that dance does for me what football does for him.

Instead, he just sees a waste of time and money for a career he doesn't think I'll ever have. I know, logically, I know that he's just worried about me, and this is how it manifests, but that doesn't stop the part of me that hopes and dreams from hating him a little.

As I'm coming up closer to Dad, he asks, "Are you tired, McClain?"

"No, sir," the guy barks back.

"You look tired."

"No, sir."

"Tired men drop the football. Tired men make mistakes. Are you tired?"

"No, sir!"

"Then do it again. Keep going until I say stop."

Even I feel sorry for the dude. He's done everything Dad asked, and done it well enough to actually impress my father (not an easy feat), and still he won't let up. But that's an aspect to my father's personality with which I am intimately familiar.

"Geez, Dad. If this is how you like to spend your birthday, maybe we should skip dinner and you could just yell at people as they walk by. Maybe chase some mailmen. Chew on a bone or two."

Dad whirls around, and he has his football expression on—

eyebrows pulled low and close together, jaw clenched, eyes even beadier than normal. He looks at me for a few long moments before I see him begin to shake off his practice persona.

With a frown, he steps up beside me and places a kiss on my forehead that's a not-so-distant cousin to a head butt.

"Am I running late?" he asks.

"Only a little."

He nods and then blows the whistle, ending the players' agony. I shoot his last punching bag, number twelve, a quick smile, and he drops the ball.

It just slips right out of his hand, bounces twice, and then rolls a few feet away.

Luckily, Dad's attention is elsewhere, or his brain might actually implode due to anger. I raise my eyebrows and glance toward the ground, and number twelve picks the thing up so fast you'd think his life depended on it. Which, honestly, it kinda does.

I walk back and out of the way as the players jog over to circle around Dad. There are so many of them that I have to resist the urge to run to avoid getting swallowed up in the crowd. They take a knee, and I lean against the wall nearby.

I feel eyes on me, too many eyes, but it takes only a clearing of my Dad's throat to redraw all of their focus. I fidget, crossing my legs and studying my toes.

Dad starts in on his wrap-up, his familiar rumbling voice carrying across the field with very little effort.

"You're getting stronger," he begins. "Quicker. Better." I can see the team collectively straighten up under his praise. "But it's not enough."

Dad is inhumanly good at that—building you up just to knock you down a peg or two.

"How many games did you win last year?"

No one answers for several long seconds, then Dad turns on Levi, who is kneeling right next to him, facing in my direction.

"How many games did your team win, Abrams?"

Levi's jaw goes stone hard, and a little warmth of pleasure uncurls in my belly to see him so agitated.

"Three, sir."

"Three," my dad repeats. Then, a little quieter, he says the number a second time. It's the second time that makes a few players drop their heads. Not Levi, though. He's staring at Dad in an angry way that makes me dislike him even more. As if I needed another reason.

"You are better than three," my dad says. "You were last year too, but there's a gap between your potential and your playing. Every second you push yourself on this field, every weight you strain to lift, every time you sit down to study plays or film, we're closing that gap. But we will only completely close that gap as a team. I can't will it closed, and a team isn't meant to be carried by one or two individuals. If even one of you doesn't pull your weight, it won't work." Dad paused and looked around the circle of players. "Don't be the gap on this team. Be the person who fills it."

I know Dad's talking about sports and training and all that stuff I don't care about, but I can't help but hear his words through the filter of our lives. There is a gap in our house. Maybe it's the mom I never knew. Maybe it's the words we never say. Or maybe it's both of us. Maybe there's a gap *in each of us* so big that we can't get past it to fill the one between us. Maybe we'll never fill it.

Well, isn't that just depressing?

You know you're growing up when you start to see more inevitabilities than possibilities.

Looking for a distraction, I scan the circle of players as Dad keeps talking. My eyes sweep over Silas, who looks at me with a carefully blank expression. I don't let myself jerk my eyes away like I want to, and instead I keep looking past him like he's any other player. I pull my gaze along, but I'm not really seeing much until ...

I freeze.

Slowly, I let my gaze backtrack to find another pair of eyes on me.

Not Silas. Not Levi.

Carson.

His hair is dark with sweat and sticking up as though he'd run his hands through it. He's kneeling, his body directed toward my father, but his eyes are fixed on me. His jaw clenches tight, and his blue eyes look like steel from here. His knuckles are curled tightly around the face mask on his helmet, and I can see the way he's pushing down on the helmet, bearing it into the ground.

He's angry.

And I feel all my earlier hope for the future, all my determination, just melt away. The gap in me stretches so big in that moment, flowing out from between my ribs and pushing up through my pores, that I forget to feel angry, too.

For a moment anyway.

Dad dismisses the team, and Carson stands. Then the fury rolls in like a storm, filling the empty with emotions too raw to put a name to. I don't wait for Dad. I don't wait for anything.

I turn and start walking off the field, wishing I could stomp my feet hard enough to make the earth shake as much as my hands. There is thunder in my chest, and I know a scream won't release it. Not this time.

It's stupid. So stupid.

He's just a guy I spent one night with.

I should not be this upset.

I should not . . . I should not have been stupid enough to let him mean anything more than that. I mean, Jesus, the guy even ignored me all weekend! So why do I feel like my ribs are trying to curl in on themselves?

Stupid. I'm chanting the word in my head as I grind my teeth and escape out of the complex and into my little maroon sedan. I turn the key in the ignition, releasing a small sob only when I know the roar of the engine will cover it.

I slap the steering wheel, but that doesn't do the trick, so I punch it instead. The car gives a small whine, in lieu of a honk, and my knuckles agree in silent misery.

Furious, I put the car in drive and take off, not knowing where I'm going. I just know that I'm on the verge of losing control in a way that I don't ever let myself. I try to just shut it off like I normally do, like I promised myself only hours ago I was going to stop doing, but for whatever reason, I can't.

Yell, always. Scream, usually. Throw something? Frequently.

Cry? Never.

I turn the music up so loud that it actually hurts my ears. I drive and drive too fast until I'm past the university bubble, past the city limits sign, and eventually . . . past the danger of crying.

Thirty minutes outside of town, I pull over at an empty rest stop. I sit in my chair, eyes closed, and I dance in my head. I imagine what it would feel like to put movement to this anger, this frustration so deep and black that it's like a creature tearing through my bloodstream. Part of me is tempted to get out of the car and do it for real, right there in the sprawling Texas countryside. I choreograph a dance that's hard, maybe too hard for me to actually perform, but when I see it in my mind, I leap higher than ever and throw myself across the dance floor with no thought to whether it will hurt. There are no pretty pointed toes or soft, arched arms. There's no build, no highs and lows. I imagine someone like Dad screaming in my ear as I dance the whole thing at full speed, as I drag myself across the floor until I just can't anymore. There is desperation and pain and when it's over, I'm emptier than I've ever been.

And I didn't even dance it for real.

I get out of the car then, not to dance but to sit on the hood of my car and stare up at the bruised night sky. They say Texas has a big sky. But I've always thought out here where there are no buildings and no people and you can see for miles in every direction, it actually feels like the sky isn't big enough. Like it's been stretched out over the land, and just barely reaches each horizon. At any minute it might peel back or tear right open having finally been stretched just a little too far.

So Carson plays football.

So he plays football *for my dad.*

It's just another truth to face, and I've had plenty of practice with that.

I just have to accept that whatever childish, hopeful fancies I'd been imagining about how things might play out between us . . . that's all they are. Imaginings. He won't want to take the chance of dating me, not when it could endanger his spot on the team. And even if he does, I've already been down that road. And though some things about the next four years are doomed to be repeats of high school, this doesn't have to be one of them. I won't let it.

Hell, maybe he already knew. Maybe he's friends with Levi and Silas, and he just did a better job of fooling me.

I take several gasping breaths, all of a sudden in danger of crying again. I breathe and breathe and breathe and wrap my arms tight around my middle like my limbs are a corset, squeezing me in tight. I hold myself together by sheer force of will.

When I climb back into my car some time later, it's just past eight o'clock, and it's only then that I remember my dad. With a groan, I dig for my phone in my purse.

Thirteen missed calls.

What must Dad be thinking? I'd run out of there with no word, no excuse, nothing. It's been *hours.*

I unlock my phone, and my jaw drops.

There are thirteen missed calls all right. But only three are from Dad.

The rest are from Carson.

Chapter 9

Dallas

Dad's truck is missing and the windows are all dark when I pull up outside our house. I slap my hand against the steering wheel, now only angry with myself. There's only one other place I know that he could be, so I head back to the university and the athletic complex.

Sure enough, his truck is there, along with half a dozen other vehicles. My stomach churns as I climb out of my car and head for the entrance.

Dad might not always be the best father, but I'm just as awful at being a daughter.

Still not familiar enough with the layout of the building to know exactly where I'm going, I head down a brightly lit, sterile white hallway, reading the plaques beside the doors. Toward the back of the building, I reach an open door and hear noises coming from the inside.

I step inside an expansive weight room, painted in Rusk University red, and then immediately wish I hadn't.

The room is empty except for two people.

One of whom is on the short list of people I would cut off my hand not to have to talk to at the moment.

Silas stands about ten meters from me, a bar filled with an impossible number of weights laid across his shoulders. He bends his knees in a squat, his face colored red with effort, and his eyes meet mine.

"You all right, pretty girl?"

His words are surprisingly devoid of flirtation, and they smack of something almost like concern. I reach a hand up to pat at my hair, wondering if he can tell by looking at me that I just had a breakdown of Britney proportions.

"Is my dad around?"

It's the trainer spotting him who answers. "He's in the office, I think. Through that door and then to the right."

I nod and head off in the direction he pointed. There's a door propped open, but the lights are dimmed inside. My feet stutter to a stop when I see Carson seated on the couch, watching game film. He has one ankle balanced on his other knee, a notebook perched on his leg, and a pencil tapping pensively against his lip. The sight of him stirs something in my chest.

I guess I didn't empty myself quite as well as I thought I had.

As if he feels my eyes on him, he glances away from the television briefly, his eyes darting back to stay when he registers who I am. He sits up straighter, dropping his propped-up foot to the floor, and the notebook follows with a thud. He's showered and changed into sweats, and I can see the number twelve printed just below his hip.

Number twelve.

I suck in a breath. The thought of him out there on that field still stings, but when I think back to the way he dropped the ball, I know that he didn't know who I was until today. I didn't realize how much that was still bothering me until I felt the relief wash over me.

He opens his mouth to say something, but then his eyes flick to my right.

I can guess who's standing there by the split second of fear on his face before he shutters his expression completely. I turn to see my dad leaning on the doorjamb to his office, the bright light behind him pouring into the dim room.

I don't know what to say . . . not to either of them.

So I stalk past Dad into the coaches' office in silence, and Dad closes the door behind us a few seconds later. The office is large, with a table in the middle, rolling chairs, a few computers, and a couch shoved into the corner. Though the comfortable couch beckons me, I take a seat at the table. It feels safer somehow. Dad sits down across from me, and the frown he fixes on me tells me I've got a lecture coming.

"Would you care to explain to me where you've been? I called. Several times."

Yeah, and you're not alone there.

"I-I'm sorry, Dad. Something came up, and I needed to . . ."

"Something came up?" he asks sternly. His elbows come down hard on the table, and he lays his forearms down flat, leaning toward me.

God, that sounded insensitive. Like running errands was more important than his birthday. *Let's try this again, Dallas.*

"I, uh . . ." I'm surprised to feel my chin tremble, and I'm reminded of why Dad and I don't talk much. He's the only person who gets under my skin, the only person I can't seem to keep my cool around. "Things haven't been easy. Starting at a new school, starting at *Rusk*."

"If this is about that New York school again, we've talked about this."

It's not about Barnard or even about dance, but for whatever reason, I can't resist arguing whenever this subject comes up.

"Dad, I get more of a challenge out of my dance lessons with Mrs. Dunlap than I do out of these classes. Do you realize what a waste of time and money it is for me to do dance here?"

"So pick a different major."

I jerk backward like he's slapped me.

"Why is it that you talk to your players about goals and living up to their potential, but when it comes to me and my dreams and what I could achieve, I should just settle for something more convenient?"

Dad bristles, sliding his chair back from the table a few inches. "These young men have scholarships. They're getting an education in addition to their role on the team. Some of them may have a chance at playing professionally, but the rest of them aren't fooling themselves into thinking that success will be handed to them."

"So you just think I'm not good enough, is that it?"

His cheeks go so red they're almost purple, and just like me, I see his natural inclination is to jump to anger. "I didn't say that, Dallas. We both know you're very talented, but—"

"But I'm not getting the chance to prove it. That's the difference, Dad, between your players and me. You never even let me apply to Barnard. You wouldn't even listen to me when I talked about auditioning at any other schools. If you had, maybe I would have a scholarship, too."

"And what would you do afterward? Hmm? Open a studio like your teacher? She's barely keeping that place afloat, and you know it."

My anger bubbles over because he's right about that at least. Dunlap Dance Academy has definitely seen better days. I teach two classes a week there in exchange for free dance classes just because I know Mrs. Dunlap can't afford to pay me, and she's getting too old to teach the number of classes she used to cover by herself.

"Central Texas isn't exactly a thriving dance environment, Dad. Why do you think I wanted to leave?"

His lips press into a thin line, curling down at the corners. He gives these tiny, hard shakes of his head, and I know he's trying not to yell at me.

"I wasn't about to let you go traipsing off to New York City by yourself. You're too young. You're not ready."

In the end, it's me who yells first. "You mean *you're* not ready!"

I stand up before I say something I'll regret. Before I say the one insult that always lurks on my tongue when these arguments get really bad. I've never said it, but in the very worst corner of my soul, I know it's the one thing I could say that would put an end to these fights for good.

Dad won't let me leave because he can't handle a repeat of Mom.

I march toward the door and fling it open, but Dad's not ready to let me leave. Even though Carson's still sitting there in the film room, he demands, "You still haven't told me where you've been tonight. You don't just take off without saying anything!"

I clench my fists, and turn back to Dad because facing him is better than facing Carson. Knowing he's here in the room, watching us, cools some of the heat in my blood. I know I'm not my most mature when I'm around my father. He treats me like a little girl, and sometimes out of habit, I find myself playing the part too well.

As calmly as I can manage, I say, "I'm sorry. I didn't mean to leave like that . . . not today. I had every intention of going to dinner with you." I can't bring myself to say it's his birthday out loud, too worried about what Carson will think of me if I do. "I . . . found out something that upset me." My voice cracks ever so slightly. "And I just needed to be alone. I went for a drive, and I lost track of time."

Dad comes to his senses then. Whether he heard the pain I tried to hide in my voice or realized we had an audience or something else, I'm not sure. But he backs off.

"Don't worry about dinner. It's fine. Are you . . . are you okay now?"

He takes a step toward me, and lifts his hands up like he's going to take hold of my shoulders or hug me even, but stops and crosses his arms over his chest instead. There's a softness in his eyes that I'm not used to seeing, and it makes the guilt rattle even louder in my chest.

I bypass his question and say, "Let me make it up to you. Tomorrow night. I'll get takeout from Tucker's and meet you at home after practice."

My diversionary tactics do not go unnoticed, but Dad's not any better at talking about emotional crap than I am. So he nods. He crosses the few feet between us, and we share one of those awkward side-hugs that are the only kinds of hugs we've ever really had.

Before I dart out the door, I say, "See you tomorrow night." Then I make eye contact with Carson, and by the slump of his shoulders, I know he'll be expecting my text message canceling our walk tonight.

I was planning to cancel that long before I ever fought with Dad.

Chapter 10

Carson

I sit stiffly in the moments after Dallas leaves, wanting to go after her. But considering her father is between the door and me, it might not be the smartest option. He stares at the door for a few moments, then huffs and starts toward me. He takes a seat on a plastic folding chair next to the couch and directs his eyes toward the film, which I have long since stopped watching.

Saturday is our season opener, an away game. And even though I'm not expecting to play, I've been squeezing in as much time watching film as possible. Hell, I don't even know for sure that I'm going to travel. Coach has been playing me second string in practice mostly because James, last year's backup QB, has been having knee problems since camp at the beginning of August. But there are four or five other quarterbacks on the roster, some of whom have been on the team for a couple years. I'm better than all of them, of that I'm fairly confident, but I don't want to get complacent and assume Coach sees me as number two.

I know Coach has been over and over these films. It's his first game, and I know he wants . . . *needs* to make a strong showing. He's got just as much to prove as me. But even so, he sits there and watches with me. I have in the tape of last year's game against our next opponent. It's not a conference game, but they're a light team that shouldn't give us too much trouble as a warm-up.

Coach sits in silence for a long while, and I resist the urge to check my watch for the time or pull out my phone to text Dallas. I'm sure that he's not even really watching until he points at the screen and says, "You see that?"

"Um . . ." I look back at the screen, totally caught unaware. "That sack?"

I try not to sound like I enjoy the sight of Abrams being flattened, but it's not an easy task.

"Do you see why, though?"

He rewinds the tape, and we watch it again.

"The safeties have his receivers covered. Moore is busy blocking for him, so he can't pitch it to him. He ran out of options."

"Except?"

"Except to run it himself, but he hesitated too long to take advantage of the gap. He relies too much on his arm, and the defense knows it. They've got his number."

"Damn right, they do. The whole damn conference has his number." I nod in understanding. No one would say it outright, but that was a big part of why they only got three wins last year.

Abrams has had a great arm for most of his career, and he's gotten lazy about all the other aspects of his game.

"He doesn't have your feet," Coach says.

I clear my throat because I'm not sure if I imagined his last words. Coach Cole has already said more words to me today than in the entire last month combined. He's apparently been watching, though. He knows me by name. He pushes me in practice.

As far as I'm concerned, that means I have a shot.

He stands and claps a hand on my shoulder. He answers my unspoken question. "I see you more than I see some of my own damn coaches, son. You're a good runner with good instincts, but you're green and your arm could be stronger."

"Yes, sir." It could. That's why I spend more than my fair share in the weight room.

"Tell me, McClain. Why Rusk? Why not stick with Westfield, where you'd play nonstop? You had a scholarship there, and you don't here. Why take all this risk?"

"Because I want to play football, sir. Really play."

"You think you can go pro?"

That's a question I try not to answer even though I get asked a lot. Truthfully, I don't, though I've never admitted it out loud and never will. But that's been the plan my father and I have had since long before I graduated high school or went to Westfield or transferred to Rusk. That's been the plan since the moment my dad realized I could play football better than I could do anything else.

"I think I can work as hard as my body allows, and then see what happens. Things might work out. They might not, but at least I'll be making a go at something I love."

My parents didn't ever say sports were all I was good at, not in so many words, but they were always pushing me toward football, always placing it above everything else. No point busting my ass to be passable at math or science when I can bust it to be great at sports. I'm not that smart, but I can run.

Neither of them went to college. Dad worked on the ranch with Grandpa until he died. He and Mom got married right out of high school. Normally, Dad would have been pushing me to do the same, but too many years spent with too little money had changed his mind on what was best for me.

"You sound like my daughter," Coach says.

I don't reply. I only heard bits and pieces of their fight, but it's not something I have any intention of weighing in on.

After a few moments of silence, he claps me on the shoulder once more.

"Go home, McClain. Get some rest. Today was supposed to be an easy day."

I resist the urge to laugh at the thought of a bleeding day being called *easy* just because it was shorter than normal. Somehow I don't think he'd take that too well.

"There are no easy days, sir."

He smiles grimly. "You are right about that, McClain. Too right."

I SHOW UP outside Dallas's dorm even though she texted me to cancel. I don't know what I plan to do there or how I'll get her to talk to me, but I can't make myself just roll over and pretend none of it ever happened.

I stand outside, watching a few people smoking just outside the doors, and I text her.

I'm here for our walk.

She doesn't reply, so after a few minutes, I call her instead.

It rings, three, four, five times, and I'm getting ready to hang up when she answers, "*What?*"

"I'm downstairs."

I'm coincidentally looking up at the building when I notice a set of blinds on the third floor being pulled up, and a familiar face peeking out of the glass. I wave, and she steps back from the window until I can't see her anymore.

"You didn't get the hint when I didn't answer any of your calls or when I texted to cancel?"

"I just want to talk," I say. If I'd had a dozen reasons before that we couldn't date, I had a hundred now. But I keep hearing what she said outside her dad's office.

I found out something that upset me.

I keep hearing the break in her voice when she said it, and it's eating me from the inside out.

"So talk."

"Can you come down?"

"No."

I sigh, but she steps up to the window again, her arms crossed over her chest, and I guess that will have to do.

Now . . . I just need to figure out what to say.

The silence stretches on for several long moments and she adds, "This is you talking?"

I snap, "I'm sorry, okay? You're not the only one who got a shock today."

"If you're worried that I'm going to tell him, don't. I know how to keep my mouth shut."

"Dallas, that's not it. I don't care about that."

"You should. You think he's tough on you in practice now? It can get much worse. Trust me."

"I do trust you."

She makes a noise on the other end that I can't quite identify.

"This is complicated, I know."

"Let me uncomplicate it. Whatever might have been going to happen between us, isn't. I don't date football players."

"I don't want to date you." I wince. "That came out wrong." And I realize when I say it, just how much of a lie it is, too. "I like you, have liked you from the moment I met you. But the whole reason I wanted to go on a walk tonight was to explain that despite wanting to date you, I can't. I decided that long before I knew you were Coach Cole's daughter."

"I have a name, you know. God, I'm so sick of just being Coach Cole's daughter."

"Before I knew you were Dallas Cole, then. I'm not a scholarship player, Dallas. I could be cut at any moment. And I'm not the best student in the world, which puts me even more at risk. If I want to stay on the team, I have to stay focused. I have to work hard. And for now at least, that means no dating."

"Isn't this kind of a moot point now? We're both well aware that no dating will be taking place."

I sigh. "I wanted to go for a walk and explain things because I hoped we could still be friends."

She disappears from the window. I wonder if she's pacing or just tired of me when she says, "Seriously?"

"I know it sounds stupid. But I told you the truth on Friday night. I'm a transfer. I'm nonscholarship. I'm an outsider on the team, and at this school. I think you're pretty great, and I'd hate to lose that because our situation is . . . complicated."

She snorts. "Complicated. Right."

I wish she would come back to the window so I could see her face.

"Is that a no?"

She doesn't say anything, and it drives me crazy not being able to know what she's thinking. Damn it, why don't dorms have balconies?

"It's an *I don't know.*"

"Can I help you figure it out?"

"No. Not tonight. I'll text you or something."

She hangs up the phone, the blinds drop, and I have no choice but to drag myself home.

I DON'T SEE Dallas again that week, not even when I stick around the environmental science building trying to catch her before whatever class she has there. She sure as hell never comes back to practice, and even though I want to obsess over it, there's no time.

On Wednesday, Coach tells me I'm traveling with the team, and the rest of the week speeds by, until I walk out on a football field in a Rusk University jersey for the first time. Mom and Dad are supposed to try to come since this away game is closer to home than Rusk, but Granny is sick again, so they don't make it after all.

It's just as well because as expected, I ride the bench the whole game, and now in the dark quiet of the charter bus on our way home, I finally have the space in my head to think about Dallas again. I sit and stare at the few texts we exchanged before everything went to shit, while the rest of my teammates are sleeping or listening to music. Most of them have a reason to be tired, though. They've actually worn themselves out playing, and I'm still keyed up with nowhere to burn that energy off. We managed a narrow victory for our first game of the season. The win wasn't pretty, especially considering it should have been a fairly easy win for us, but it didn't feel nearly as ugly as the feeling in my chest reading those damn texts.

Why can't I stop thinking about her?

Why does the one night I had with this girl suddenly hold more weight in my mind than relationships that lasted months of my life?

When we get back to Rusk, we pile out—a long line of sleepy guys in sweatpants with duffel bags.

We all have Sunday off, and I know a few of the guys are going out tonight despite their sleepy appearances at the moment. They'll want to celebrate the win while they don't have to worry about enduring an early morning workout with a hangover.

I stop to drop off a few things in the locker room when I hear someone mention Firecracker. It's the team's nickname for Dallas.

"Heard she and the Asian chick might be at that party on ninth tonight. You gonna try again, Moore?"

I am so sick of hearing them talk about her that I have half a mind to anonymously tip the coach off about *Firecracker*. Let him hear their conversations and take care of it.

Instead, I grab my shit and head out without saying goodbye. And once I'm in my truck I text Dallas.

> *You going to a party tonight?*

She hasn't answered by the time I make the five-minute drive back to my apartment. I didn't expect her to, not really. But the thought of one of them making a pass at her for some stupid bet sends my muscles into a fit of rage that could rival tetanus for tension.

> *I'm not asking you out, Daredevil. Just answer the question.*

No. I'm not. Why?

> *Good. Just . . . Don't let Stella drag*
> *you to another party tonight.*

Why?

> *Nothing. Just stupid shit going down.*
> *You don't want to be around it.*

It's a mostly honest answer.

Oh. Thanks.

> *No problem.*

I'm pretty sure that's the end of it as I throw myself down on my couch and turn on the TV. But my phone buzzes with one more text.

Congrats on the win.

And there's my subtle reminder of my position on the team and everything that means for us. Too tired to put up a fight or feign gratitude, I don't answer her at all.

Chapter 11

Dallas

Why don't you just tell your dad?" Stella asks.

I sigh and haul myself up onto one of the uncomfortable stools in front of a library computer. "Because we had another argument, and I'd have to apologize to get him to buy me a new computer, and I'm not there yet."

"Oh, big deal. Say you're sorry. You guys will fight again next week, and you can be mad at him all over again. With a new computer."

"I'm tired of pretending we're okay only to end up at each other's throats again. It's not healthy."

"You really want to have a conversation about what's not *healthy?*" She leans on the high-top table next to me and mimics, *"Oh, Stella, he's so sweet and so nice. And I think I really like him. OH . . . JK HE PLAYS FOOTBALL HE'S DEAD TO ME."*

"That's not how it happened!"

It's kind of how it happened.

"Oh, sweetheart. The denial is squeezing all the fun out of you."

"Nothing is *squeezing* me. You know I'm not the romantic type."

"All that denial is like a pair of Spanx around your heart. You're not romantic because you don't let yourself be."

"That's a lovely visual. So what? I'm the Grinch? My heart is three sizes too small?"

"Not three sizes too small. It's just cranky. As anyone or anything would be after being corseted up for years on end."

Stell's an art major. And she's always talking about my life in terms of metaphors, most of them depressing.

I ignore her and finish logging on, so that I can print my GCE assignment. Gender, culture, and ethnicity in dance. Surprisingly, with how weak my studio classes are, it has ended up being my favorite class, in part because the professor, Esther Sanchez, is the most legit dance professor on staff. I would have loved to have a studio class with her, but after an injury a few years back, she doesn't teach them anymore. She's in charge of all the theory, composition, and history courses.

"At least tell me that you're gonna try to meet someone else, then? We could go out this weekend. One of the art history majors is having a party at his place."

I ignore Stella in favor of plugging in my USB drive.

It's been two weeks since the catastrophe with Carson, and he's texted me twice since then to ask me if I was going to a party. Or more correctly, He'd told me *not* to go. Each time I've asked around the next day, trying to discern if any parties got busted or had major drama, and both times I've come up empty.

Other than that, he hasn't texted me, and I haven't contacted him. Despite saying I would.

A small part of me wonders if he tells me not to come because he's going to be there, and then I get irrationally furious over a party I really had no desire to attend anyway. Especially considering he was the one throwing around the F-word like it was actually a possibility for us.

Stella straightens up beside me and grins in a way that cannot mean anything good. Before she can unleash whatever maniacal plan she's formulating, I say, "There's this guy in my English class who I'm kind of interested in."

And by *interested in*, I mean he doesn't make me want to bang my head into solid objects.

"Dallas." Her tone is almost warning, and I know she doesn't believe me.

"What? He's nice. His name is Louis, and his family is from Latin America somewhere. He's quiet, but really cute. And I bet he'd be a fantastic dancer. So really, you can stop bringing up—"

"Carson!" Stella chirps. I shoot a glare at her, but she smiles sweetly back at me before directing her gaze behind me. "Nice to see you again. Congrats on the second win on Saturday. 2–0 is a big deal."

I stare at my computer, knowing that if I look at Stella, she'll read the absolute terror in my eyes far too easily. I look over my shoulder at Carson, not turning around enough to look at his face.

I only catch sight of his broad chest and the sexy stubble along his jaw before I turn back to my computer.

"Hey, Carson."

I say it like I would say hello to anyone else I saw in passing around campus. Then I hit print and slide off my stool to escape to the printer.

When I turn back to my computer, Carson is sitting on my stool and Stella is halfway to the door, giving me a sly wave.

Damn you, Stella.

"'Gender Neutrality in Modern Dance'?" Carson asks when I stomp up to my computer.

"Yep." I end the word with a crisp pop, and I don't even acknowledge him as I lean in front of him to grab the mouse and close out the document. I feel him suck in a breath beside me, and his muscular chest brushes my shoulder.

Either I forget how to use technology or the stupid mouse hates me, because I can't get the arrow to move more than an inch or two at a time toward the button to log out at the bottom. I'm practically banging it against the table by the time I get the arrow where I want it.

While the computer logs me out, I tap my papers against the table to align them and then turn to leave.

I don't get more than a few inches before Carson grabs my elbow.

"Can we talk?"

My eyes land on Katelyn Torrey watching us from one of the study tables. Katelyn is on the Wildcat Dance Team, and she's hinted before that she'd like to see me try out for the team next year. But there's a rumor that she and Levi hooked up on a few away games last year. The cheer and dance teams often stay in the same hotel as the players, and even though the guys have a curfew, everyone knows they sneak girls in.

As fun as a dance team might be, that is not a world I want to live in. Those girls . . . their whole lives revolve around the team. And I'd spent enough of my life with football as my unforgiving sun. And I certainly don't need my private life whispered about all over campus like Katelyn's is.

"I need to grab a book before class. You can talk while I find it."

I pull my elbow out of his grasp and don't wait to see if he follows as I make my way back into the stacks. I don't actually need a book for class, and if I did, I sure wouldn't find it in the reference section, where I slow to a stop and face him.

He picks a book on copyright off the shelf. "Planning to patent that angry look you're giving me?"

I deepen my glare even as a flicker of worry at the back of my mind wonders how unattractive my expression is.

"Talk, Carson."

"You don't need a book?" he asks.

"I don't need people gossiping about seeing us together, and neither do you." First it would get back to Levi, and I could only imagine how obnoxious he would be. Then Dad would hear, and I didn't have the energy to fight wars on two fronts with him.

He scoffs. "You severely overestimate my importance on the team and at this school. No one gives a crap who I am."

"I do."

When he looks at me with darkened eyes, I realize my response could mean two things, and I rush to correct. "I care that you're on the team. I told you I don't date football players."

"And I told you, I'm not *asking* for a date. And technically, I am a football practicer. I've yet to step a foot on the field during a game. Shouldn't that get me a little slack?"

He grins cheekily at me, and I hate that even with all the anger I can muster, it's not enough to keep one corner of my mouth from pulling up in a half smile. When his eyes drop to my lips, I slam my walls up as fast as I can.

"Doesn't matter. Say what you want to say, because I need to go."

I've got class, and then I'm starting a new job at the campus Learning Lab. Basically, I'm a tutor, writing and Spanish mostly (since those are the two things I tested out of and am good enough at to provide help), though from what I hear, more often than not I'll end up helping people figure out how to work the lab computers.

Whoop-de-doo.

It's a start, though. If I want to save money to get away from Rusk and go somewhere with a decent dance program, I've got to begin somewhere.

Carson runs a hand through his hair and sighs, drawing my attention back to him. My eyes scan the way his body tapers out from his waist to his strong shoulders. God, his arms are my weakness. I remember how one of them slipped up the back of my shirt, surrounding me and pinning our bodies together.

Too much. Abort. Abort.

He says, "I just want you to know that I get it. I get why you want nothing to do with me or football. I've seen enough from guys like Abrams and Moore to get your hesitance." I lift my chin to show their names don't bother me. "So anyway, I just wanted to let you off the hook. I understand, and . . . it's cool."

He pauses for a few moments, then nods his head and walks away. It's not until he's completely out of my sight that I let myself acknowledge the disappointment weighing heavy on my chest. A part of me had wanted him to push again, to poke and prod my reasoning until I had a decent excuse to give in.

When Katelyn's eyes meet mine as I cross the library toward the exit, I straighten my shoulders because, disappointment or not . . . this is for the best.

I SPENT AN hour whining to Stella about how boring my first day at the Learning Lab was, only to find myself wishing for more boring when Carson McClain walks in on my second day. It's late, with only an hour left before we close for the night, and there are only three tutors working. I'm the only one not already with another student. He's wearing university sweats and a Rusk T-shirt. His hair is wet, and I'm willing to bet he just came straight from the practice. I don't think he sees me. He just checks in at the front, stalks through the room, takes a seat at the station in the far corner of the lab, and starts pulling out his books and things.

I hesitate . . . just for a moment. Then I suck it up and go do my job.

"Can I help you?"

He doesn't look up as he opens an English textbook and flips through a spiral covered in chicken-scratch writing. He smells fresh and clean and masculine, and I tell myself I should take a step back. I don't.

"Yeah, I have to do an outline for my . . ."

He looks up and trails off.

He doesn't say anything, but his expression tightens and his light blue eyes don't dance the way they usually do.

"Hi," I say, since he doesn't seem too keen to begin the conversation.

"Never mind," he says. "I think I've got it on my own."

He looks down, and those words are like a punch to the chest. So much for him being "cool" with it. I look down at the page he's turned to in his textbook.

"Working on an outline?" That's right up my alley. If he'd been doing math, I'd have a good reason to walk away. "What kind of paper is it? Persuasive? Informative?" He doesn't answer. "Did the professor say if the outline required complete sentences or just subjects?"

He stops writing whatever illegible thing he's been scratching out in his notebook. "Dallas. I've got this. I don't need your help."

Stupid stubborn boy.

"Yeah. Riiiight. That's why you came to the Learning Lab instead of just going to the library. Listen, we're only open for another"—I checked my watch—"fifty minutes. And both Elizabeths are busy helping other students. You can wait, but there's no guarantee either will be done in time to help you."

"Both Elizabeths?"

I point to the other tutor closest to us, a pretty Latina girl with the longest eyelashes I've ever seen in my life. "Elizabeth A." Then I gesture to the petite blonde on the other side of the room. "Elizabeth B."

"How did you decide which one is A and which one is B? That seems a little unfair."

I raise an eyebrow and point at the girls again. "Elizabeth Alvarez. Elizabeth Banner." Then I cross my arms over my chest and give him my best smirk.

The corners of his lips tug up toward a smile for half a second before his mouth goes flat again.

He closes his spiral and his textbook and says, "I'll just head home."

"Seriously?"

"I'm pretty tired from *practice*." He emphasizes the word, and I know he's trying to get me to back off.

But . . . well . . . I do stubborn like Lady Gaga does weird, and the fact that he wants me to leave him alone makes me even less inclined to do it.

"Don't be stupid, Carson."

His jaw tightens, and he begins stuffing his things back into his bag.

Okay . . . so maybe calling him stupid when he came for tutoring help wasn't the *best* word choice, but I'm not exactly known for being sensitive and polite.

"I'm sorry. That came out wrong. Just . . . stay."

"It's fine, Dallas. I'll see you around."

Then he's gone.

And I want to punch myself in the jugular.

Chapter 12

Carson

'm fine with my decision to walk out, right up until the moment I sit down on my couch and attempt to resume working on my outline by myself.

The professor has us doing outlines for an informative paper on a current event of our choice. I picked a random headline off CNN.com, and after I type up all the notes I'd scribbled down by hand, I'm left with a bare-bones outline that I may or may not have done correctly. I still have no idea what to put for all the *A* and *B* and *C* lines, let alone the *i*'s below those.

And it's due tomorrow.

That's a big giant *fuck* if there ever was one.

I pick up my phone and dial Ryan. He's taken to showing up during most of my extra workouts, and we talk during those. I'm not sure I would really qualify us as friends yet. But he's my only choice, really.

It rings and rings, and I'm left with his voice mail.

Damn.

"Hey, man, it's Carson," I say into the speaker. "If you get this tonight, give me a call back. Nothing big, I just have a question. If you don't get it tonight, don't worry about it."

I hang up and slump back into my couch, exhausted.

Levi's pulled off two wins in a row. They haven't been pretty. Too many errors, but he's had just enough impressive plays to make my chances of taking his spot even slimmer. And if I'm honest . . . I'm not sure how long I can keep this up.

I've almost dozed off when my phone beeps and I jerk upright. My eyelids are heavy as I grope for my phone to read the incoming text.

It's not from Ryan, but Dallas.

So I've been thinking about this whole friendship thing . . .

I blink a few times to make sure I'm really awake.

And?

And I think I can handle it.

If you can.

I can't tell if her second text is just an additional thought or a challenge. Not that it matters. My response is the same. I didn't want to embarrass myself in front of her. I'd told her I wasn't a good student, but giving her a front row seat for it was different. But tonight, I didn't have much of a choice.

> *Are friends allowed to help other stubborn friends with essay outlines?*

Sure. I'm working tomorrow morning from 8 to 11 if you want to swing by.

> *I can't. It's due tomorrow, and I have classes then.*

And I'm the idiot who procrastinated. I start typing out a message asking if I can call her when she replies.

What's your address? I'm already out. I'll just swing by.

Oh shit. Shit taking a shit on a shit.

I jump off the couch and take a look around my messy living room. There are free weights strewn around the open space on the far side of the room. Sweats and towels and balled-up socks are strewn all over. And yesterday's dinner still sits on the coffee table in front of me.

I throw the old food out quickly before answering her text. Then I'm in a mad dash to make the place at least somewhat presentable. With sweatpants thrown over my shoulders, my arms full of miscellaneous things, I kick a stray pair of shoes back toward my bedroom and hide it all there. My phone buzzes with another text, but I don't look at it. There's too much to do in too little time. I throw the weights in the corner, gathering a few more pieces of dirty laundry to stash in my room. I don't get time to address the bathroom or the kitchen before a knock sounds at my door.

Damn it.

"Just a second!"

I pull the shower curtain closed and flip off the lights in both the bathroom and the kitchen. I'm left with only the lamp beside my couch on, and I think maybe the low light will help hide whatever I didn't manage to straighten.

I take a few seconds to calm my breath before I open the door.

It doesn't help. Not when I see her. Her hair shines in the light cast by the porch light outside my door. Her long legs are crossed at the ankle, and she's fidgeting with the hem of her shirt in a way that makes me smile.

I school my expression so I don't look too eager and say, "Hey. Come on in."

She steps inside, but she stays near the door. She looks around, and her eyes fall on the lone lamp, and I can tell she thinks I'm using the low light for something other than hiding my lack of cleanliness.

"I can't stay long," she says. "But I was on my way back to campus after a quick run to the store, so I thought it couldn't hurt to swing by. Especially after I ran you off earlier."

I shrug, still gripping the open door.

"It's my fault. I don't like asking for help."

She laughs. "Join the club."

Her shoulders relax, and I take that as my cue that it's safe to close the door.

I move toward the couch, straightening the cushions before I take a seat in front of my English homework piled on the coffee table.

"Thanks for doing this. Next time I won't wait until the night before to try and get help."

"It happens. Procrastination is my natural state of being." She sits down on the couch with nearly a full cushion between us. "So tell me what you're working on."

I slide my computer over so she can see what I have so far, and hand her the CNN article I printed out. I fill her in on what I've already outlined and explain that I'm having trouble filling out more of the outline.

She looks it all over in silence for a minute or so, then pulls my computer off the coffee table and onto her knees.

"Well, your first problem is that your roman numeral two should really be your *A* point under roman numeral one. They're too closely related to be separate informative points."

Damn. That means I need to come up with something else I can write a full paragraph about.

"The roman numeral is the broadest way to describe the topic. The letters break it down into more specific key points, and the lowercase roman numerals are for supporting details like statistics, quotes, and examples."

I love how she just rattles off the information with no problem, when I find myself looking back at the textbook example every few seconds. She must read the frustration on my face because she turns toward me, her knee brushing my thigh.

"Think of it this way. If you were to write a paper informing someone who knows nothing about football how to evaluate the skills of a quarterback, you might choose to use your three paragraphs to evaluate his passing game, running game, and decision-making. Under each of those headings, you'd use a letter to explain the various skills that contribute to a good passing game, running game, etc. So, let's say under 'passing game,' strength is your *A* point, accuracy might be your *B* point. And then for supporting details you could give player statistics or even discuss drills that are designed to improve strength or accuracy. You can include as many points and details under each heading as you want. The more you have, the more comprehensive your outline will be, and the less trouble you'll have writing a decent-length paper when the time comes."

There's something really fucking sexy about listening to a girl like her talk about football and actually know her stuff. I'm used to having to explain what a first down means to most girls.

"You make it sound so easy. If only I could write about football instead of current events."

She grins at me. "Yeah. I'm sure you would *love* that."

"Hey, you're the one who brought up football. Not me. I wasn't going to even utter the word for fear that it would scare you off."

Now that I've brought attention to it, she looks a little like she wants to bolt, but she doesn't.

"The trick with papers like this is to pick a current event that interests you or that connects to a subject you're familiar with."

"I don't know anything about anything but football."

"That can't be true. What kind of stuff were you interested in growing up?"

"Girls," I answer.

She rolls her eyes. "I don't think *girls* count as a current event."

"I didn't do anything growing up except work for my dad and play football. That's all I know how to do."

"What does your dad do?"

"He's a rancher."

"Why don't you write about the drought? I saw a thing on the news just this morning about the decline in the number of cattle in Texas. If it's on the news, I'm sure you could find an article somewhere about it."

"I can talk about that?"

She smiled. "Yeah. As long as you find some articles and more official information to back it all up."

"I could write about that in my sleep. I've got my dad's whole rant about it down pat."

"Then do that."

She does a quick Internet search and on the first page alone, she points out three or four articles that would make good sources. And in five minutes, I've got all my main points mapped out.

"I think once I've read a few of these articles, I should be able to wrap up the rest of this pretty quickly."

This would have taken me hours by myself.

"Yep. I think you've pretty well got the hang of it."

I look up from my computer to face her, and I notice that she's closed the gap between us on the couch, leaving a scant few inches between her leg and mine.

"Thanks for this, Daredevil. You're a lifesaver."

She shakes her head.

"I'm no daredevil."

"Any girl who can jump off balconies and hold her own in a fight with Coach Cole is a daredevil in my book."

Her face falls, and I immediately regret bringing up that night.

"Like father, like daughter, I guess."

"It's not such a bad thing . . . being like your dad. Yeah, you're both stubborn and proud. That's for sure. But you've both got big hearts."

She looks at me like an extra head has just sprouted from the socket of my shoulder.

"No one in my entire life has ever told me I have a big heart."

I touch the hand she has braced on her knee, just for a few seconds, and say, "Then no one in your entire life has been paying much attention."

THE NEXT MORNING Ryan approaches as soon as I enter the weight room. He doesn't ask if I need a spot; this has become our routine since the first time he helped me.

He helps me load weights on the bar over at the bench press, and he wordlessly adds an extra ten pounds.

I might have mentioned Coach's words about improving my arm in passing, and Ryan has unofficially taken on the role as my trainer.

I'm not as chatty today, not with an extra ten pounds to worry about, and not with my head still dissecting every moment I spent with Dallas last night. But Ryan picks up the slack.

"You're later today than usual."

I push out a breath as I lift the bar away from my chest.

"Up late," I breathe.

"Something to do with the message you left?"

"Oh, that. I just had a question, but I worked it out."

"Okay," he says, but doesn't comment further as I finish out my set. When I rack the bar and take a quick breather he adds, "I hope you're coming during your lunch break today."

I had been thinking of trying to catch Dallas after environmental science to thank her again for her help, but that will just take a few minutes.

"I'll be here."

"Good. Otherwise I would have two pissed-off receivers on my hands."

I take the bar again, readjust my grip for a second, my hands burning slightly where some new calluses are forming. Then I start another set.

"What do you mean?"

"Torres and Brookes are meeting us at one. Thought we could spend some time throwing today. Work on that arm. It will give you a chance to get to know them, too. Build a rapport."

Torres and Brookes? They're both first string.

Ryan sees my expression. "They're good guys. And they're taking shit from Abrams about not being able to get open, so they've been hanging around, putting in some extra work. Seems stupid not to take advantage and let you guys work each other."

"Yeah. It does. Thanks, man."

"Don't mention it. Now tell me what was so important that you broke your strict schedule for a late night."

"Eh." My hesitation turns into a groan as I struggle with my next to last rep. Ryan touches two fingers to the bottom of the bar, letting me know he's there.

"One more."

I take a few ragged breaths, and then I let my shaking arms lower toward my chest.

"Tell me this," he says. "Was it more important than outplaying Abrams? Because that's what all this is for, right? No one works this hard to ride the bench."

Sweat runs in my eyes as I began to push up one last time. Ryan's two fingers under the bar disappear and now both his hands grip the bar, pushing down just enough to add resistance.

I growl as I try to push past him.

"Was it more important?" he asks slowly, enunciating each word by letting me gain just a centimeter. My arms are shaking badly now, and the ache extends from my wrists to my shoulders.

I think about Dallas, and rather than answering, I grit my teeth and push up as hard as I can, dislodging Ryan and depositing the bar on the rack. I sit up, and my arm screams with the effort to even just lift up the hem of my shirt and wipe at the sweat on my face.

"Anyone ever tell you that you're a bastard?" I say.

"Once or twice. Who is she?"

I stiffen and stand up, stretching my arms above my head. "What do you mean?"

"If it were anything else, you would have just said yes or no. When guys start having trouble giving straight answers, I find that it's usually about a girl."

"For your information, I was up doing homework."

"Riiiight." He raises his hands does those lame air-quote things. "*Homework.*"

I shake my head, pushing the sweaty hair off my forehead. "Doesn't matter. We're just friends."

"I knew it!"

"Watch it, Blake. Don't make me shove that dumbbell up your ass to keep your head company."

"Fine. Fine. Go shower. Rest up so you don't embarrass yourself in front of Torres and Brookes this afternoon. Then you can just concentrate on the friend zone . . . I mean end zone."

I shove him, and he just laughs in response.

"Bastard."

"Yeah, well. Let's both get our heads out of our asses before this afternoon, hmm?"

Chapter 13

Dallas

'm heading out when Stella comes home that evening.

"You going to the cafeteria? I'm starving!"

"Uh . . . no. I already ate. Sorry."

She nods, stripping off a paint-covered T-shirt. "Dance class or work?"

God, why couldn't I have just left five minutes earlier?

"Neither. Studying."

She gives an exaggerated snore. If she knows where I'm actually going, she'll never let me hear the end of it.

"Fine. Go do your thing. But first . . . I made something for you." She drags her large portfolio bag that she uses to carry her artwork onto the bed. She unzips the top and reaches inside. "Ta-da!"

She thrusts a small canvas painting in my direction. In the center in thick, deep red is a heart (the metaphorical, not anatomical, kind). It's painted so that it looks three-dimensional, like

I could pick it up off the page. And down the center of the heart are black, string laces, pulled tight, and squeezing the heart, exaggerating its shape.

"It's your corset heart. Remember?"

I remembered our discussion in the library before Carson had interrupted us, the one all about how I am laced too tightly to ever let myself fall in love. When I really think about it, that oppressed heart is a pretty damn accurate depiction, but as I hold it in my hands, I feel my stomach toss. I might be sick.

"You hate it," Stella says.

"No, it's really pretty. I love the colors."

"But you're not exactly a hearts-and-flowers kinda girl. I know. It's fine." She moves to take it back. "I'll just paint over it. Try something new."

"No!" I jump back, holding the small painting away from her. I clear my throat. "No. I'd like to keep it . . . if that's okay with you."

Stella looks even more shocked than I feel. "Really?"

I nod.

"Yeah. It's all yours."

I slip it in my oversized purse, say goodbye, and walk out the door.

I'll keep the painting because it's pretty, because Stella made it and against all odds, I love her. I'll also keep it as a reminder of the person I've let myself become.

I DIDN'T LIE to Stella, not really. I just didn't elaborate on what *studying* meant. Or more specifically, with whom I'll be studying. I ran into Carson earlier today on my way to my geology class as he was leaving. He asked what I was doing tonight, I said homework. I asked him, and he answered the same. And when he suggested we do our homework together . . . at the same time . . . in the same place . . .

I agreed.

I volunteered to meet him at his apartment again because I still am not ready for the ramifications of hanging out with him in public. It seemed like a reasonable, harmless way to spend the evening.

Wrong. Oh so very wrong. In fact, I keep hearing that word, echoing like a gong in my head. I changed probably half a dozen times before settling on a simple pair of shorts (the longest pair I owned) and a V-neck tee.

And as I pull up outside his apartment, I am a mess. A hot mess. A steaming pile of . . . mess.

I know how dangerous this is. The potential stupidity of this night is epic in nature, but I still don't turn around and get back into my car (even though I really should).

Between our interactions so far and the unfamiliar rawness in my chest that's been chafing at me since Stella gave me that painting, I am not at all in control.

I should walk away. That's what I do when I find myself in an unpredictable situation with immense potential for pain.

Most of the issues in my relationship with Levi had stemmed from the fact that I was always willing to be the one who walked away. We'd get in these awful fights (not unlike Dad and me), and they only ever ended in one of two ways—Levi backed down or we broke up.

Not normal, I know. But we always got back together. It had always felt like a given, until suddenly it stopped feeling that way. He set a state record for our conference; he and my dad started talking about playing college ball, and suddenly it felt like I wasn't the only one willing to walk away if I didn't get what I wanted.

So rather than walking away after our last fight, I gave him what he wanted. In the back of his pickup truck, parked in the lot at the football field of all places.

He walked away anyway.

I will never be in that position again. I will never be the person who cares more, because that person is always the one who hurts more.

And yet here I am, knocking on Carson's door, telling myself that my heart is only in my throat because I'm out of practice at making new friends.

Yeah right.

"Just a second!"

I almost run. But then I imagine how ridiculous it will look when he opens his door and I'm sprinting down the stairs and across the parking lot like the crazies on Black Friday.

He opens the door, and if I hadn't already sucked in a breath, I would have had to do it again. He's wearing university sweatpants, hung low on his hips, with a thin white cotton T-shirt. His hair is wet like he's fresh from a shower, and in a few places his shirt is damp and see-through, stuck to his skin.

I can smell him. Over the sticky September air, over the chlorine from the pool that his apartment overlooks, over everything.

"Hey. Come on in."

This is such a bad idea.

But when I peek inside, his coffee table is covered in papers and books, and the pencil in his hand tells me he was working when I knocked on the door.

He really does just want to study. I can do this. I can. And if at any point it gets to be too much, I always have my trusty backup plan.

Walk away.

I step just far enough inside for him to close the door, but when he heads to the couch, I stay where I am. He has the overhead light on tonight, so the room is brighter, less intimidating. He looks up and in the well-lit room his blue eyes look almost electric.

"If we're really going to be friends, I need some ground rules first," I say.

When I was just stopping by for a few minutes to help him with homework, it wasn't a problem. But hanging out two nights in a row is *definitely* a big deal. And big deals require rules.

His head tilts to the side, but he puts down his pencil and leans back on the couch.

"Okay. Whatcha got?"

"We don't tell anyone we're hanging out. Not yet." Not until I know for sure this is something I can do without getting in over my head.

After a moment, he nods. "Okay. I won't mention it to a soul until you're ready to come out of the closet as my friend."

I wince. "It's not like that. I just . . . I can't trust it won't get back to my dad. You know what gossip is like here. And when he finds out, it should come from me."

"Fair enough." I swallow, acutely aware that it sounds like I'm negotiating the terms of a relationship that's much more scandalous than a friendship.

"No questions about my dad. This should go without saying, but no using me to spend time with him. If you want to get on his good side, do it on the field, not through me."

His eyes soften, and I swear my heart constricts like those imaginary strings around it have been pulled tight.

"I want to get to know *you*, Daredevil. Not your dad."

I nod, glad to hear it, even though I've heard similar over the years from guys who turned out to be lying.

"If it gets to be too much, if it goes too far . . . either one of us just has to say the word, and it's done. We walk away, and that's that."

His eyebrows knit together in an almost-scowl.

"You have this kind of contract with all your friends?"

"No," I answer simply.

He waits, and I'm sure he's expecting an explanation, but I don't give it.

"Fine. Then I have a few stipulations of my own."

I nod for him to go ahead. It's only fair.

"Stay away from the other football players. Abrams, Moore, anyone who comes up to you in class or a party or whatever. If we're keeping our worlds separate, then they need to stay that way. Completely."

His voice is firm, an almost growl, as he says it. I don't let myself think about the possessive edge in his tone. That's a rabbit hole I can't fall into.

"That's an easy yes."

He nods, but the troubled expression on his face doesn't go away with my acceptance.

"We're honest with each other, no matter how hard or awkward it is to say whatever needs to be said. We"—he uses a hand to gesture between us—"are a safe space. You can say anything to me, and I promise I'll hear you out. I'll listen. No matter what it is."

I swallow, wondering just how honest he plans on getting, but I don't refuse.

"Okay. Is that it?"

"You don't walk away without an explanation. An honest one."

"If that's what you want." It's likely to be a brutal truth; it always is, but if he can take it, I can say it.

"All right, then. Come sit down."

He scoots over, repositioning some of his papers so that there's room on the coffee table for my stuff.

Last time, I was so caught up in keeping my cool and getting out of here as quickly as possible that I didn't really look around. But this time I take a bit more liberty. The furniture is all older and generic, and I wouldn't be surprised to find that it came with the apartment. The living room is dotted with athletic items— free weights in the corner, at least three footballs in various spots around the room, a basketball, an extra pair of tennis shoes. His playbook lies open on the coffee table next to his homework.

I sit down beside him gingerly, unnerved by how cool he is with all of this. Most guys would call me a nutjob and send me packing, especially when all those hoops to jump through are just for friendship and nothing else.

"What are you studying for?" I ask.

"Spanish," he answers in a near-groan.

I laugh. "I take it foreign languages are not your thing."

He pulls a pillow into his lap and lays a textbook across it. With his eyes on the page, he replies, "*School* is not my thing."

He keeps scanning the page, so I take that as my cue that it's not a subject that he wants to talk about. I bend over to rummage through my backpack for the book of essays I'm supposed to finish by tomorrow. It's a thin book, not more than a hundred pages, but it's drier than Dad's attempts at cooking, and I've yet to manage to read more than one essay at a time.

I look over at Carson as I sit back, and catch him staring at the strip of skin on my back where my shirt has ridden up.

I raise an eyebrow. "You're a little slow on the uptake when it comes to this *friendship* thing, huh?"

He grins. "Practice makes perfect."

I roll my eyes and pull my legs up onto the couch, balancing the book on my knees and flipping open to the dog-eared page where I left off.

We work in silence like that for a while, and when I sneak the occasional look at him, he's concentrating hard on the page in front of him, mouthing words silently. Verb conjugations, I'm guessing.

After I've read three essays, my brain feels like mush. Really boring mush. When I let out what is probably my fifth or sixth annoyed huff since I started reading, Carson's eyes lift to mine.

"You want something to drink? Or eat?" he asks. "We could order in if you're hungry."

I wave a hand at him and stand up to stretch. Carson doesn't try to hide the way his eyes follow my movement. "I'm fine. Go back to your Spanish. I just need to stretch a bit. I had a dance class this afternoon, and I stayed after to work on a piece of my own. Then I had another class tonight at my old dance studio." Not to mention waking up bright and early for my shift at the Learning Lab. "I might have gone a bit overboard."

He laughs and rolls one of his shoulders back. "I know the feeling."

After laying his book on the coffee table, he stands and comes toward me.

"I think we've probably earned a break. What do you think?"

I watch him warily. "What kind of break?"

He moves close to me, and suddenly my muscles are tense for an entirely different reason. He reaches out, and I think he's going to touch me, but instead he reaches past me and opens a cabinet next to his television that houses a few DVDs.

He doesn't have to search long for the one he wants, plucking it right off the top shelf. He holds it out to me, and I laugh. "*Aladdin*? Really?"

"We could always watch *Die Hard*."

"So we can listen to people shouting out your last name? No thanks, Bruce Willis."

He shrugs. "I like *Aladdin*. It reminds me of the good old days."

"When we were kids and our idea of homework was multiplication tables?"

"Nah. I meant the good old days when you were jumping off balconies and into my arms instead of down my throat."

He's teasing, and I'm glad for it because it loosens some of the remaining pressure in my chest.

I hold up my hands and give him an offended look. "Oh, excuse me! Next time I jump off a balcony, I'll make sure I do more damage when I land on you."

"Yeah, yeah, Daredevil. I know you're capable of inflicting all kinds of damage. Now sit down and let's relive our childhood."

He doesn't have to tell me twice. I'm so sick of reading those damn essays, I would take just about any kind of distraction. He turns the TV on and gets the DVD ready while I grab a blanket off the back of a muddy brown recliner beside the couch. I toe my shoes off, then snuggle into the arm of the couch. I stretch my legs out just a little, leaving a comfortable space between myself and where Carson will sit. He stays standing as he clicks past the previews and to the menu. He starts the movie, and while the familiar Disney castle is forming on the screen, he switches off the light and returns to the couch.

In the dark, the space I left between us doesn't seem like nearly enough. The opening music starts, casting the room in a soft red light, and his hand rests on the couch next to him, inches away from my feet.

My heart beats faster. Over feet. How stupid is that?

I chastise myself for being an idiot, but don't feel quite so stupid when Carson takes hold of my feet and tugs them into his lap, making me slide off the armrest and plop down on the regular cushions.

"What the crap, Carson?"

He smiles, leaving my legs draped across his lap and spreading out the bottom of the blanket.

"It's the only blanket I have, Cole. Friends share things."

I grumble, "I am not a football player. Please don't call me by my last name."

He smiles and makes that universal sound that means *Too bad.* "Just treating you like any other friend, Cole."

I scoff and jam my elbow under my head in an attempt to get comfortable, refusing to let myself glance at Carson even though I swear I feel him watching me. I'm also *seriously* undone by the feel of his muscled legs beneath my shins. Just when I've got myself propped up the way I like it, my phone buzzes on the coffee table.

I reach forward to grab it.

It's from Carson.

You've got some janked-up feet, Cole.

Chapter 14

Carson

Her reaction is about what I expected, though a little more violent. But at least it gets her to loosen up.

"You are such a jerk!"

One long foot nails me right in the stomach, and I catch her by the ankles before she hits me in a more unforgiving, more sensitive place.

"Hey! I'm just speaking the truth. That's one of our deals, right?"

"I don't want to hear those kind of truths! If you have a problem with my feet, then you should find a friend who isn't a dancer."

She tries to tug her ankles out of my grasp, but I jerk them back, sliding her a few inches closer to me on the couch.

"I didn't say I didn't like them, Cole. They have *character*."

She turns her face down into the couch cushion and lets out a groan. I know it's a groan of agitation, but that doesn't stop my body from reacting to the sound.

She lays her cheek against the cushion and says, "*Character* is just a nice way of saying they're ugly."

Her attempts to kick herself free have left the blanket up around her knees, so I slide my hands down from her ankle and grasp the foot closest to me.

"What are you—"

The breathy moan she releases when I push my thumb along the sole of her foot just about undoes me.

"Oh God, Carson."

Think nice, clean, friendly thoughts, Carson.

Yeah. That's about as effective as ordering myself to know Spanish. In other words . . . impossible.

"You sit there and watch Disney while I prove I have no problem with your feet."

They do look kind of tortured, like my hands when I go too long without lifting weights and then pick it up again. She has numerous calluses and a blister on the side of her big toe. And the joint below that toe looks like it wears a permanent red mark. I avoid it as I rub her feet, worried it's a bruise and will be painful. I alternate between digging at the muscles with my thumb and running my palms over them softly.

Dallas is uncharacteristically still and silent. I could almost believe she's asleep, except for the way her fingers are curled around the edge of the couch cushion in a death grip.

I switch to the other foot for a little while, relaxing back into the couch and watching the movie with lazy interest.

I don't let go of her feet, but as my hands grow tired, I switch from a focused massage to unhurried caresses. When we get to the balcony scene, I tickle the foot I'm holding, and she digs her other foot into my thigh in warning.

Chuckling, I move my attention off her feet to her calves, and she flinches and breaks her silence with a gasp.

"That hurt?" I ask, circling my hands around her shins, and gentling the push of my thumbs.

It's several long moments before she answers, but when she does, I know it's my honesty rule that made her hesitate.

"No. It doesn't hurt."

She doesn't tell me to stop, so I take that as permission to keep going. Her calves are lean and strong, and her skin is so silky smooth that I don't want to ever stop touching it.

She turns her head away from the television, pressing her forehead down into the couch cushion, and I know she's just as affected as I am.

Even though I don't want to, I take pity on her and stop my ministrations. I rub my thumb over her skin one last time, not kneading, but just a light goodbye touch. Then I leave her legs in my lap and prop my arms up along the back of the sofa, and try to return my attention to the movie.

Out of the corner of my eye, I watch the rise and fall of her back as she breathes. As the minutes tick past, the movement becomes less pronounced and her breathing calms. When she's completely in control, she sits up. Since I dragged her closer earlier, she's now sitting on the middle cushion directly beside me. I could drop my left arm forward off the back of the couch, and it would land around her shoulders.

While I'm debating whether or not it will be worth the elbow to the ribs it will surely earn me, she stands and looks down at me. "Right or left?"

I don't know what she means, and the first conclusion my mind jumps to is that she's asking which side of the bed I prefer.

She's not. I know she's not, but my brain seems to be at least a little divided on that conclusion. My voice thick with all the things I won't let myself say, I ask, "What do you mean?"

"Your throwing arm? Right or left?"

Oh. I clear my throat and answer, "Right."

"Scoot." She pushes at my knees, and mechanically I slide over, making room for her on my right side. I'm only halfway on the middle cushion when she slides in beside me, deliciously close.

She's facing me completely, her back pressed against the armrest. She has one leg pulled up on the cushion, bent at the knee and touching me from my hip to midthigh. Her touch is tentative, and she can't decide exactly how she wants to go about doing this. Eventually, she pulls her other leg up on the couch, leaving it propped upward. She lifts my arm and lays my elbow on her knee so that my upper arm and shoulder are completely open to her. I let my forearm hang down on the other side of her knee, my fingertips brushing both her calf and her thigh at the same time.

Her touch is light and exploratory at first, tracing the dips and curves of my muscle. I drop my head back against the couch and concentrate on keeping my breathing even. But it's a battle

I'll never win, not with her touching me. One warm hand curves over my shoulder, slipping underneath the sleeve of my T-shirt. I groan, and I let the fingers brushing against her leg grip just above her ankle.

She freezes, and I wonder if she'll repeat the question I asked her, if she'll make me admit the noise had nothing to do with pain.

She doesn't.

Instead, her touch turns firm and she expertly works my sore muscles. She starts at my shoulder, pressing her thumb hard against the knots she finds there. It hurts in the most perfect way, not dissimilar from the way this night as a whole feels.

"You've got a lot of tension," she murmurs.

You have no idea, Daredevil.

But at the moment, my mind is on a different kind of tension. With my fingers wrapped around her ankle and the way she's positioned, I know that one well-placed pull would have her across my lap just like the night we met.

But I told her that we could just be friends, so I'll have to settle for my imagination. In fact, I might have to settle for my imagination several times tonight before I'll be able to go to sleep.

She pushes my sleeve up, tucking it into the neck of my T-shirt, so that my shoulder is bared to her.

"How many hours a day are you working out?" she asked.

I shrug, and her hands stay with me through the movement.

"Depends on the day."

"How many hours today?"

"Somewhere between six and seven."

"Seven hours! Carson, are you crazy? How are you not dead asleep right now?"

I throw her a sly grin. "There are other things that are more appealing than sleep at the moment."

Her lips fall open just barely, not in shock, but just for a slow inhale.

"Are most days like that?" she asks.

I shrug again. "Give or take. Not game days, obviously. And less on Fridays when we have to travel. But I try to squeeze in at least five hours on most other days. Since it's open week, and there's no game to worry about, I've been going extra hard the last few days."

Her hands slip down and circle my bicep, just holding on to me. "Carson, you're going to wear yourself out. Or injure yourself. No one can keep up that kind of schedule, especially not when you've got school and homework on top of that."

"I'm okay, Dallas. I promise."

Her lips purse, perfectly kissable.

She kneads at my muscles, and I flinch a little, sore and caught off guard. Her touch softens, and she leans down to brush a light, apologetic kiss across my shoulder, and I release her ankle immediately, not trusting myself to keep from flipping her over until her back is against this couch and her legs around my hips.

My voice is little more than a growl as I say, "You cannot do things like that, Daredevil, and expect me not to pull you onto my lap and kiss you senseless."

Her answering look is contemplative. Her gaze drops to my

shoulder again, and damn it, I can see her thinking about it. That right there is almost enough to make me say screw it all and take as much as she'll give me.

But the moment passes and she just replies, "Okay."

Then she goes back to working on my arm, and I continue my slow descent into madness courtesy of Dallas Cole.

Chapter 15

Dallas

In hindsight, it might not have been the best idea in the world to give Carson a massage. I already knew his arms were my weakness, and if seeing them filled me with lusty thoughts, touching them made my previous urges saintly by comparison.

Two days have passed, and I *should* have my head on straight. I should not still be obsessing over how strong and devastatingly sexy he is.

I should be kicking in that backup plan and walking away for good.

Tomorrow, I will likely need another powwow with my old pal's hindsight and stupidity, since I just ditched Stella at her art party in favor of hanging out at Carson's place again.

I just . . . I was sitting there at that house party listening to discussions on artists and techniques that sounded like gibberish to me. A pretty cute guy in thick, black-framed glasses and a mop of curly brown hair was hitting on me, and I was bored out of my ever-loving mind.

When I started thinking about one of the history essays I'd read two days prior at Carson's house, that's when I knew I was in trouble.

It's the team's open week, so it's the only Saturday for a long while that Carson won't be busy, and I want him to spend it with me.

Insane! Of the certifiable sort.

He doesn't answer when I text, even though he told me earlier today I could come over if I got bored. His apartment community is gated, but the gate automatically opens if a car pulls up close enough. Not exactly a stellar security measure. He's in building ten, and there must be a party happening in one of the other apartments, because the parking lot is completely full. I have to circle back around and park down by building six just to find a space.

I should probably be nervous, but somehow in all the jumble of things I'm feeling . . . nerves are nowhere near the top of the list.

Stella's stupid painting is in my car, and really, I blame it for the reckless way I'm feeling. Well, it can share the blame with Carson's killer arms anyway.

When I pass building eight, my suspicions of a party are confirmed. There are half a dozen people outside on the sidewalk smoking, and I can hear music trickling out of a closed door behind them. One of the guys smoking catches my eye and nods a hello as I pass. I smile, but then focus my head forward and down toward the sidewalk, walking a little faster.

I don't expect anyone here to recognize me, but I'd prefer to get to Carson's quickly all the same. There had been one too many times in my life when a complete stranger had approached me at the mall or the grocery store or wherever to proclaim, "You're the Cole girl, aren't you? Spitting image of your dad."

I'd never understood that. I didn't think Dad and I looked anything alike. My red hair came from the mom I never knew. Dad's is a dark brown, peppered with strands of gray. He is hulking and huge, and my figure could barely rival that of a telephone pole. Our height, I guess, could be it. I'm tall for a girl. And maybe our noses and eyes are similar, but how that could allow a total stranger to pick me out in public as his child, I'll never know.

My phone buzzes with a text as I come up on building ten. I drag it out, expecting it to be Carson. It's Stella.

Would you hate me forever if I hooked up with Silas Moore?

> *Silas? As in, the dude who's friends with Levi and tried to sleep with me at the frat party, Silas?*

Yep. That's the one.

Jesus Christ.

> *Did he show up to your art party? I don't understand.*

Nah. I got bored after you left, and hopped to another party.

You do know he's slept with like half the girls on campus.

And I've not heard any of them complaining.

Are you kidding? I've seen at least two girls cry over him, and I don't even do the party scene.

They're not crying because he's bad in bed. They're crying because they thought they'd be the one to tame him. I have no such illusions.

You're crazy.

I know. But will you be mad?

I hesitate and then reply.

Of course not. I can't stand the dude, but do what you want.

She sends back a fist-pump emoticon followed by a smiley blowing me a kiss.

I'd halted at the bottom of the stairs to Carson's place, not trusting myself to climb and text at the same time. I jog up them quickly now, feeling a slight chill creep through my leather jacket. Even though a couple weeks have passed since the the first game, it's just now starting to smell like football season, that slightly damp, grassy smell that most people probably just call fall.

I knock, and then shove my fists into my pockets, glad at least that I didn't give in when Stella tried to push me to wear a skirt to that party. The only noise that follows my knock is the whining chirps of a dozen or so crickets huddled close to the wall of the building. I shiver. Crickets. Just another reason to despise fall. They come out in plague proportions.

I knock again, bouncing on my toes, finally feeling those nerves.

I pull out my phone to text him, but suddenly don't want him to know that I came all the way over here without actually knowing for sure that he wanted to hang out. I head back down the stairs and back toward my car, nursing my disappointment. Even if Stella weren't currently trying to score with douche-lobster Silas, I still wouldn't feel like joining her at another party. I love her, but I'm not much of a drinker, and the only other thing to do there is listen to drunk conversations that I find only slightly less annoying than people's compulsion to post pictures of their food online.

I'm two buildings away from my car when I pause by the party I noticed on the way in. Maybe that's where he is? Maybe he didn't hear his phone over the music?

I hesitate just long enough for the smoker I smiled at on my way over to notice me. He's alone now, a cigarette still dangling from his mouth.

"Back so soon?" he asks.

He's wearing a beanie that it's not quite cold enough for, but with his scruffy jaw and surprisingly pretty curly black hair, it works. He's also one of those guys with impossibly pretty eyes and long eyelashes. He puts the cigarette to his lips and takes a slow drag.

"Looking for a friend, but he's not home."

Smoke curls slowly out of his mouth, and he smiles. "You could make some new friends. We're a friendly bunch. Promise."

I'm the one who has friendliness issues.

I contemplate how I might find out if Carson's inside without actually admitting that I'm looking for him.

"You live here?" I ask.

He shakes his head, tapping at his cigarette to release some ash from the tip. "Nah. But I'm here a lot." He nods at the apartment behind him. "This is my friend Ryan's place. You live around here?"

"No. I, uh, live on campus."

He hums around his cigarette before giving a close-lipped smile. "Freshman."

"Yeah, so?" I'm defensive, which is stupid. I mean, the whole *freshmen are so lame* tripe is annoying, but I could care less. I'm just annoyed that I don't know where Carson is. And I'm *annoyed* that I care enough to be annoyed.

I'm kind of annoying myself.

He chuckles. "Easy, girl. I couldn't care less how old you are. Want one?" He holds up his cigarette carton in offering, and before I can decline (because blech), an arm drapes over my shoulder, and I'm pulled in close to a very sweaty, very hard body.

"You looking for me?" Carson asks.

His chest rises and falls rapidly, and I know he's been running. He's smearing sweat on me, and my reaction should be similar to Beanie Boy's cigarette offer (blech). Instead, I find it kind of . . . hot (brain = broken, clearly).

I narrow my eyes on him. "Aren't you supposed to be taking the night off? How long have you been running?"

He brushes a strand of hair off my face, and thumbs my nose in a gesture that feels both affectionate and condescending, like I'm a little kid.

"I don't need a mom, Cole. Got one of those."

"I'm not your mom. I'm your friend." I shoot him a challenging look, and all he does is grin in response.

"Right."

He stretches out the word like I've just said something delusional, and when he glances at Beanie Boy, it's with hard eyes that don't seem very friendly.

"Have a good night."

Then his arm tightens around my shoulder, and he starts steering me back in the direction of his apartment.

"Hey!" I stick my elbow into his ribs and use it to pry myself out of his grip. "I was talking to him! What if I liked him? You can't just go steering me around like I'm your pet."

Apparently, I didn't wait until we were far enough away, because Beanie Boy shouts after us. "*Do you like me?*"

I flounder for a response, my mouth doing that unattractive open-and-close bit that makes me look like a fish.

"She doesn't. Sorry, man," Carson says, grabbing my wrist and pulling me along a little faster.

"Seriously? I get mad at you for controlling me, so you decide to do it some more? You are really not getting this whole friendship thing."

"You gave me rules for a friendship. Stealing you away from some guy obviously not worth your time was not mentioned anywhere in those rules."

"You don't even know him! How could you possibly know if he's worth my time?"

He stops and steps close enough to me that I have to tip my head back to see his face. Momentarily, I think about how much I love that he's actually taller than me. My head is perfectly aligned with his chest so that if I leaned into him, I could lay my head in the crook of his shoulder.

"I don't know if he's worth your time, but I do know he's not getting it. You came here to see me, which means your time belongs to me for as long as I can manage to keep you here."

I'm beginning to see why other people find my honesty off-putting. There's no good way to reply, so I change the subject.

"You're lucky. You weren't home, so I was about to leave."

He hooks his arm around my shoulder again, and this time I manage a more appropriate response.

"Gross, Carson. You're all sweaty."

"Am I?"

He pulls me into him and buries his face in my neck, wiping his damp hair across my skin. He smells salty and masculine and delicious and gah—seriously, what is wrong with my brain?

"Carson!" I push at his shoulders, trying to stifle a laugh and failing. "What's got you in such a good mood?"

He stops rubbing his hair against me, but doesn't unwrap his arms from around me.

"Just celebrating my luck."

He holds me for a few seconds longer, and I can feel his tantalizing breath against my neck. I dig my fingernails into his arms, but that only makes me more conscious of how close he is. He pulls away one torturous moment later, his arm still over my shoulder, but otherwise not acknowledging that anything more than friendly had just happened.

"So what do you want to do tonight, Daredevil?"

It takes me a second longer than I'd like to find my voice. "Doesn't matter. I was just bored of the party Stella dragged me to."

"Well, we can't have that."

We approach his building in silence, but as we take the stairs he asks, "So, what was this party?"

I shrug. "It was at another art major's house."

"And you weren't having fun? Not even with your friend? I guess that means you don't want me to shower and take you back to the party we just passed. I know the dude who lives there."

"Uh, no thanks. I just never feel comfortable at parties. If you're not drinking, it just seems like work—all the get-to-know-you chats that are painful on a normal basis, but straight-up miserable as the other person gets progressively less coherent."

"No personal conversations, huh? You're not the easiest person to get to know, Cole."

I roll my eyes. "It's different at a party. Most of those people, I'll never see again, so it just seems like a waste of time. I don't mind talking with you. You're different."

"I'm free to ask invasive, get-to-know-you questions? Why didn't you tell me?"

"Within reason," I hedge.

He opens the door to his apartment, and I step inside without any hesitation this time.

"Make yourself at home," he says. "I'm going to rinse off in the shower, but I promise I'll be fast. There are food and drinks in the fridge if you want anything."

I take a seat on the couch and tell him that I'm fine. He disappears down the hallway, and as soon as I hear his bedroom door click shut, I throw myself down face-first on his couch with a silent scream, and do my best not to think about him getting naked in the other room.

I fail.

And my imagination is surprisingly vivid.

Chapter 16

Carson

I take the coldest, fastest shower that I can manage, and I run plays in my head to keep from thinking about the girl just on the other side of the wall. I'm pissed at myself for not taking my phone on my run. I damn near missed her completely because I'm too insecure to take a night off.

I'm getting better. That much is for sure. I've had three sessions now with Torres and Brookes, and I'm finally starting to see the payoff of the hours I'm putting in. The receivers are jokers too, which makes the time fly by. Unlike a lot of the crap I hear on the field and in the locker room, their jokes are genuinely funny. Most of the time.

But while I'm getting better, so is Abrams. Maybe it's being back under the demanding eyes of Coach Cole or maybe he's just got his head on a little straighter after having played for a year. Either way, I'm losing ground as fast as I gain it, which means there's no time to take it easy.

The cold shower means there's no steam to fog up the mirror, and I have to look myself in the eye during that last thought, knowing that spending time with Dallas sure as hell falls into the category of taking it easy.

But she's too damn hard to resist.

I pull on a pair of clean jeans and a gray T-shirt instead of the sweats I would normally don for the night. She's dressed for a party in dark, slim jeans, a tiny leather jacket, and a long green shirt that matches her eyes.

I take a second to collect my thoughts before I leave my room, but all my thoughts about her are stubbornly polarized. I want to be the friend she's asked me to be. I want to convince her we can be more. I want to run in the other direction. So I push all those things aside and just decide to do whatever feels right.

As I walk into the living room, she's sitting sideways on my couch, my playbook resting on her knees, chewing on her thumbnail as she surveys the page.

"I thought this was a football-free zone," I said.

She jumps and practically throws the thing off her lap. Then, with a little more composure, she says, "I was bored."

"And that was the best snooping you could do?"

"I wasn't *snooping*. I was just mildly curious to see how Dad has changed things up."

I pick up the playbook and sit beside her, resting one of my elbows on top of her knees.

"You know you could ask him if you really wanted to know."

She dons a look of horror. "I said *mildly*. If I mentioned it to Dad, he would talk my ears off for hours."

I pick up the book, full of combinations and variations that I'm busting my ass to memorize should I ever actually get a shot to play. "So you can actually make sense of this?"

She scowls. "I'll have you know, I knew that thing backward and forward when I used to help . . ."

She trails off, wiping the scowl and every other hint of expression off her face.

If I were a nicer guy, I'd let her get away with it.

"When you used to help Abrams? You guys used to be together, right?"

She crosses her arms over her chest, and in that leather jacket she looks as intimidating and sexy as I've ever seen her.

"Fantastic. What is he telling people now?"

"Nothing."

"Yes, I'm sure Levi just casually dropped into conversation that we dated over two years ago with no ulterior motive. Sounds just like him."

I let my arm slip off her knee, wrap it around her legs, and give her a squeeze. "I heard you'd dated. I didn't bother listening beyond that because, frankly, I didn't want to. He's a dick, and I don't like him. I sure as hell don't like thinking about you and him even in the same sentence."

"Welcome to the club," she mutters.

"Okay. Enough of that. Someone promised me I could ask personal questions."

"What? My love life wasn't personal enough for you?"

My jaw tenses when she says *love life*. Of all the words she could choose to describe her past with Abrams, that one is way, *way* down the list of what I prefer to hear.

And since I don't have any right to feel territorial, over Abrams or that hipster outside that party or anyone, I choose a very different subject.

"Why dance?"

"Why football?"

"Because it's the only thing in my life I haven't dreaded or hated or failed miserably at. It's what I'm good at, in comparison to everything else anyway."

Her head tilts to the side, and she sits up, leaning toward me. Her stomach grazes the arm I have wrapped around her legs, and that brief touch is all I can think about.

"Do you love it?" she asks.

"Cole, you're the one griping at me for working out too much. What do you think?"

She doesn't miss that I haven't answered the question, but she sits back against the armrest anyway, taking away any chance that she'll brush up against me again.

"Your turn," I say. "You love to dance?"

"Yes," she answers firmly. She arches her brow like a challenge and continues. "I have fun when I'm dancing, but I also, I don't know, feel more intensely there, too. When I dance, it's like I finally have everything figured out, like I've crossed over from the ordinary and am on the verge of discovering something wonderful. Inspiration, I guess. But it's bigger than that. *I am bigger* when I dance, like my heart fills my whole chest, and it's leaking out of me with every step and every breath."

Her green eyes are lit with such passion, and the smile playing about her lips is the most gorgeous one I've seen yet. I think I feel more exuberance and life just radiating off of her than I've ever felt about something myself.

The way she talks about dance is a little like how I feel when I look at her. Overwhelmed and fulfilled and falling apart all at the same time.

I climb off the couch and pull her to her feet, suddenly desperate to see it.

"Show me."

She's still in a bit of a trance, caught up in her thoughts and emotions, and it takes her a few seconds to say, "What?"

"Show me. I want to see you dance."

Her eyes widen, and she chokes on a laugh.

"I can't just *show you* in your living room, Carson. I'm in jeans and boots and there's no room and no music and—"

I grip her arm and tug her away from the couch and out into the open space where I occasionally work out at home.

"To quote your dad: don't give me excuses, Cole. Give me results."

Irritation blooms across her face. "Ugh. Why did you say that? I *hate* when he says that."

I laugh, and move my hand in gesture that tells her to get to it.

"I'm waiting, Daredevil." I stick out my arm, closing my hand in a fist. I throw her a playful smile and add, "You can use me as your bar thing, if you want."

"You are not seriously making me do this, are you?"

"Come on. What are you afraid of?"

"Making a fool of myself, twisting an ankle, splitting these ridiculously tight pants, giving you material to mock me for the next century . . . should I keep going?"

I shake my head, unable to contain my wide smile.

She sucks in a deep breath and starts in again. "Falling on my face, disgracing dancers everywhere, failing to impress you—"

I cut her off, getting right in her face.

"Hey." I take hold of her chin for extra emphasis. "You don't ever have to worry about impressing me."

"Just because you tell me not to worry about something doesn't mean I can stop. It's not a switch I can turn on and off."

"Then teach me something. I'll do it with you, and I promise I'll be the only one disgracing dancers everywhere."

She hesitates, and I can see her weighing her own dislike for the situation against the desire to watch *me* make a fool of myself.

Finally, she huffs, "Okay. I'll show you the basics. But I'm not dancing for real for you in your apartment. That's just weird."

She squares her shoulders and shakes her hair out of her face and begins. "So, there are basic positions for your feet and arms and then basic orientations, and everything else in ballet sort of works off of those."

"And that's what you do? Ballet?"

She sighs. "Yes and no. I do ballet. I love it. But I don't really have the training to be as good as I would need to be to do it professionally, and I'm not going to get it here. So mostly I do lyrical or contemporary, which is a little less rigid and more about the movement as a whole rather than body positioning and technique. But most people learn the basics of ballet first. And that's what I teach, too."

"You teach? You didn't tell me that."

"It's just something I do to help out my old dance teacher. I teach a couple classes of little kids with five-minute attention spans. It's . . . interesting."

"Okay then, teach. Show me what to do."

"This is first position."

She stands with her heels touching and her feet spread so wide they're practically in a straight line.

I try to copy her, but lose my balance when I try to push my toes that wide and my body protests. She catches one of my flailing arms and smirks at me as I get my feet into the widest V I can manage.

"Close, but now you need to straighten your legs."

I do as she says, and the muscles of my calves and my ass pull uncomfortably tight. She's still holding on to my arm, and she releases it to place both hands on my midsection, one on my stomach and one on my back. I'm hunched over slightly, and she pushes against me. "Stand up straight."

I do, but I have to hold on to her to manage it, which leaves her tucked under my arm, still touching my waist.

"Maybe we should have done this by a wall," she says.

"I'm a slow learner. The hands-on approach works best."

"Could you be any more obvious?"

"Sure."

I let go of the crazy foot position and use the arm around her shoulders to wrench her toward me. Then, just to make sure she doesn't wiggle away, I drop my arm down until it circles her waist and draw her closer. Both her hands have migrated to my lower back, so I don't feel *too* guilty.

"Do you ever dance with a partner?"

She doesn't meet my eyes, staring straight ahead at my neck instead. Then slowly, she bends her head until her forehead rests on my chest just below my collarbone. Beneath my hands, I feel her body curve on an inhale. She turns her head, shifts a little closer, and lays her cheek against my shoulder as she answers.

"No."

Chapter 17

Dallas

One of Carson's hands slips up my spine and curls around my shoulder, holding me the way he did the night we met. But now his hand is only under my jacket, not my shirt. His hold now is softer, sweeter, and surprisingly sexier.

"Someday I'm going to see you dance, Cole."

I close my eyes, humming my acceptance, and just let him hold me, his thumb smudging up and down the back of my neck in a way that's both comforting and incendiary.

We've passed the point where this is acceptable for a hug, but I just don't feel like letting go. And I'm scared to push it any further because if I don't feel like letting go of a hug, how much harder will it be to stop something more?

"I hate to break it to you," I begin, and his head tips down to hear me better. His lips graze my forehead lightly, then rest there for good, pushing my heartbeat into a breakneck pace. "But I don't think you have a future as a dancer."

He laughs. "No, probably not."

It makes me laugh too, and I take the opportunity to slide out of his grasp, to gain some distance. His hand trails down my back as I step away, and that slow glide makes me shiver.

"Can we just watch another movie or something?"

"Sure."

He picks up the blanket from the recliner and hands it to me before heading to the TV.

"Any special requests?"

"Something that doesn't suck."

The smile he sends me makes me collapse on the couch a little harder than necessary.

"Comedy? Action? Drama? I don't have much in the way of chick flicks."

"Whatever you like."

I don't think I'll be able to pay attention enough for it to matter anyway.

In the end, he picks a television show on Netflix instead of a movie . . . something British about time travel. He doesn't start it at the beginning, but instead starts me on an episode from one of the later seasons that he says can stand alone.

It's a little cheesy, with some kind of techno sci-fi introduction music, but he seems excited about it.

While the beginning of the episode starts, he walks past the couch and back toward his bedroom. I take the opportunity to slip off my jacket and shoes, leaving me in a short-sleeve shirt. He returns a few seconds later with a pillow in hand and flips off the light.

He drops the pillow against the armrest and then leans back against it.

"Come here, Cole." He opens his arms to me, his voice deep and soft.

I only hesitate for a second before I get up, shake out the blanket, and lie down in front of him, my back to his chest. He shifts the pillow diagonally so that both of our heads can lie on it, his a few inches above mine. I can feel his breath ruffling my hair, and I feel a little light-headed. He situates the blanket over both of us, his hand brushing up against my legs a few times and making me jump. When we're both comfortable, he drapes an arm over my waist and pulls me in until our bodies are curved together from head to toe.

I shut my eyes tight, and an irresistible smile starts pulling at my lips. I could fool myself into thinking that this is something that friends do, that it doesn't mean anything, but I'm not so sure that I want to be fooled anymore.

I've spent my whole life following along with whatever Dad wanted me to do. And when he wasn't busy constricting my life, I was doing it for him.

And now . . . I think it might be time to loosen the reins and let myself breathe.

Cautiously, I lay my arm over the top of his that's draped over my waist. He doesn't bother with caution. Boldly, he laces our fingers together before tucking both our hands between my side and the cushion, his arm wrapped firmly around my middle.

The show is interesting . . . with angel statues that come alive, basically ensuring that I'll never be able to turn my back to any statue again. Ever. But I'm more concerned with the person at my back now.

Halfway through the episode I say, "Carson?"

"Hmm?" He lifts his head off the pillow, leaning down and resting his chin against my shoulder.

I don't breathe before I ask, "Could you walk away?"

He locks up behind me and the hand still holding mine flexes. I find myself glad for the way we're lying because I know I couldn't have asked this with him looking at my face.

"Are you asking me to?"

There's a hint of emotion in his voice that makes me wish I could see his face without having to return the favor.

"No. I'm just asking if you could."

He exhales, his breath hot against the skin of my neck, but he doesn't relax.

"I don't know how you want me to answer this, Dallas. I'm scared I'm going to give the wrong answer, and you're going to be the one walking away."

"Just tell me the truth. Honesty, right? This is a safe space."

I didn't think there was any more space to be had between us, but he tugs me back forcefully, plastering our bodies together. I can feel his body's answer against my behind before he whispers against my ear, "No. I can't walk away from you."

It should scare me, but mostly I'm just glad I'm not the only one.

His lips touch my neck, and I want him so badly that my body arches into his from that tiny connection.

"I can't walk away from you because I don't want to. There are a thousand things I want and need to do, but you trump all of them. You drive me to distraction, and all I want to do is get lost in you. All I want to do is make you lose it, too."

His lips skim up my neck, not quite kissing, just teasing before he plants a firm kiss on the corner of my jaw.

"Is that the answer you wanted? Or have I scared you off?"

"You definitely scare me." His head falls back against the pillow, and his hand releases mine. I grab hold, not letting his arm fall from around my waist. "But I'm not walking away either."

His arm tears away from me anyway, but it's to lift himself up off his side. I roll onto my back to look at him; he hovers above me, his arms braced on each side of me.

"Do you know what you're saying? Because you're not exactly free of mixed signals, Cole. And I don't think I can take kissing you again if you're just going to turn around and tell me we can't."

I slide myself back a little, propping myself up on the pillow he vacated. His eyes watch me, hungry and hooded, and nerves dance low in my belly. I touch his forearm, now lined up with my hips since I moved. I trace my fingers up his arm, past his elbow, following the path of his muscles up toward his shoulder. Then, remembering the massage I gave him the other night and the warning he gave me about kissing me senseless, I lean forward and place an identical kiss on his arm, just below his shoulder.

The sound that rumbles in his throat immediately takes me back to our first kiss. And when his lips slam into mine, my mouth is already open.

His tongue sweeps in, demanding and daring, pushing just hard enough that I know how very serious he is without overwhelming me. I angle my head farther to the side, kissing him deeper. He lifts himself a little higher, kneeling on the couch, and I sit up more to follow. Without warning, his hands curl around my knees, and he yanks me down off the pillow, pulling my knees apart and settling all his weight down on me.

I gasp into his mouth, and his hands encourage me to wrap my legs around his hips. I do, and I'm drowning in him. His taste. His scent. His sounds. They swarm around me, dousing me in desire, and I welcome his weight.

With his chest and hips crushed against me, it's almost like he's pushing out everything else but him. All those niggling little fears and doubts and what-ifs are buried beneath the ache he's spinning in me.

His hands run down the outsides of my thighs, curling around my ass and lifting me up just a little while his hips bear down into mine, and I swear my vision goes a little fuzzy. For the first time in a long time, I think about what it would be like to be with someone again, to be with him. I imagine our clothes disappearing, skin sliding against skin, the noise he'll make when he slides into me.

I haven't had sex since that one time with Levi. I haven't wanted to. But now I want it so badly that I'm shaking. I lower my hands to the hem of his T-shirt, and at my tentative tug, he lifts up just enough to help me pull it off.

I swallow and stare and swallow again, because dear, sweet

Jesus riding a unicorn, he's perfect. Hard contoured muscles slope toward the broad plane of his chest. And I have this sudden unfamiliar longing to taste the muscled ridges of his abdomen.

"I will never gripe about you working out too long ever again."

His answering smile is toe-curlingly brilliant, and the warmth that had been building in my center erupts into a flame. He leans down to nuzzle his lips against my neck, and I grip his waist, my hands sliding perfectly along the V of muscles above his hips. One hand brushes the line of hair leading down from his navel, and he groans, nipping my neck in response.

Shuddering, I want to pull him back down onto me, wrap my arms around him, and feel the heat flowing off his skin. But he disappears from over me, sliding down until he's hovering above my hips. He lifts up my shirt, not taking it off, but just pushing it up enough to bare my stomach. Then he settles down onto his elbows and lays his open mouth against my hip.

The warm touch of his tongue draws a moan from my mouth, and he glides his hands up, slipping beneath my shirt and curving around my ribs. His fingers are so close to my chest, and if the fiery path of his mouth along my belly didn't have me so rigid, I might have been tempted to arch my chest toward him.

His eyes glance up to meet mine when he places a hot kiss directly above the button of my jeans. The possessive way his body is caged around mine, coupled with a greedy look in his eyes, makes my spine seem to twist in my body. It coils and tightens, spreading to my hips and creating an unfamiliar ache between my legs that terrifies me.

I'm uncomfortable, miserably so, barely resisting the urge to writhe beneath him, and I know it won't stop. Not until he touches me. Really touches me.

But I can't ask for that. I'm not sure I can *have* that.

Sex and regret have always been intertwined for me, and if I sleep with Carson and regret it tomorrow, I think it might kill me.

I know now that with him, there will be no walking away. If it comes to that, I'll be dragging myself away in pieces.

Chapter 18

Carson

I reach for the button of her jeans, and I see it in her eyes before she says it.

"I can't do this."

For a second, I think she means all of it, and I want to scream. But then she smooths a hand through my hair and pulls me up toward her mouth for another kiss, and I get it.

She just can't do *this*.

I pushed things too fast. I seem to do that with her a lot. But as long as she keeps being honest with me, as long as she doesn't run away, I can fix that.

"Okay," I say, laying a series of kisses on her forehead, cheeks, and mouth. "That's okay."

"You're sure?"

She looks like she expects me to fight her on it or kick her out because of it.

"Very sure." I kiss her again, the compulsion to taste her too strong to deny. "This is more than enough."

At her suggestion, we watch another episode of *Doctor Who*, the first one this time. She smiles at me as she pulls her long hair up into a ponytail while the new episode loads.

I want to pull her to me and wrap my arms around her again, but I also need the separation to calm myself down. I don't need anything more than she's given me, but I would like to be able to hold her without my raging hard-on making me miserable.

"I'm going to get some water. You want something?"

She shakes her head no, and I use the spare minutes standing in front of the ice-cold refrigerator to finish talking myself down. I come back with two water bottles, just in case she changes her mind.

This time I lie on my back, and she snuggles up close to me, resting her head on my chest. I run my fingers through her ponytail, and the scent of vanilla settles over me.

I fall asleep that way—my hand in her hair, her body draped over mine—and I can't remember a more peaceful moment in my entire life.

I WAKE WHEN Dallas shifts next to me, lying almost completely on top of me as she reaches for the phone silently lighting up on the coffee table. She rests her chin on my chest once she has it, eyes heavy with sleep. She yawns and puts the phone to her ear, laying the opposite cheek down against me.

"Hello?"

She's silent for a few seconds, and then she jerks upright.

"Shit! What time is it?"

I squint at the red lights on the cable box. 3:17 A.M.

"You called him? Are you kidding me, Stella?"

Damn. That didn't sound good. Not at all.

"I was asleep. I didn't hear the phone ring. No. I know." She sighs and looks at me briefly before closing her eyes. "I'm at Carson's."

Stella says something, though really it just sounds like shrieking to me, and Dallas replies emphatically, "No, of course not! We were watching a movie and fell asleep."

She struggles to pull herself up with one hand, so I help, getting us both up into sitting positions. She perches the phone between her shoulder and her ear, and then drags her shoes on.

"Stella, can we talk about this when my dad doesn't think I'm lying dead somewhere in a ditch?"

She shrugs on one arm of her jacket and then the other. "I'm on my way now. Call him back and tell him . . . I don't know. Tell him I sent you an e-mail to say I accidentally locked my key and my phone in our room and was crashing at a friend's, but you just now saw it. And apologize like you've never apologized before in your life. I'll text you when I get there. Can you come let me in through the east stairwell so the dorm monitor doesn't see me come in? Yeah. Yes, I will. I promise." She covers her eyes with her hand and mutters, "Bye."

Still sitting on the couch, I perch my elbows on my knees and tell her, "Sorry. I didn't mean to get you in trouble."

"It's my own fault. I lied and told Stella that I was leaving that party to go back to our dorm. When she got home and I wasn't there, she panicked."

"What did your dad say?"

"He's freaking out, of course. He didn't want me to live in the dorms in the first place, so this will be another addition to his list of reasons I'm not mature enough to handle going to school in New York."

New York? I'm guessing that's a dance thing, and I don't like the way that thought leaves me feeling. I don't like feeling like she's about to fall through my fingers at any moment.

"Why don't you stay? If Stella's calling back your dad, there's no reason for you to rush back in the middle of the night."

She frowns, coming closer and pushing her fingers through my hair. "I can't. Knowing Dad, he's probably already had my RA and even the dean on the phone. I need to be there in the morning in case anyone decides to check up on our story."

"Can't you just tell the truth?"

"Carson." The look she gives me is sharp.

"I don't mean about me. Just say you were at a friend's place and fell asleep watching a movie. It happens. You're not a kid anymore."

"As nice as it is to hear someone else make that argument, it won't work. I don't really have any friends besides Stella. And you."

I stand and fold her into my arms. "Okay. But text me when you get there. And in the morning, after you talk to your dad."

"I will."

She pulls back to leave, grabbing her purse, but she doesn't make it to the door before I stop her again. I cup her face in my hands and kiss her, slipping past her lips for one last sweet taste.

"I know it was on a couch and only a few hours, but that was the best sleep I've had in a long time."

After she leaves, I don't bother going back to my bed. I fall back down on the couch where it still smells a little like her, and stay awake just long enough to get her text that she made it safely back to the dorm.

I DON'T SEE Dallas for the rest of the weekend or on Monday or Tuesday. On Wednesday, I take it out on the weight room and everything in it, including Ryan.

"You have really got to get that friend-zone shit under control, man. You're distracted, and I'm not too keen on being the dude you drop hundreds of pounds on when you're not paying attention."

I shake my head and stare at the floor, then do as he says, picking up the bar and throwing it above my head in a dead lift with all the strength I've got. Then I drop it back to the mats several feet away from where Ryan is leaning against a weight machine with his ankles crossed.

"Friend zone isn't really the problem anymore."

"Oh, do tell."

I roll my eyes while he grabs a nearby chair and straddles it like he's settling in for story time.

"I can't really talk about it."

He nods and makes a sound of affirmation. "Gotcha. She's in the CIA, right?"

"Oh yeah. CIA agents really have a thing for college students."

"Do *not* mess up my fantasy, man."

"You're such a geek. Of all the fantasies in the world, that's the one you choose?"

"Hey, we're talking about you here, not me. So, if she's not CIA . . . let me see. She got a boyfriend?"

I shake my head, going for another dead lift. I grit my teeth and growl as I struggle to lift the weight all the way up. The moment that I drop it is almost as bad as the lift itself—that lightning-fast transition between holding all that weight and releasing it, makes my joints twinge.

"No boyfriend. Hmm . . . former lesbian too ashamed to admit you dragged her back into the closet?"

I bark a laugh, not even bothering to tell him no.

"I got it. You're banging Coach Cole's daughter."

He laughs, and I drop the bar I'm holding before I ever get it past my waist, surprised.

Ryan has to jump out of the way to avoid a few crushed toes and his laugh trails off into dead silence. His face morphs into an expression that makes me want to drop that damn bar on my own head.

"Fuck, man. You are . . . Fuck! Are you crazy?"

"Yes," I answer, because really, that's all there is to it.

"You just . . . you're . . . Oh my God, man. You better be wearing a rubber. I'm picturing your mangled body if you ever knock her up and the big dude finds out."

"Shut up." I cut my hand across my throat in a warning gesture.

There's no one near us at the moment, but I'm paranoid. Dallas's rule strictly forbids me from telling anyone. I've already botched that up and don't need someone else accidentally stumbling on to the knowledge. "We're not . . . I'm not *banging* her, as you put it. We're just seeing how things go."

At least, I'm pretty sure that's what we're doing. We texted back and forth over the weekend, and she didn't seem like she'd changed her mind, but she said she had church with her dad on Sunday and some dance thing on Monday and work on Tuesday. A small part of me is worried that she's blowing me off. Okay, a big part.

"Seeing how it goes with the *coach's daughter* . . ."

"You're going to take a dumbbell to your balls if you say that out loud one more time."

He knocks on the back of the metal chair he's straddling like it's armor, and I'm moving forward to rip him off the chair when he holds his hands up.

"Relax, man. I won't say a word. But you know"—he coughs instead of saying Coach's name—"won't be the only person you have to worry about. There's Abrams, too. The guy's an asshole, but no one talks about an ex as much as he does unless part of him still wants her."

"I don't give a fuck what Abrams wants. He's not getting anywhere near her, whether we work out or not."

Ryan nods, and after I do my last dead lift, growling a little more than is probably necessary to get me through it, he mercifully changes the subject.

"Speaking of Abrams. Dude is finally figuring out how not to shit the bed every other play."

I stretch my neck from side to side, and then roll out my shoulders. "I know. I don't know what it is, but he's kicked it into another gear."

"Maybe he felt you breathing down the back of his neck."

"Maybe."

Ryan checks his watch. "I gotta get to class, but let's get lunch before you come back here this afternoon. What's the closest cafeteria to your class?"

"Schaefer," I say, and my stomach flips. That's Dallas's dorm.

"All right. I'll meet you there. Try not to injure any pedestrians in your frustrated state."

The only person I'm really in the mood to hurt is myself. If I didn't have to get to Spanish, I'd stay and punish myself for another couple hours. I have a feeling I'm going to have to do more than my usual run to clear my head this afternoon.

Chapter 19

Carson

It quickly becomes clear that I should have just stayed in bed today when my Spanish professor lays my failing test on my desk just before the end of class. I shove it in my bag and make a beeline for the door.

It stays there, taunting me through my next two classes. Those taunts merge with all my thoughts about Dallas, and Ryan might actually be right about me posing a risk to strangers.

I don't say a single word when we meet up outside Schaefer for lunch, and he must sense my mood because he doesn't say anything either. I don't let myself think about Dallas's dorm somewhere in the floors up above me as I stalk down the stairs to the cafeteria in the basement.

I grab my tray and for today only I forget about eating healthy and what will give my body the best energy. I grab anything that looks good to me, and I've filled two plates by the time I'm done.

I see Stella first. She's laughing loudly, drawing attention in a way she seems to relish. Dallas has her back to me, and she's sitting straight in her chair because I know she'd never slump. All the same, she's very still and has her head down like she wants eyes to just pass right over her.

Mine don't. They never could.

Which is why I don't realize that Stella has spotted us until she steps directly into my line of sight.

She steps up beside me under the pretense of refilling her drink.

"You do realize that if you hurt her, I'll castrate you long before her dad gets to you . . . right?"

I punch my cup against the ice dispenser a little too hard to be casual.

"I'm not going to hurt her."

"You forget I saw you that first night, all over her. She's not like that, if that's why you're in it. She's sweet and innocent." Her voice falters on that last word, and she looks like she wishes she could take it back. "She's not a hookup is what I'm saying. So if that's what you're after, get it somewhere else."

"Do you really think I would risk my spot on the team just to hook up with her?"

She shrugs. "You wouldn't be the first stupid one to try."

My anger is too close to the surface today, and her words mixed with the thought of Dallas's relationship rules make me so irate, I actually crack the plastic cafeteria glass I'm holding.

Soda pours out over my hand, and I curse, rushing to dump it out in the machine grates.

Ryan's quiet mutter of "Incoming" is the only warning I get before Dallas is there beside us, drink in hand.

"You idiots do realize you're holding up the line, right?"

I don't look at her as I grab another glass and start to fill it up.

Stella leaves to head back to their table, and Dallas moves in closer to me.

"What's up with you?" she asks.

"Nothing. I'm just having a fucking terrible day."

I turn to go, and she grabs my elbow. She lets it go almost as fast, and if I weren't so aware of her, I could have convinced myself that I imagined it.

"Sit with us," she says.

I glance around the cafeteria briefly.

"What happened to not hanging out in public?"

"Sit beside Stella. No one will think anything of it."

I don't want to fucking sit by Stella, but I'm not stupid enough to pass up time with Dallas if I can get it.

Stella's expression when I sit down beside her is the icing on the cake.

Ryan sits his tray down next to Dallas, but with one look at my face, he slides it down one spot and sits with one chair between them.

I wouldn't have made him do that, but I like him all the more because of it.

"This is Ryan," I say.

Dallas's face is carefully blank. "I didn't realize you had anyone with you."

"It's okay," Ryan whispers. "My lips are sealed."

When Dallas's mouth falls open, and her green eyes catch mine, all that extra admiration for Ryan flies out the window.

"I didn't tell him. He just kind of—"

"He didn't," Ryan says. "I'm just an intuitive genius. Probably going to get recruited by the CIA any day now."

Stella snorts a laugh next to me, and at Dallas's glare, she says, "What? I can't *laugh?*"

"This isn't funny!" Dallas's tortured expression almost makes me wish I'd never sat down.

Stella is unperturbed. "You're the one who brought him over here. If you're that paranoid about gossip, there's an easy solution. I don't know how you thought it was going to play out."

I can't tell whether she's more distressed by my presence here or Ryan's, considering her *rules.*

"I wasn't thinking! He just—"

She looks at me, and I really wish I'd never sat down. I want to spend time with her, not be the object of pity that I currently am.

"Are you okay?"

"I'm fine."

She arches an eyebrow in a challenge because she knows I'm lying. I arch one back because I don't think our agreement of honesty extends to this weird four-way conversation where both Ryan and Stella are watching us with barely concealed expressions of interest. Besides, the conversation I want to have is unlikely to be something she wants to have in public.

Her eyes soften, and I think she gets it.

"Ugh. Dallas, just take him up to our room already and make out or something. These soulful, searching looks are going to give me hives."

I would not want to be on the receiving end of Dallas's glare, but Stella must be used to it.

"I have a solution!" Ryan says. "You guys don't want to be seen in public together in case someone gets the wrong idea. Or really, the right idea, but you don't want them to know it's the right idea."

Stella leans her elbows on the table. "Get to the point, 007."

"Go out with me," he says.

Stella looks at Dallas, but when Ryan keeps his eyes on her she says, "Wait . . . me?"

"Yeah. If we're dating, then Carson and Dallas can just tag along with us, pressure-free."

"One problem there, bud. *I don't date.*"

"Not yet. I could be the one to sweep you off your feet."

Her snort of laughter could have taken any guy to his knees, but not Ryan. He just continues grinning, completely unfazed.

"It's a good idea," he says.

She laughs even harder, and I think there might actually be tears in her eyes when she finally settles down.

"Yeah, well, listen." She turns to Dallas. "I have to get to class. Sorry I can't continue to be your buffer." She slips her purse over her shoulder, and before she picks up her tray, she leans across the table toward Ryan. "If you want to ask me out, you're going to have to man up and do it for real."

As she walks away, he calls out, "I thought you don't date."

"I thought you were going to sweep me off my feet."

Dallas stays picking at her food for a minute longer, then she says abruptly, "I need to go, too." I sigh, and she adds, "I'll text you."

I don't let myself watch her leave because that would just be the torture cherry on top of an already shitty day.

When Dallas said she'd text me, I didn't think she meant immediately.

Third floor. Room 43. Take the stairs.

I take one look at the two plates of food that I barely touched, then switch my gaze to Ryan. He waves a hand. "Yeah, yeah. I'll finish my lunch alone."

"I forgive you for all your bastard moments."

"Good. Means I get to rack up some more."

I'm in such a hurry to leave that I almost forget my tray.

"Don't forget, you're working with Speedy and Blocks in an hour!"

Almost forgot about that, too. I roll my eyes because he's been trying to make those nicknames for Torres and Brookes stick for weeks now, and he just can't accept that it's not happening. "I'll be there."

I'm glad he's not there to see how quickly I take the stairs to the third floor, otherwise he might start calling *me* Speedy.

I try not to look too impatient as I knock on the door to Dallas's dorm room.

She opens the door just a crack at first, then when she sees it's me, she opens it wide.

"I'm sorry about downstairs. Now tell me what's wrong. Did something happen with—"

As soon as she closes the door, I push her against it and crash my mouth to hers. Her fingers thread through my hair, gripping it tight, and we're on the same page in seconds.

These are no soft kisses.

We touch lips and tongue and teeth. When she pulls on my hair and moans, I take that as my permission to be a little rough. I lift her up by the hips, and she wraps her impossibly long legs around me, squeezing me between them. I slide my hands around to cup her backside, and she arches out from the door. Her hands leave my hair to wrap around my shoulders, fingertips kneading and pushing at my muscles in a way that releases all the stressful tension and replaces it with the want barreling down my spine.

She is the most intoxicating mix of hard and soft—lean, strong muscles covered in silken skin. That's her personality, too: combative and shy, bold and insecure.

She pushes off the wall in favor of leaning on me completely. I stand there, completely wrapped up in her, and she clings to me so fiercely that she wrings every bit of frustration out of me.

Gradually, our kiss slows from punishing to exploratory. Her breath is sweet against my mouth, and I relish every slow slide of our tongues together. I loosen my arms. Now that she's not locked against me, the rise and fall of her breath morphs into a sensual push and pull as she rocks against me.

Every other kiss I've ever had is wiped away because this . . . her rubbing herself against me, trusting me completely and abandoning every thought but how to get closer—it's the hottest fucking moment of my life.

I slip my hand under her shirt and up her spine in what is quickly becoming my favorite way to touch her. She makes a mewling sound, and her back straightens, pulled tight like she's stretching. Then she melts against me, completely mine.

"That's what was wrong," I whisper against her lips.

"Oh." Her eyes are lazy and hooded, and they remind me of waking up to her lying against me. "Better now?"

"Should tide me over for a few hours at least."

I leave Dallas's dorm on a high (and through the back stairwell she says never gets used). And it lasts all the way to the athletic complex, where I enter the locker room with a stupid grin on my face.

That grin disappears immediately when I walk into a freaking circus. All the coaches are there, a few players, two police officers, even more campus police, and several stern-faced suits that can't mean anything good.

Coach Cole catches sight of me, says something to one of the police officers, and then starts my way.

I really, *really* should have just stayed in bed today.

Chapter 20

Dallas

It's never a good thing when you walk into your dorm lobby and there are swarms of people in groups talking hurriedly and staring at their phones. That should have been the first thing to tip me off.

I hear people whispering about the football team behind me before class starts, but I try not to listen because in my gut, I'm terrified someone saw Carson coming out of my room. Surely that wouldn't cause this kind of buzz. I mean, he's not even a starter, and it's not like we did anything crazy scandalous in public.

But our dorm does have windows, and sits directly across from another dorm. I can't remember if I had the blinds closed or not. But surely . . . surely that's still not big enough news to have the campus going this nuts.

I get my answer when my phone buzzes.

It's a text from Stell with a link to a Twitter post.

Under my desk, I follow the link, and my jaw drops.

There's a slightly blurry picture of Levi in handcuffs, being placed into the back of a police car.

Levi Abrams, @RuskUniversity's star quarterback, arrested. #theregoestheseason

People are posting theories—everything from drugs to prostitution to murder. Other rival universities have picked up the thread, and it's been retweeted hundreds of thousands of times.

Holy crap. No *wonder* everyone is whispering. We have a game on Saturday, the first true conference game and potentially our biggest game of the season just because it's with the Dragons, our rivals. It's a home game, and people always turn out in huge numbers. Even during the school's worst seasons, that game is always a big deal.

And Levi . . . what the hell did he do?

After class lets out, I try calling Carson, then Dad, then Carson again.

I text and call for the entire ten minutes that it takes me to walk to the fine arts building.

Finally, as my dance professor, Annaiss, calls us to our positions at the barre, my phone vibrates.

It's from Dad.

Can't talk. Come by my office after your
classes are over, and I'll fill you in on
what I can.

Shit. That doesn't sound good. Surely if it were all some stupid misunderstanding, he'd be able to just say that.

I'm distracted, but Annaiss doesn't say anything. Everyone is distracted. Every time we line up on one side of the room to take turns doing different passes or combinations, the whispers begin.

No one tries to ask me anything. I don't know if it's common knowledge everywhere that Levi and I dated, or just on the team. Whether they're considerate or clueless, I'm glad for it.

I don't like the guy. I've not made that a secret to anyone, Levi included. We barely spoke at all during the four months between when we broke up and he graduated. And I pretty much avoid him at all costs.

But once upon a time, I think I loved him. It's hard to tell now. There are too many other messy feelings clinging to those memories, but until he broke up with me, I had thought we'd end up together. Everyone thought we would. We talked about college, and what I would do if and when he got a scholarship. We even talked about what would happen beyond that . . . if he went pro. I don't necessarily think that's an option for him anymore (especially not with whatever was going on today), but back then things looked like they were heading that direction.

Then he got hurt. Not on the field, but on the court. Like a lot of the guys at our school, Levi did pretty much every sport. And when he fractured his ankle playing basketball, everything kind of changed. He had surgery, and the recovery time was minimal. Just six to eight weeks. But it was enough to jeopardize his negotiations with a lot of the universities that had approached him.

He still got a scholarship with Rusk, but it wasn't what he wanted. And we fought more and more. Over everything. Other girls. Other guys. My dad. Sex.

Mostly we fought about sex.

I don't know whether he always had that bitterness and arrogance in him or if it bled out of the dismantling of all of our plans, but I'd like to believe that he didn't completely fool me. I'd like to believe that the boy I originally fell for was just as sweet and genuine as I remember him being.

But if that's true . . . it's crazy to think that one tiny event can derail your entire life, derail who you are. If he'd sat out of basketball that year, would we still be together? Would we both even be at Rusk? Would dad have let me go to school out of state if I was going with Levi?

What if?

I could waste a lifetime thinking about what-ifs, and that's all I would ever have—hypotheticals and hopes pinned on a plan that crumbles when dragged into reality.

It's nearly four o'clock when my last class lets out. Normally that would be right in the middle of Dad's practice, but he didn't give me a specific time to come by, and I've been going crazy reading all the theories online. Most of the theories now are focused on drugs, but the specifics all vary.

Annaiss stops me before I go. She's in her early thirties, the youngest professor on staff, and though she doesn't have as much experience as most of the other professors, she at least feels a little less out of touch with the real-world business of dance than the rest. She has thick, glossy black hair and exotic eyes that are soft as she looks at me.

"Are you all right, Dallas?"

Maybe she's not as oblivious as I thought.

"Yeah, just distracted, I guess."

"You know you can come talk to me about anything. Dance related or otherwise. My office is on the second floor."

God, I must look a wreck if she's this concerned.

"Thanks, Annaiss. I'll keep that in mind." I still feel a little weird calling a professor by her first name, but she insists.

She lets me go after that, and in a daze I change out of my dance attire into jeans and street shoes.

When I get to the athletic complex, the parking lot is filled with cars, but the halls are oddly silent. I step into the weight room, and it's completely empty, weights left out, clearly strewn about from an interrupted workout.

I step through the door that leads to the film room and Dad's office. It also apparently leads to the locker room, because the door is propped open, and I see the team sitting at their cubbies. Still. Somber. Silent. A smattering of coaches are walking around the room, carrying papers and looking busy.

I look for Carson, but I don't see him.

I don't see Levi either, but I didn't expect to.

The office door is closed, and I knock.

A different coach opens the door. One I don't know.

I haven't exactly gone out of my way to stay in touch with my dad since school started. I'm a little ashamed to admit that I have no idea how he's settling in here.

"I, um, I'm Coach Cole's daughter. Do you think I could talk to him?"

"He's in his office, but he said you might be coming by. Come on in."

The coach is young, maybe thirty, with sandy blond hair. He holds out a hand and says, "I'm Coach Oscar. Most everyone calls me Oz."

I shake it, feeling strangely . . . adult.

"Dallas," I reply. "Like the Cowboys. Unfortunately."

He laughs. So do the two other coaches sitting around the office, which is more like a conference room now that I look at it.

He points to a door on the far side of the room that I didn't notice last time I was here. "There's your dad's office."

I cross the room, nodding to the other coaches, and knock on the door. Dad takes a while to answer, and I stand there awkwardly, not sure if I should ignore the coaches behind me or talk to them or what. Luckily, I'm saved by the turning of the doorknob. Dad opens the door an inch, and then when he sees it's me, he opens it wide.

"Come in, Dallas. We were just about finished."

I freeze as Carson looks over his shoulder at me. He's sitting in one of the chairs in front of Dad's desk, and when he sees me his blank expression cracks just enough to reveal the worry and stress lurking beneath.

I almost reach for him.

"Hey," I say before I can stop myself. Quickly, I redirect my gaze to Dad, hoping he'll think that was for him.

I shouldn't have worried. Dad doesn't notice.

"Carson, why don't you stop by and talk to Oz on your way out. He'll make sure you get set up with a solid tutor and anything else you need."

The faintest blush runs across his cheeks, and he ducks his head.

"Yes, sir."

His eyes meet mine briefly on the way out, and I can tell . . . things just got significantly more complicated.

The door clicks closed, and Dad slumps into his seat. He looks . . . sad.

With his eyes closed, he leans his elbows on his desk and runs a hand through his hair. It's going gray at the temples. When did that happen? He looks older, too. There are lines on his face and hands that I can't recall ever seeing before.

Has this job or this thing with Levi taken that much out of him or have I just not really looked at him for that long?

I stay silent, knowing instinctively that he needs it. This is probably the first quiet moment he's had since Levi was arrested.

Again, I'm struck not just by how much older he feels, but how much older I feel, too.

"What have you heard?" he asks finally.

I clear my throat. "Nothing concrete. I saw the pictures. People are talking, but no one knows for sure what happened."

Dad straightens up, sliding his chair closer to the desk, and suddenly he looks all business again. When he starts talking, I get the feeling that he's said this speech several times today. "Earlier today, Levi was arrested when he attempted to sell marijuana and other pharmaceutical drugs to an undercover police officer."

"He *what?*"

That . . . that didn't sound anything like Levi. The old one or the new one. Sure, he partied, but what reason could he possibly have to sell drugs?

"I know." Dad sighs. "It gets worse. When the police executed a search warrant on his apartment, they found more drugs, including anabolic steroids and HGH."

"HGH?" It sounded familiar, and as soon as Dad opened his mouth to answer, I remembered. "Human growth hormone?"

Dad nods.

"Was he taking it?"

"We're not certain yet. It appears likely. Along with the vials, they found syringes, both used and new. We think that might have been why he was selling the other drugs in the first place. HGH is an expensive habit."

"That's crazy. Why would he do something so stupid?"

I've heard of athletes, dancers included, taking the stuff to get over injuries quickly. But supposedly there are all kinds of possible side effects. Serious ones.

"When people are desperate, it distorts their view of the world, of what's right and what's smart. If you're desperate enough, it will distort who you are in addition to what you see."

"I can't . . . " I shake my head, not knowing where I am even going with the sentence. I don't know a lot of things in that moment.

"Dallas, I don't want to ask this, but I know that you and Levi are close. I need you to tell me that you didn't know about this, that you weren't around him or drugs or anything else he was involved in."

"No! Dad . . . no." I want to be angry that he could even think that of me, but mostly I'm too shocked. "Levi and I are *not* close, Dad. We haven't been since before he graduated high school."

"I know you guys had a rough breakup, but when I started this year, he led me to believe that you two were past that. That you were friends."

I scoff, and I feel so sick that I have to stand up and walk around and just breathe.

"We are not friends. I can count on one hand the number of times we've spoken in the last few years. Dad . . . I *hate* him. I don't know any other way to put it . . . " Angry tears swim in my eyes, and panic paints Dad's face. "There are things you don't know . . . that I never want you to know. But suffice it to say, I hate him."

I can tell Dad wants to ask despite my assurances. His knuckles turn white as he grips the desk, and I can see the confusion and frustration battling in his eyes.

"Why didn't you tell me?"

"What? That your favorite player turned out to be an awful human being? That the guy you called *son* the entire time we were dating is an asshole, and I wish we'd never met?"

"Dallas," Dad's voice is sharp.

"I've earned the right to call him that, Dad. Trust me. God, even now you're defending him."

"I'm not defending him." There's the stern, angry Dad I know. He's the one I know how to talk to. "Clearly, there are many aspects to his character that I didn't see, but that doesn't explain why you didn't tell me that he hurt you."

"Gee, Dad. I thought you would have picked up on that by yourself. What with all the crying and general misery."

"That's not fair. You kept to yourself. You never talk to me. And I was—"

"Busy, I know. *Trust me*, I know."

Dad looks almost hurt. For a second.

"I was going to say that I was trying to respect your space. I thought if you'd wanted me to know, you would have told me."

"Well, you got that part right."

"Damn it, Dallas. I don't know what you want from me. I'm trying here."

"Too little, too late, Dad. It's been years, and honestly, it's not a conversation you really want to have. Just . . . don't accuse me of doing drugs with him or wherever this conversation was heading. I'm not giving you another reason to call me irresponsible or to tell me I'm not ready to be an adult. Because whether you like it or not, I *am* one." I think of just how drastically Levi has changed since the moment I first met him. He was sweet and shy and so good to me. "I've realized something . . . We don't get to know what's going to happen to us. And anything can come along and ruin our plans, change our world, change us. I've given in to you on so many things because I just keep telling myself that I have time. But I can't keep planning for a future that might never come. That's not living."

For the first time in my entire life, Dad doesn't have an immediate counterargument. He just asks, "So what are you going to do?"

I make this weird noise somewhere between a laugh and a sob because, ironically enough . . . I don't know.

Chapter 21

Carson

We don't even have a real practice, and yet by the time I head out to the parking lot, I feel more exhausted than I have in weeks.

They're worried about other team members being on drugs, both recreational and performance enhancing. So we all took a standard drug test, and it looks like they'll be bringing someone in to do blood tests for HGH, too.

I should probably stay and work out considering I've done nothing since this morning, but I just can't find the energy. Barring some other crazy happening, I'll most likely be starting on Saturday in Levi's place. That should be motivation enough to get my ass in gear, but it's just . . . not.

I wanted that starting spot, had worked hard for it. But a part of me had accepted that I would never get it, and I think that I was relieved.

I certainly never thought to get it like this.

When I get to my truck, Dallas is there waiting for me, sitting on the hood. I look around. She's not exactly being covert. Most of the team left before I did, but there are still people heading to their cars and leaving for the night.

"Hey. You didn't have to wait for me. We could have met at my place. Or I would have come to you."

She shrugs. She's wearing that leather jacket again, her hands stuffed in her pockets. Her long legs are crossed at the ankles, her feet dangling off the hood of my truck.

"I didn't really feel like going anywhere."

I step closer, running my hand from her ankle to her knee before holding it out to her. One hand appears from her jacket pocket, and she laces her fingers with mine.

"I'm not complaining. I just thought you didn't want to advertise this."

She sighs. "I don't. I was angry and feeling a bit reckless."

"You and your dad?"

She nods. "He just makes me so angry sometimes."

"Come on." I help her slide down off the hood, my hands lingering on her hips for just a second. "Let's go to my place, and you can tell me about it."

I help her into my pickup, mostly as an excuse to touch her, and then I drive over to where her car is parked at the edge of the lot, then we head to my place separately.

Once we're both inside, she sheds her jacket and shoes, and my body kicks back into normal gear, alerting me to just how hungry

I am. I had barely anything at lunch, choosing Dallas over food. I'm tempted to do it again with her sitting on my couch, relaxed and perfectly at home, but one loud growl of my stomach tells me that she's not going anywhere. Food first.

I order pizza and eat a sandwich while we wait. I offer to make one for Dallas too, but she laughs. "I think I'll be fine with just the pizza, thanks."

I sit down on the couch, sandwich in hand, and say, "Okay then. Tell me what happened with your dad."

"Ugh. He's just clueless." She scoots closer and lays her head on my thigh. "He thought Levi and me were still friends or something, and wanted to know if I knew about the drugs or was involved. I don't even know. Most days, I swear it's like he doesn't even know me. You'd think he would have at least picked up on a few things since I was in diapers, but nope."

I let my sandwich-free hand drift through her hair, wrapping the deep red strands around my fingers.

"Do I still get to ask personal questions?"

She leans into my hand and says dramatically, "I suppose."

I pause for a few seconds, brushing my thumb across her temple, wondering if I really want to go there. In the end, my need to know everything I can about her wins out. "Where's your mom?"

She purses her lips, and her feet point, then flex, and point again before she answers. "I don't know. She left before I could walk. They met in college. Dad played football. She was a cheerleader. She had me their first year out. Dad's first year coaching.

They weren't married. They were going to after I was born, but then she had really bad postpartum depression, so they just kept putting it off, and then one day . . . she left. She never came back. Dad never looked for her. That's all I know."

"Do you think he misses her?"

She shifts uncomfortably. "I don't know. He doesn't act like it. It's always just been about football. He'd pick us up and move us to wherever. He gets this high from fixing programs, turning them around. You'd think after he was done we could just stay and enjoy it. Enjoy the things he built, but no. It's always off to the next place."

"You don't think he's doing it on purpose?"

"What? Like he's looking for her?"

I shake my head. "Like he's fixing everything else so he doesn't have to fix himself or fix your relationship."

She stays silent for a few moments, her eyes directed at the ceiling, while she chews on her lower lip.

"Do you ever think that maybe that's all people do? Fix some things and break others? And we all just live in this giant cycle where we screw things up and hurt people we love, and then we turn around and try to atone for that by fixing others things. And maybe we're all just waiting on our turn for a broken heart and the person who will fix it."

"Are we still talking about your dad?"

She sits up, and her hair falls around her slumped shoulders. She stays silent for so long that I'm pretty sure she's done answering my questions for the night. Just when I'm about to pull her to me again, she says, "I think I break more than I fix."

Her voice is low and hollow, and it kind of echoes in my ears, until I feel sick with pain for her.

"You know what you need to do?"

"Grow up?"

I brush all her hair to one side of her neck and lean down to kiss her shoulder.

"You need to dance."

She shoots me a look over her shoulder. "This again?"

"I'm serious. It's what fixes you. I can tell by the way you talk about it."

Her answering smile is sad. "How is it that you can see that when you've known me for so little time, and he can't?"

I know she's talking about her dad.

"Sometimes it's hard to see past our own broken pieces."

I want to say that they're really not all that different. They've just found different ways to heal themselves, but I'm not sure it's the time for her to hear that. I think she might need to figure that out herself.

"Come on." I take her hand and pull her to her feet. Together, we walk over to the open space in my apartment where she wrapped her arms around me in a hug not that long ago. I pull us back into that position, but this time I keep her hand in mine. It's nothing complicated, but she lays her head on my shoulder and we sway together. Someday, I'll learn how to do more, but for now I hope this is enough.

"What fixes you?" she asks.

A month ago I would have said football. I would have answered her immediately and automatically. But now, if I'm honest, and she always makes me want to be . . .

"I don't know."

THE ATMOSPHERE IN the locker room the next day is downright arctic. No one likes our chances for Saturday, me included. And when you stick dozens of young guys in a room, most of whom prefer to deal with their feelings through aggression and physicality, too many of us are itching for a reason to break something.

This morning, Maz, a massive offensive lineman from Alabama, put a hole in the wall in the weight room. Well, two holes technically, one with each fist. And the locker room is short two chairs—one broken by a player and the other by a coach.

I've managed, just barely, to stay above it and stay focused, and I suppose that pisses some people off.

Carter, the defensive lineman who I already couldn't stand for talking about Dallas a few weeks ago, is the first to push me.

"Saw Firecracker sitting on your truck last night, McClain. What's that about?"

"It's about being none of your business," I answer, lacing up my cleats.

"Wasn't enough for you to take over QB from Abrams, you had to go for his sloppy seconds elsewhere, too?"

I drop the cleat I'm holding, and I slam him hard into the wood bracing between cubbies. Something splinters, and the uneven edge probably hurts like hell, but I don't care.

"Say one more fucking word about her, and I swear to God,

I'll lay you out, Carter. And once I'm done beating every ounce of shithead out of you, I'll hand you over to Coach and see what he thinks of my work."

He snarls, "Fuck you."

I'm ready to slam his head against the wood frame behind him when someone grabs me and pulls me off. Strong arms loop under my armpits, forcing my arms up.

Whoever's holding me growls, "Get that idiot outside. All of you, go."

Torres and Brookes both step toward me, but they hesitate, look at whoever has me, and then leave with the rest of the team. Only when everyone is out does the guy release me. And when I see who it is, I'm ready to go postal all over again.

Silas Moore.

He's too fucking close, and I push him back, struggling to stop myself from doing more.

"Don't you say a fucking word about her, Moore."

He holds up his hands in surrender.

"I get it. I'm not exactly at the top of your list right now. Understood."

"Try right at the bottom."

"I'm an asshole. I know it. You know it. But I've got nothing against you, and I'll stay far away from Firecracker."

"*Stop* calling her that."

"Done. I'll make sure the rest of the team lays off, too."

I grit my teeth because even though he's not said anything wrong, I've got nowhere for all the anger to go.

"Why are you doing this?"

"I might have been friends with Levi, and sometimes we might have gone too far with some things, but I'm not him. What he did was stupid and careless, and it makes us all look bad. I'm not going to tank this team over some misguided loyalty to him. I care about this team, and we all, myself included, need you to be on your game. So if you need something from me, it's yours. Whether it's to shut up idiots like Carter or run plays or lift—whatever it is, I've got you."

"I still think you're an asshole."

"Yes, but I'm an asshole who's got your back."

He holds out a hand, and after a few deep breaths, I take it.

"Let's go to work."

Chapter 22

Dallas

I didn't think there would ever come a day when I would willingly step foot into another football stadium to watch a game. Add to that the red Rusk T-shirt I'm wearing (which clashes oh so horribly with my hair) and the fact that I'm kinda, sorta, definitely dating another football player (which I swore I would never do) . . . and yeah, it's a day of improbable things.

The crowd is absolutely huge. It took Stella and me nearly an hour just to drive the few miles to the stadium, and then another forty-five minutes to park and walk to the nearest entrance.

Between our fans in red and the Dragons' in green, it looks like Christmas threw up all over everything. I could have gotten tickets from Dad to sit with all the other coaching families and school administrators, but I didn't want to tell him why I was coming. There are plenty of things my dad hasn't picked up on over the years, but my abhorrence for football is not one of them. My sudden interest wouldn't go without questions.

I think I might actually be ready to tell Dad about Carson, but that's not just my decision to make. Carson has enough on his plate at the moment without worrying how my father will react to the news of us together.

One thing at a time.

That's what I've been telling him since the news broke about Levi.

We've both just got to take it one thing at a time.

It's still over an hour before kickoff, and the student section is basically full. Stella and I cram ourselves onto the edge of a bleacher right next to the band. We won't be able to hear ourselves think, but we're only ten rows up, and we've got decent visibility as long as we stay standing up.

I pull out my phone to text Carson, but I don't know what to say. I want to tell him something that matters, something big, but the only thing that comes to mind are those three little words that we are so, *so* not ready for.

I tell Stella as much, and she pauses in unwrapping a piece of gum to say, "I've got three different words for you. Winning = BJ."

"Stella!"

She pops the gum in her mouth. "You said you wanted something big that matters. I think that qualifies."

"You're terrible. And no help whatsoever."

"Speaking of big things . . ." Her slow-spreading smile reminds me for the thousandth time how different we are. "How big is it? You can tell me." She bounces her eyebrows a few times.

"We're not there yet."

"You spent the night last night."

"Yeah. But we just slept."

"I mean, I know you're not having sex. You would have told me that. But you haven't done . . . like anything?"

I wince. I really do need to tell her about Levi, but at this point, I've lied for so long, I almost think it will cause more damage to tell her the truth.

"We've both been a little preoccupied with other things."

"All the more reason to find a little distraction in each other. It's good for the mind. And the body. And the personality. Just about everything, really."

I ignore her and stare at my phone.

I type out a text.

Sending you all my daredevil vibes. I'll wait for you at your place after.

"Naked," Stella says, reading over my shoulder. "Tell him you'll wait for him naked."

"I'm going to have to lock my phone, aren't I?"

"Jesus, you don't lock your phone? What century are you living in?"

"Not all of us spend our days sexting."

"Oh my God, speaking of sexting. Carson's friend Ryan is surprisingly dirty."

"*You're sexting Ryan?* Seriously? I thought you weren't interested."

She shrugs. "I'm not. But he's fun. That's all it is."

My phone buzzes.

I wish we were already there.

"He'd be wishing a lot harder if you'd added my suggestion."

"Why don't you go mentally scar a band member or something?"

She takes me seriously and starts scanning the bleachers next to us for potential victims.

I want to keep texting Carson, but I don't want to distract him. This was going to be a tough game to win before everything that's happened. The whole team will need to really focus and come together to pull it off.

So I shove my phone back in my pocket and sit down. I bounce my knees and force myself to think about something else.

I'm really close to mastering the dance I choreographed on the night of Dad's birthday. I've been working on it gradually, trying to re-create the piece that I imagined in my head.

It hasn't been easy. In my imagination, I was stronger and more flexible. But I've almost got it down. And when I do, I think I'm going to show it to Carson. He's been bugging me to dance for him, and that piece was inadvertently inspired by him.

Between thoughts of dance and Stella, I manage to keep from texting Carson before kickoff.

The Dragons win the coin flip, and they choose to receive first. As the guys line up, everyone in the student section raises their right hand, shaped like a claw for our mascot, the wildcats. They shout and scream and *go wild*, and the sound races around the stadium, filling up the entire space with noise. I pick out Carson on the sidelines, number twelve. He's bouncing back and forth on his toes, shaking out his arms, trying to stay loose.

If the first run of the game is any indication, we're in for a world of hurt.

The opposing team breaks through our defenses, finding every hole and returning the opening kick sixty-eight yards all the way to our thirty-yard line. I squeeze my fist tight and press the back of my hand against my mouth. They get two first downs in a row, and then score on the third play. The kicker makes good on the extra point, and just like that Carson's going in, and we're already down by seven.

Stella holds my hand, and I resist the urge to close my eyes.

He can do this. He works so hard. He's got it.

He takes the snap, looking to hand off to Silas. But when the defensive end crashes down on him, Carson keeps the ball and makes a break through the gap, surprising everyone with his speed. The safety takes him down with a hard hit that makes me grip Stella's hand a little tighter, but not before Carson's pulled in a twelve-yard gain.

I breathe a little easier.

On the next play, the defense has wised up to the fact that he can run, and they're more conservative in the options they give him. He gets a decent look with one of his receivers, but the pass goes a little too far left and ends up incomplete. He shakes it off and follows it up with a handoff to Silas that gets a small gain. It's third down, five yards to go. When he drops back, he doesn't have more than a second to scan the field before a Dragon player breaks through the line like it's nothing. He slams into Carson from behind, and he hits the ground so hard I gasp.

He gets up and he has held on to the ball, which is something, but I can tell from the way that he holds his body that he felt that one. And we lost ground on the play, too.

It's fourth and twelve, and we're still deep in our own territory.

Dad opts for the punt, trying to get the ball as far away from our end zone as possible.

On the sideline, Dad looks like he's tearing the offensive line apart. His arms are waving so wildly that no one has to hear him to know he's pissed. Carson is farther down the field, bouncing on his toes just like he was at the beginning.

Please don't let this affect you. It wasn't your fault. You've got this.

While the band blares away beside us, the Dragons score again. The crowd around us grows restless. I hear Levi's name a few times, and my stomach clenches.

Before Carson takes the field again, Dad stops him with a hand on his helmet. He leans close, talking to him for a few seconds, and I hope Dad knows what he's doing. I hope he's as good as people have always said he is.

"Go Carson!" I scream.

I know he can't hear me, but it's more for me anyway. I just want to feel like I'm *doing* something.

Whatever Dad said, it works.

Right out of the gate, Carson hits one of his receivers for a forty-yard gain, putting us in Dragon territory for the first time.

He follows it up with his own carry for fifteen, and all the douche-bags who've been grumbling around me are cheering.

Next, he hands off to Silas, who skirts two, three, four defenders before he finally gets dragged down by two guys on the fifteen-yard line.

The screaming around me is so loud, I swear I can feel it vibrating the metal bleachers. The student section starts chanting "Go Red. Fight Red. Bleed Red." And even though it's morbid, I scream along with them.

And when we score with a reverse pitch to Torres, a wide receiver, the sound is deafening. The band immediately picks up with the RU fight song, and for a few seconds, I remember what it was like to love football. Before Dad and I fought so much and before Levi ruined me more than I already was, there had been something special about the game for me. I loved the way one person could start a chant, and soon a stadium of thousands had picked it up and were screaming in unison. I loved that kids who didn't give a crap about school were suddenly belting the school song from the top of their lungs. I loved those tense moments before the start of a play when everyone is wishing and hoping exactly the same thing, and the whole stadium holds its breath.

Even now . . . I can admit that there's something a little bit magical about it.

And I get why Dad does it. Not just football, but his whole thing. To take a team and a town that doesn't believe and bring them together, I can see how that would fill him up, to the brim, just like dance does for me.

Chapter 23

Carson

I taste blood from a busted lip. Nausea rolls in my stomach. Every part of me aches . . . inside and out.

Because we lost.

I know we all went into this expecting it, but . . . I still hoped. And now all that hope sits rock hard in my stomach, rotting and gnawing at me, asking, *What if?*

What if Levi had been here? Would we still have lost?

I sit at my cubby, a towel over my head, while sweat drips down from my forehead and stings my eyes. I hear a pair of pads crash into the wall, and guess that it's Silas, but I don't know for sure.

"Listen up." It's Coach's voice, and even though I want to stay huddled beneath my towel so I don't have to see my teammates' faces, I know I can't. I push the towel back around my neck, but stay leaning on my knees. Coach is silent for too long, and when

I glance up, I realize he's been waiting for my eyes. I sit up a little straighter.

"I've been here before," he says. "Which is how I know that none of you are in the mood to listen, but you need to. So put aside what you're feeling for just a few minutes, and hear me out. No one was expecting you to win this game." I wince. We'd all been thinking it, but it was worse hearing it out loud. "No one was expecting you to come out and rush two hundred yards and pass two hundred and fifty, which for those of you paying attention is the most this team has had in any one game in over two years. It also happens to be more yards than your competitor put up tonight. That scoreboard might have had us losing by three tonight, but one look at the stats proves that you fought harder, played stronger, worked better than you ever have before. No one was expecting you to give that team a fight, but I promise you that people will sit up and pay attention now."

He pauses and moves toward the wall where he lays a hand against the painted wildcat, beside which it reads, "Bleed Rusk Red."

"You know, a few weeks ago, I stayed at the office late. And when I went to leave, I didn't expect to see a player sitting in the film room, still hard at work hours after practice had let out. I asked why he hadn't gone home for the night, and do you remember what you said, Carson?"

I know what night he's talking about—the night he fought with Dallas—but all I can remember is thinking about her, wanting to go to her.

"You told me that there are no easy days. And I've been thinking about it ever since. Today was not an easy day. This *week* was not an easy week. But every single one of you fought through it. I've coached and played against every kind of team, and I'm telling you now, this team will be the kind that takes no easy days. This team will be the kind that fights every last second for every last yard until we see that win on the board. And for days like today, when we lose, I promise it will be the hardest damn win that other team has ever had. That's the kind of team we will be. It's the kind of team we are as of tonight. And I tell you, I'm damn proud to be your coach."

No one is slumping or frowning anymore. Everyone looks deadly serious, like we'd go out and play another game right now if we could.

"No easy days?" Coach says.

And together we repeat, "No easy days."

He tells us to hit the showers, and before we do, I feel a hand on my shoulder. It's Silas, and he nods at me once before walking away. Torres does the same, followed by Brookes. I lose track, but it must be at least twenty players who throw me a nod before they strip and head to the showers.

As I stand to do the same, I see Coach is still standing at the edge of the room. His eyes meet mine, and I get one final nod before he turns and disappears in the direction of his office.

DALLAS IS WAITING at my apartment like she promised when I pull up later that night. She slips off the hood of her car, where she was lying staring up at the sky, and comes over to me.

She kisses me. Firm and sweet, and I notice she's wearing a Rusk Wildcats shirt. I grin.

"Never thought I'd see the day."

"Yeah, well, only for you. I might have something else you've been wanting to see, too."

That definitely piques my interest, and I raise my brows.

She laughs, and the sound is so light and perfect that I could listen to it all day long. "Not that. Well, at least not right now anyway."

Dear God.

She takes my hand, and leads me over to a basketball court that sits between my apartment building and the one next to it.

"Tonight, I got to see you play. So I figure it's only fair you get to see me dance."

She's uncharacteristically shy, and I'm beginning to realize just how much I like every version of her—from daredevil to demure.

"That sounds . . . perfect."

"Now, there's still a part or two that I'm not as solid on as I'd like to be, but I think you'll get the idea." She hands me her phone with a song pulled up. "Press play when I tell you?"

I nod.

She has on these weird black sneakers with no sole in the arch that I guess are some kind of dance shoe. She pulls off the red Rusk T-shirt, leaving her in a tight gray tank top and black stretchy pants. She walks to the center of the court and takes a deep breath. She nods her head at me, and I press play.

The music starts soft, and with her hand stretched straight

up, she spins a few times, her movements smooth and graceful. She lands, feet apart, her head tipped back, and she is stunning. Then the music changes, picks up, and her body lurches backward like she's taken a punch to the stomach. She reaches out, running forward, and she leaps into the air. Somehow, she manages to look like she's straining to fly while some imaginary thing holds her back.

She lands, crumpling, and the emotion in her face and body is so strong, so raw that I have to resist the urge to go to her. But then she lifts herself up. The entire dance oscillates that way between soft and hard. Her body spins and moves beautifully, and then it turns to hard angles, bent limbs, desperate jumps. At one point she throws herself down on the ground, rolls a few times until she lands on her back, and then she arches up, supported by her shoulders and her toes, and I swear it looks like she's just had her soul ripped out. The music seems to bleed out of her, matching perfectly with her movements. On and on the song goes, and she beats herself down and down. But as the song comes to a close, she gets up one final time. Her legs shake, then straighten, and she lifts her head up to the sky, and even just standing there, her body tells a story.

The song ends, and I stand staring at her, absolutely dumbfounded.

"Well?"

I blink, light-headed, and I don't know if I remembered to breathe at all the entire time she was dancing.

"You are incredible."

She smiles and dips her head, and I know she's doing that thing she does where she's trying to look smaller, look less, so that people will pass on. But there's no fucking way I'm letting this go.

"I'm serious, Dallas. That was . . . You did that? You came up with it all?"

She nods. "The night that Dad and I had a fight, and I found out you were on the football team."

Now it's my turn to feel like something's been ripped out of me. There was so much pain in that piece. I hate that I had any hand in it.

"I'm sorry," I say.

"What?" She crosses to me. "What could you possibly have to be sorry about?"

"I made you feel that . . . that ache."

She smiles. "Only because I was stubborn enough to think I couldn't have you."

"You have me. Completely."

She lifts up on her toes and kisses me, and she's the sweetest damn thing I've ever tasted.

She says, "You were so good tonight." I exhale, dropping my shoulders. "Stop that. You were. It's all anyone is talking about. You did everything you were supposed to do. Our defense just wasn't as strong as theirs."

She shivers, and I grab her Rusk T-shirt off the ground. "Let's get you inside."

I hand her T-shirt back to her, but she doesn't put it on. So I wrap my arm around her shoulder to keep her warm until we get to my place.

I lay my keys on the table just inside the door, and we both slip off our shoes. I stretch my neck back and forth, knowing I'm going to be sore tomorrow. I take a step toward the couch, but she grabs my hand.

"You're tired."

I nod. And step toward the couch again for just that reason, but she pulls me straight ahead instead, back toward the bedroom. My heart rolls over in my chest, and my blood pumps a little faster, and I am suddenly not as tired as I thought.

She's stayed the night twice since this started, but both times we fell asleep on the couch after a movie. We never talked about whether or not she was going to stay, it just happened.

The door to my bedroom is open just a crack and she pushes it a little farther with two fingers. It's dark, but she makes no move to turn on the light. The light from the hallway is enough to cast a glow on the bed, and she steps up beside it.

"I'm not ready to have sex," she says quickly. "I mean . . . I want to, but I also don't, so for now, can we just sleep together in the normal sense?"

I work to keep my expression clear of any disappointment. I want her to be ready, but I also can't deny that seeing her beside my bed makes my whole body buzz with want.

"Of course. I'll take you in my bed however I can have you."

I can see the blush burn across her cheeks even in the dim light. She places a hand on my shoulder and says, "Sit down."

I do as she asks, and she steps between my open knees. She fingers the sleeve of my T-shirt and adds, "Take this off?"

I reach back and grab the fabric behind my neck, pulling it over my head. I feel the light touch of her fingers helping to pull it off the rest of the way. Instead of letting my hands drop, I rest them on her hips and pull her a little closer.

Her fingers are warm on my bare shoulders, and she sighs at the contact. She moves both hands to my right shoulder, and starts working the tight muscles. I groan and drop my head down, resting my forehead against her stomach. She kneads at my shoulder, skating down to my biceps on occasion, her fingers strong and sure. I close my eyes, and try to keep from getting too worked up. I try for about a minute before I give up and let my hands slide down from her hips to her thighs. Her breathing picks up as I run my palms up and down, curling my fingers around the backs of her legs.

I don't push any further than that, though, letting her stay in control. And she's completely in control when she pushes me back on my unmade bed and straddles my hips. She runs her hands up my abdomen, first soft and then harder, pushing on my muscles there like she did at my shoulder. I let her explore my chest while every ounce of blood in my body heads south. She leans down and presses a kiss on my sternum. She hovers there, her hot breath making all my muscles tense. She drags her mouth from the center of my chest to where my heart beats wildly beneath my skin. Her tongue peeks out tentatively as she does, and I fist my hands in my sheets to keep from grabbing her and flipping us over.

She looks up at me, her pupils deep and black. "Not sex. But maybe we could . . . Maybe we could do other things?"

I growl and roll her beneath me, pressing my hips down into hers. She moans, and with her stretchy pants and my gym shorts, I can feel the heat of her through the thin material.

"Other things sound pretty damn perfect."

Chapter 24

Dallas

Kissing Carson McClain has officially become my favorite hobby.

His lips are soft even though he kisses me hard. I curl my legs around him, and a masculine noise of approval sounds in his chest. I thread my fingers through his hair, and my blood is rushing so fast that my limbs feel both light and heavy at the same time.

His lips leave mine to slide over my jaw, and the rasp of his stubble sends shivers down my spine. His elbows rest on either side of me, and his hands slide under me to curl around my shoulders. The heat of his breath touches my neck before his lips do, and I grip his hair tight.

I lean my head to the side to give him more room, and his lips burn a line down to my collarbone. Then he dips lower, down to the top of my strappy camisole. His hands smooth from my shoulders down to my ribs as he skims his lips over the curve of my breast peeking just above the fabric. He places a kiss on my sternum, and I shift my hands from his hair to the bare skin of his shoulders.

"Carson," I breathe.

His eyes lift to mine, hooded, dark, and questioning. I don't know what I was planning to say or that I had anything to say at all. I just needed to say his name. I let my fingertips travel down his back as far as they can reach, playing over the taut muscles and warm skin.

He surges back up to take my mouth in a bruising kiss, shifting to lie beside me as he does. When his hand slides along the waistband of my yoga pants, I'm not sure whether I want to lock up or arch into his touch.

He pulls back to look at me, and though I'm mildly terrified, I don't close my eyes. His gaze roams my face as his fingers slide beneath the fabric into a territory we've not covered yet.

He's slow, waiting for me to say no, I think. But no matter how many pieces of me want to say no, there are far more begging me to say yes.

His fingers slide against me, teasing sensitive flesh. He pushes one long finger into me, grinding the heel of his hand down at the same time, and I dig my nails into his muscled shoulders. I tilt my hips up, moving on his finger, and he moans.

"God, Dallas, if you only knew how much I wanted you."

I slip a hand between us, finding the hard ridge of him through the fabric of his shorts, and he hisses out a breath.

"I've got some idea."

His mouth covers mine—wild and hot and greedy—and he

bites down on my bottom lip at the same time that his finger curls inside of me. I arch up, lost in the sensation, and his mouth moves down to my chest. I feel another graze of his teeth and squeeze his length in response.

"Oh fuck, baby." His gruff words, spoken against the sensitive skin of my breast, make the heat between my legs turn molten.

This . . . *this* I can handle. His sure, sensuous touch. Tendrils of a new kind of trust.

I pull him up to me for another kiss, and together we spend time exploring, touching, and tasting before exhaustion takes us.

IN THE WEEK before the team's next game, the entire university transforms. There's red and black everywhere—banners and T-shirts and signs and sidewalk chalk. The energy is electric and powerful, and I can see the way it changes Carson. He's tired. He's been putting in crazy hours all week—on the field and with his tutors. I've spent almost every night at his apartment because otherwise, I'm not sure I'd get to see him. But even through the fatigue, he wears a constant smile, and I think that finally he's beginning to believe in himself.

It's our last game before homecoming, and then we've got three away games in a row. When the buzzer sounds and we've won by fourteen, the student section of the stadium pours down from the bleachers, and fills the field with red and black. Some overzealous fans make a dash for the goal posts, but the crew is already busy collapsing them before they can get there. Instead, everyone just stands there screaming and shouting like we've won a national championship.

It's not that. But it is an upset, and not by a small margin either. It's a solid win, and the fans aren't the only ones that are ecstatic. I stay in the stands because I still haven't told Dad about Carson, but I watch him on the field. He smiles widely, sharing crushing hugs with player after player before finally my dad stands in front of him.

It's not the team's first win, but it's Carson's, and that seems more important.

Dad slaps a hand on his padded shoulder, and they talk for a few moments before they hug like all the rest.

I decide that I'm telling Dad this week. I need to if I want to road-trip with Stella to the next away game.

I expect to meet Carson at his apartment again, but he texts asking if I'd be open to going to a party, and I say yes because he's earned the right to celebrate. I tell Stella and she's all over it, dragging us back to our dorm to get prettied up.

Even though it's chilly outside, I pull on a formfitting purple dress. It has long sleeves, and I decide on some black tights and my black leather jacket to go with it. I leave my hair down because I know Carson likes it like that, and I put on a little more makeup than normal.

Stella whistles. "Damn, girl." I take that as her approval. She drives to the party, and in the car on the way she says, "I'm going out on a limb and saying you're going home with Carson tonight."

I nod. We haven't talked about it, but all the energy of this week and the win has me anxious to touch him, to soak up the way he makes me feel.

"So are y'all just giving up the whole incognito thing?"

I shrug. "I don't know. I was going to talk to him about it to-night."

"What do you think your dad will say?"

"He'll be pissed. You remember how long it took him to be okay with me dating Levi, and he loved him. I think, though, after the whole drug thing, that he's even more wary. But Carson is a good guy, and Dad likes him, and I think as long as I ease him into it that he'll be fine. Eventually."

"Good luck, sister."

The party is at a house where a few teammates all live together, and as soon as we enter, I can see Stella sizing up the room.

I laugh. "Good luck to you, too."

Hands on her hips, she scoffs. "Luck has nothing to do with it."

I follow her lead, and scan the room looking for Carson. I find him almost immediately. He's sitting on a huge sectional, sur-rounded by players and cheerleaders, but his eyes are on me. He's wearing a charcoal gray shirt that hugs his body and makes his eyes stand out. He's so incredibly sexy, and the hungry look he fixes on me makes my legs feel like Jell-O.

My phone buzzes.

You have no idea how
badly I want to kiss you.

I smile.

*About that. I was thinking that
I might tell my dad this week.*

*I'm glad I kept it tame and only
said kiss.*

I roll my eyes.

*You know what I mean. About us.
That is . . . if you're okay with it.*

*Am I okay touching and kissing
you every time I see you, no matter
where we are? Hell yes.*

*He might be hard on you. He's not
always most logical person when it
comes to treating me my age.*

I can take it.

*Is there somewhere we can be
alone? For just a little bit.*

To my surprise, he leans over to Silas and the two talk quietly.

Upstairs. Second room on the left.

I'll go up first. Give it a minute or
two, and then you follow.

Done, Romeo.

Romeo, huh?

I might have changed my mind
a little about chance romantic
meetings at parties.

Well, here's to romantic party meeting number two.

I duck into the kitchen to get a drink and to kill some time. Someone must have been feeling especially celebratory, because in addition to the keg, there's liquor and mixers set up on the bar. I fill up my cup with mostly cranberry juice, and a splash of vodka, while two minutes stretches into an infinity.

I'm counting the seconds in my head when a body leans on the bar next to me, too close.

"You're Coach Cole's daughter, right?"

I manage a thin smile. "Yeah."

The guy is massive, tall and blond and probably closing in on three hundred pounds.

"Jake Carter." He holds out his hand. "I'm on the defensive line." I take his hand, and he shakes mine a little too long for my comfort.

"You talked to Levi since everything went down?"

I jerk back. "Um, no. I haven't. Why would I?"

"I just thought you might since you guys have a history."

"Yeah." I roll my eyes. "*Ancient* history. I am miles past moved on."

"McClain, right? You must have a thing for QBs."

"Excuse me?"

I grab my drink and turn to leave.

"Wait, I'm sorry. That came out wrong."

I don't even bother concealing my annoyance. "Yeah. Don't worry about it."

"Before you go . . . there's something you should know." I raise a brow, remembering why I don't come to parties like this. "I like your dad a lot. He's a good coach. I would have told him, but I don't want to mess with the team dynamics when everything's going so well."

"Just spit it out," I say.

"There's a bet going around the locker room. Levi started it at the beginning of the year. Silas and a few other guys are in on it. Whoever hooks up with you first wins."

"Hooks up with me?" Despite all the noise and laughter of the party, the world is oddly silent around me.

"It's stupid. Levi . . . He was just saying how you . . . well, you weren't that easy, and it became this thing to joke about who could nail you down. I just . . . I thought you should know. You being here at a football party and all."

"Who can nail me down, huh?" I laugh and it tastes bitter on my tongue. "Thanks for the tip, Carter."

I add a little more vodka to my drink before I turn and leave. This isn't new territory for me. After Levi graduated, I was the frigid bitch who wouldn't give any guy a chance, especially football players. And the scum at the bottom of the male barrel always seem to think a girl who says no is just a girl who's a challenge.

I tip my cup up, and swallow steadily as I climb the stairs. I didn't really mix in that last pour of vodka, and the first few swallows burn. But I keep going, and my cup is half-empty by the time I'm outside the door that Carson mentioned.

He's pacing when I enter, just the lamp on beside the bed.

He looks gorgeous, and I wince.

I gulp down more of my drink and tell myself that there's no way Carson is in on that bet. He's been entirely too sweet and patient and caring.

"Hey." He folds his arms around me and presses his face into the crook of my neck. "I missed you."

Maybe he's *too* sweet. Is that a thing? Are there actually guys like him that are really this great? Or do they all have some ulterior motive?

I tip my head back to sip more of my drink, and his mouth opens over my pulse. "You taste so fucking good. You drive me crazy."

"Are we in Silas's room?" I ask.

He nods before trailing his lips down to my collarbone.

"I know. Not exactly the most romantic place, but we'll just stay standing and not touch any surface."

Silas and a few other guys are in on it.

He can't be. He just . . . He can't be. He said he didn't listen to the locker-room talk about me.

He lifts his head up and cups my chin. "Hey. Where are you?"

I finish off the last of my drink and say, "Sorry. I might have poured a little more vodka than I thought into that."

He presses his forehead against mine and says, "You okay?"

"Yep. A little vodka never hurt anyone."

He grins. "Famous last words."

My heart twinges at that grin.

He has nothing to do with the bet. I repeat it in my head until I'm sure I believe it.

And yet . . . I'm so sick of being the frigid freak. So tired of being the kind of girl targeted for shit like this. Maybe it's time for me to get over the thing with Levi. I'm certainly not the first girl to lose her virginity and regret it.

I just need to let it go.

I put my cup down on a dresser, and wrap my arms around Carson. I move my mouth to his, and he wastes no time dipping his tongue inside. His hands start at my hips, gripping me firmly. They slip up under my jacket, stopping around my rib cage as his lips tease mine.

"It was a stupid idea coming to this party," he says. "All I want to do is be with you."

I step back, smiling like I know what I'm doing.

"So be with me."

"You wanna leave?"

I shake my head and peel off my jacket, tossing it on the floor. Silas's bed is made, and I take a quick glance at the comforter. "As long as we don't get under the covers we're probably safe."

"You love testing my control, don't you, Daredevil?"

I think back to the night we met. There's no way he knew who I was . . . right? But he heard me arguing with Silas. If he and Silas are friends, wouldn't he have recognized his voice?

I shake my head and force myself back into the present.

"I love it when you call me Daredevil."

That's the girl I want to be—the girl who doesn't give a damn about football or bets or sex. I want to be the girl who takes what she wants. And right now, bet or no bet, truth or lie . . . I want Carson.

And I want to stop being scared that everything will hurt me. I'm stronger than that.

I crawl up on the bed on my knees and crook my finger at him, and he practically jumps on the bed.

We both laugh, and I smooth my fingers through his hair. He does the same, combing softly through the strands and then settling his hands on my back.

He makes me happy. I'm comfortable around him. No one is that good of an actor. Even when I'd had sex with Levi, I could tell he wasn't all the way in it. Everything was too mechanical. It hurt, but I went through the motions.

It wouldn't be like that with Carson. It would be hot and sensual, and it would get me past this hang-up.

I tip my lips up, capturing his. But everything about the moment is a little too soft. I thrust my tongue against his, press my chest into him, and then lie back, pulling him on top of me. I need him to lose himself in me, so that I can lose myself, too.

Chapter 25

Carson

I know that this isn't the best place for this. I'd rather be home in my bed, but I can't bring myself to pull my lips away from hers long enough to actually put those thoughts into motion.

Her lips move fast and hard against mine, and I think maybe we're both a little high off the night's victory. I try to slow her down because if I don't, it's going to be mighty uncomfortable heading back downstairs. But she's not having it.

She pushes on my shoulder, and I roll to my side, thinking that finally one of us has the sense to suggest we leave, but then she presses me back and straddles me. I groan, the sight of her above me taking me back to the first night that we took things a step further. She's nothing if not determined, and with just our hands and mouths, that night was the best sex of my life, even without the sex.

Her hips circle above me, and in that purple dress and tights, I know she can feel me straining against my jeans. She rubs herself against me and I gasp, "Fuck, Dallas." I want to get her out of here right now, but I can't seem to get anything but those two words out of my mouth.

I'm squinting up at her, wanting to close my eyes, but unable to stop watching her. She reaches for the hem of her dress and pulls it up and over her head, baring her slim waist and a black bra.

Fuck. This has gone too far.

"Dallas." I sit up and her hand darts to the hem of my shirt, tugging it up. I push her hands away. "Dallas, stop. Not here. I won't be able to stop."

"So don't."

She reaches behind her for the clasp of her bra, a line we haven't even crossed back at my place, and I seize her hands to stop her.

"Dallas, why don't we just go back to my place?"

She slips her hands out from under mine, leaving mine against her back. She runs her hands up my arms to my shoulders and rocks her hips into mine.

"Please," she murmurs, diving down to drag her lips across my neck.

"Please what?"

She grasps one of my forearms, pulling my hand off her back and guiding it to her breast. She closes her mouth over mine, rocking harder against my dick, and whispers again, "Please?"

I break away, groaning, capturing her shoulders in an attempt to hold her still. "I don't get what is happening here, babe. Just tell me what's going on."

She makes a small cry of frustration and tries to kiss me again, but I've got her held tight.

"This is what you want. It's what I want."

"This is *not* what I want, Daredevil."

She jerks in my arms, and I can't tell whether she's trying to get closer or pull away. "Please. Just help me," she demands.

"Help how?"

Her fingernails dig into my shoulders, and I can't tell what she's thinking. Not at all.

"Fix me," she whispers.

"Baby . . ." I release her shoulders to cup her face, and her hands go back to wandering along my chest, but I can tell she isn't even really feeling it. I shake her, just enough that she stops for a second and looks at me. "You are *not* broken. And even if you were, *this* would not be the way to fix it."

She starts to cry, and it's just like her laugh—silent, only her expression doing the work. Her lips tremble and tears crawl down her cheeks. I press my face close to hers, forehead to forehead, so that I can feel some of her tears against my own skin.

"I want you, Dallas. I have since the moment I met you. And when you're actually ready, I won't waste one moment before I take you to bed. But you're more than this. *We're* more than this."

She collapses into my arms, crying, and it's the most emotion I've ever seen from her. In fact, other than her dance and the emotion that I see in her gaze when she looks at me, I've only ever really seen anger from her. Nothing like this.

"Sorry," she whispers. "I'm sorry. This was stupid. I just . . ."

Her chest shakes as she struggles to breathe. "I thought this would help."

"Help what?"

"It's stupid."

"Nothing that makes you feel like this is stupid."

She scrambles back off of me, grabs her dress, and bolts for the door. As soon as she has the dress over her head and chest, she pulls open the door, still tugging the dress back into place. I tear after her, catching her just before she hits the top of the stairs.

"What the hell, Dallas? Talk to me."

"I can't. I just need to be alone for a little while. We can talk later."

"No." I wrap my hand around the back of her neck and pull her so close that our lips would touch if she just tilted her head up. "You promised me you wouldn't run. Not without an explanation."

"Carson, please just don't."

Her expression is angry, but her voice just sounds sad.

"*No*. I am not letting you walk away from me."

"Maybe you should let her walk away, man."

I jerk back to see Ryan at the foot of the stairs. Stella and Silas are beside him, and the three of them are doing their best to block us from the dozen or so people behind them, craning their necks to see what's going on.

"Shit."

I let go of her, even though I don't want to. I look down and see that her dress is stuck up over one hip. You can't see anything because of her tights, but I reach out and tug her dress back into place anyway. I hate that people have already seen us arguing, but I sure as hell don't want them to see any more.

I step back, but I keep my eyes fixed on hers. "You promised. You have to talk to me."

Her voice is small and her eyes wide. "I will. Tomorrow."

I breathe a sigh of relief and watch, aching, as she flees down the stairs. Ryan and Stella walk in front of her, pushing their way through the people, and when they move out of my line of sight, I collapse against the wall and slide down to the floor.

I don't know how much time passes before Silas grips my elbow and pulls me up. "Come on, man. Just go home and sleep it off. Whatever it is, isn't helped by sitting up here. Plus, you've got fangirls at the bottom of the stairs planning how to fix your broken heart."

That pulls me out of my funk, and sure enough, he's right. There's a group of girls not-so-casually hanging out at the bottom of the stairs. I turn my back on them and scrub my hand over my face.

"I just don't know what happened. We were fine and then . . ." I don't say any more, knowing Dallas wouldn't want me to. But everything just happened so damn fast, my head is still spinning.

Silas holds up his hands. "There are plenty of things I know about women, but how to deal with an angry one is not in my skill set."

The thing is . . . I don't know if she *was* angry. I don't know anything

"She's gone?" I ask.

"Yeah. Your boy drove them home 'cause Stella already had too much to drink."

I grab my phone and text Ryan. I keep texting him all the way down the stairs, past the group of girls, and out the front door. I'm probably blowing up his phone, but I don't care.

When I get to my truck and don't trust myself to text and drive, I call him. He answers on the second ring.

"Relax, dude. She's fine."

"No, she's not."

Ryan sighs.

"She's *going* to be fine. She and Stella are back at her dorm, and they're talking some things out."

"Why can't she talk to me?"

"She will. Just give her some time."

"I can't." Or I don't want to. All I can think about are her damn rules. What did she say? If either of us thinks it's too much, then we just say the word, and it's done. We walk away.

What if that's what this is?

"You can." Ryan's voice is surprisingly firm. "She doesn't want you to see her upset. She's not going anywhere, man. Just wait and talk to her tomorrow."

He hangs up on me then. And I barely resist the urge to throw my phone against the windshield.

I drive around for a while, getting closer and closer to her dorm each time before I convince myself to stay away. I'd be there in a heartbeat if I were certain it wouldn't push her away faster. Finally, I head back to my place and do the only thing I can think of.

I run.

Chapter 26

Dallas

I make a beeline for the shower as soon as Stella and I get inside our dorm. She tries to stop me, but I can't talk right now. I don't know how to deal with stuff like this. I've spent my entire life actively *not dealing*, and now I'm ripping at the seams because of it.

It's a Saturday night after an incredible victory, so the dorm is pretty much a ghost town. I have the shower all to myself, so that even if anyone could hear me crying over the water, it wouldn't matter.

What scares me more than anything is that I don't know who the girl at that party was. She sure wasn't me.

I know my tendencies and my faults. I know that I jump to anger first, and when that doesn't work, I walk away instead.

That girl? She was throwing herself into the fire instead of trying to escape. And that's not a version of myself that I've ever had to face.

I don't think Carson had anything to do with that bet, not with the way he reacted, the way he stopped things from going further, but that doesn't help with the humiliation burrowed so deep beneath my skin that even the scalding-hot water of the shower can't touch it.

God, what he must think of me.

At least I didn't mention the bet. At least he doesn't know just how little I trusted him for a few moments there. Because the only thing that hurts more than my own pain is the idea of causing his.

But when I finally pull myself out of the shower, wrap a towel around my frame, and face my bloodshot eyes in the mirror . . . I have to ask myself—

Regardless of how much I like Carson, do I like the person *I* am with him?

It would be an easier question to answer if I had any idea who I really was.

Back in the room, I tell Stella everything. Including the fact that I slept with Levi. As I predicted, she's hurt. I can see her questioning our entire friendship. What else haven't I been telling her? But I promise her that I have no other outstanding secrets. Not after I tell her everything about Carson and me, too.

When I finish, I'm furious to find myself crying again, but at this point, it's not something that I can turn off or stuff down anymore. I'm not sure if I'll ever be able to do that again. She pulls me into a hug, and together we lie on my tiny twin bed until I've gotten it all out of my system.

"Everything is going to be okay," Stella assures me.

"Is it?"

"Of course it is. That guy is head over heels for you, and this is just a bump in the road."

"It's not Carson I'm worried about. It's me. I trust him a hell of a lot more than I trust myself."

She pushes my hair back out of my face and sighs. "Oh, sweetheart. You're going to be just fine. You're nowhere near as screwed up as you think you are." I know that's a dig at herself. I recognize the self-loathing because I am a master at it. "This is just what it feels like to get older. It won't be the last time you look back at your life and realize just how stupid or naive or terrible you've been. I'm pretty sure that's a reoccurring thing until death do us part. The truth is . . . we're all a little screwed up. If humans were capable of being perfect there would be no such thing as *Jerry Springer*, and the world would be filled with unicorns and fairies, and families would never be broken, and children would never disappoint their parents, and things wouldn't hurt as badly, but it also wouldn't feel so damn good when things go right. And friends wouldn't have anything to stay up late and talk about because everything in the world would be too boring to matter. The only thing we can do is try to find people whose scars compliment our own. And I'm pretty sure Carson McClain would carry your baggage around the world and back if you asked him."

"You think?"

"In a heartbeat."

We fall asleep that way, two grown women in one twin bed, like we're still freshmen in high school having a sleepover, whispering about boys and gossip so my dad won't hear. Things were so much less scary then. We were rushing headfirst into the future with no idea just how complicated things would get on the way.

WHEN A KNOCKING at the door wakes us, the sun is bright and bleeding through the blinds. Stella mumbles a "Go away" and burrows deeper under my covers. How the two of us managed to sleep through the night in one twin bed is one of the great mysteries of the universe, but when the knocking gets louder, I snap to attention.

Carson. It has to be Carson. I scramble over Stella trying to get out of my bed, and my knee accidentally sinks into her midsection.

"Easy on the bladder, Dallas, unless you want a mess in your bed."

"It's Carson," I whisper. "Just a second!" I call toward the door.

Stella props up on an elbow and says, "I'm guessing you want me to make myself scarce?"

"Just for a little bit? Please."

She nods. "I'll go take a shower."

While she gathers her things, I take a quick moment to look in the mirror. I pat down my hair, tucking stray strands behind my ears, and resituate my pajamas so everything is covered.

When it's as good as it's going to get, I open the door.

My stomach plummets.

"Dad?" I glance at him in confusion, and only after a few moments do I realize he's dressed for church. "Oh my God. I forgot about church." I had no idea he cared strongly enough about my attendance to drag himself to my dorm. I've never skipped before, but clearly it matters to him. "I'm so sorry, Dad. I had kind of a rough night last night, and I fell asleep without setting an alarm."

"I know."

His expression is so neutral that I'm jolted by the barely concealed rage I hear in his voice. He can't be that mad about church.

"You know *what*?"

He doesn't say anything for a moment, just swallows, his thick neck bulging with strained muscles.

Stella pops up by my side with her towel and shower basket. "I'm just gonna go take a shower so you two can talk."

When she's gone, I step back to let Dad into the room. He takes a seat on Stella's fuchsia bedspread because her bed is still made. He's so big that he makes the dorm bed (hell, the whole dorm room) look miniature. And he's wearing some expression that I have never seen on his face before. Not normal, not pissed, not football, but something that scares me far worse.

"Dad. What's going on?"

He wraps the fingers of his left hand around the fist of his right and squeezes until I hear a few pops.

He swallows and his voice is scratchy and uneven when he speaks. "I realize that I have not always been there when you needed me, and I'm sorry. I won't make excuses because none of them are good enough. But I can do better."

I keep waiting for his yell to break loose, for this to turn into a fight. We're in uncharted waters, and I'm in danger of drowning.

"I never wanted you to feel like you couldn't talk to me. But I let my unwillingness to talk about how I was feeling dictate how our relationship worked, and I'm sorry."

I feel tears prick my eyes, and I'm shocked that I even have liquid left in my body after last night.

"So I'm telling you now that you can talk to me. Whatever is going on in your life . . . I'll listen. And I will always, *always* take your side."

"Dad," I start softly. "No offense, but you're kind of scaring me."

He chokes on something that might be a laugh, and drops his head down, pushing his thumb and forefinger against his eyes. "At least we're on the same page there."

When he finally looks back up at me, I raise my eyebrows and shake my head because I have no idea what's happening here.

He sighs. "You're really going to make me be the one to say it?"

"Considering I have no idea what *it* is . . . yeah. It's gonna have to be you."

He unlocks his phone and after a few taps and swipes, he hands it to me.

It takes a moment for my eyes to focus and process what I'm looking at. It's blurry around the edges, but there in the center is me against a wall, looking up at Carson. The purple dress I wore last night is bunched up around my thighs, and he has his arm around my neck in a way that looks painful because of the expression I'm wearing, but I know for a fact that his touch was as soft as could be. His jaw is a hard line, and if I hadn't been there myself, I would swear it looks like he's hurting me. And with my dress all skewed, it looks even worse than that.

"Oh God. Oh my God. How did you get this?"

"Since the thing with Levi, I have a grad assistant keeping an eye on the players, their online accounts and stuff. I want to know what they're getting into before it's too late. He called me this morning to tell me he saw this popping up all over Facebook."

I need to sit down, but my bed is too far away, so I just plop down on the floor at Dad's feet.

"This is my fault," Dad says. "I should have kept you away from athletes. They can be volatile and unpredictable, and now because of me you've been hurt by two of them."

"Dad, no." I pull myself up on my knees so that I'm nearly at eye level with him. "This is not what it looks like. Carson didn't hurt me."

His mouth twists like he's tasted something sour.

"I know you don't want to talk with me about these things, but I can't ignore something like this."

"I swear to you. I know this looks bad, but Carson is a good guy."

He grabs the phone out of my hand and holds it up. "However you may feel about him, *this* is not a good guy."

I can't breathe. I might actually hyperventilate because this . . . this is worse than any outcome I could ever have imagined.

I grab Dad's hands in mine. They're big and warm and callused, and they're *shaking*. "I swear to you, Dad. Carson was trying to *help* me. I'm not making that face because of anything he was doing to me, but because I was upset. He was trying to talk to me, to get me to calm down."

"Your—" He hesitates, like he can't even manage to say the word. "Your dress."

I blanche. There's no good way to explain that, and I'm too much in shock to think of something clever, so I settle for the truth.

"Carson and I have been seeing each other. I was planning to tell you this week, today even. I met up with him at a party last night after the game, but before I could see him, someone told me something, a rumor, that upset me. I thought . . ." Oh God, how could I say this? "I was stupid, and I thought that sleeping with Carson would make me feel better." Dad's hands jerk in mine, and I grip them tight enough to hurt. "He stopped me. *He* told *me* no. He knew I was upset, and I wouldn't tell him why, and that picture is me trying to run away before he could make me explain. He's the good guy in this. I promise. I *promise*."

"There are rumors. People are saying—"

"I don't care what people are saying! People are stupid. You said you would believe me and be on my side. Believe me about this."

He turns his head away from me and clenches his eyes shut.

"The boy has only been here since August. You can't have been dating that long because he hasn't *been* here that long."

I let go of his hands, sensing the shift in his anger.

"You're right. We've been friends, I guess, since the first week of school. We've only been dating since right before the Levi thing."

We've not actually said the word *dating*, but considering neither of us wants to spend time with anyone else, I figure we qualify.

He stands up abruptly, and I scuttle back out of his way. "A couple weeks, Dallas? Christ, you were going to sleep with that boy after two weeks?"

The look of disappointment he levels on me makes me feel so small, like I'm shriveling right there on the spot.

"It was stupid. I know that."

"Damn right, it was. I raised you better than that."

My first inclination is to get mad, to sling back insults and tell him that in fact, he did very little to *raise* me at all. But I swallow those words down. Push them so deep that I hope they'll never see the light of day because I know he's only yelling because he doesn't know what else to do.

I know that because that's what I do, and he must have raised me, because I ended up exactly like him. Terrified of the things I can't control. Desperate to subdue all the things I can. Frightened of my own feelings. Frightened of everyone else's, too. For all the teams he's built, and games he's played, and championships he's won—deep down, we're both just afraid to lose.

And if I fight now, neither of us win.

"You're right," I say. "You did raise me better than that. I'm sorry, Dad. So, so sorry."

He purses his lips and swallows, paces back and forth a couple times, and then repeats it all over again. After he's done that a few times, he takes a deep breath and says, "I want you to move back home with me."

"What?"

"Don't argue with me right now, Dallas. I've made mistakes. We both have. And I've still got time to fix them, and that starts with you moving back home until you can prove to me that you're responsible enough to handle this." He gestures around me at the dorm, but I know he means all of it. School. Dance. Work. Carson.

And even though it kills me, rips me into pieces, I nod and say, "Okay, Dad."

Chapter 27

Carson

I wait as long as I can bear, and when I show up at Dallas's dorm on Sunday evening, it's to find out that she's gone, moved back home, and apparently the whole university thinks I'm abusive, possibly worse.

I get sick in the bathroom down the hall from Dallas's room, literally sick over what she must think of me, what everyone (my coach included) thinks of me. Stella tries to convince me that Dallas isn't mad, that she's just placating her father, but I don't hear her.

She went home with him. She hasn't called or texted. It's pretty clear what she thinks, so first thing Monday morning, instead of getting dressed for my usual workout, I walk into Coach's office with my head held high and tell him, "I'll quit the team."

His head jerks up from where he was slumped over some paperwork, and the look he fixes me with is damn near stone. He doesn't say anything, just stands up, walks around his desk, and closes the door connecting his private office to the coaches' lounge.

He gestures for me to take a seat, but I shake my head, too keyed up to do anything but stand here. He crosses in front of me and leans back against the edge of his desk, pinning me with his stare.

"Why would you go and do a thing like that?"

"To save you the trouble of having to find a reason to cut me, sir."

He crosses his arms over his chest and asks, "Did you hurt my daughter, McClain?"

I jerk back, but manage to keep my feet planted and my chin up. "No, sir. Never."

"Did you sleep with my daughter as part of some bet?"

That time I do lose my footing. Is that what she thinks? That I'm part of whatever twisted thing Abrams and Moore had going at the beginning of the year?

"No, sir," I say as firmly as I can.

"Did you sleep with my daughter, period?"

I'm still too caught up in unraveling his last question, wondering how Dallas could ever think that, but I answer him, "No, sir."

"Then I think this is all just a misunderstanding, and we can move past it."

"Move past it?"

"Yes, McClain. That's what I said. Think you can do that?"

No. No, I can't. I have never let anything in my life slow me down. Not failure, not money, not missed opportunities. But this? It has me flat on my back, and I'm not sure how I'll ever get back up.

He lets me sit in silence for a while, but when I still haven't answered, he shoves off his desk and pulls open the door.

"Blake!" he calls.

A few moments later, Ryan's head pops into the entryway of the coaches' lounge.

"Yes, sir?"

"McClain is going to need a little help getting focused this morning. Think you can help him out?"

He steps fully into the coaches' lounge and answers, "Yes, sir."

He turns back to me. "It's done, son. Put it to bed. We've got homecoming this week, and I need you thinking clearly."

I might say, "Yes, sir." I'm not actually sure. But a few minutes later I'm out of the office and staring at my usual treadmill with Ryan by my side.

"You okay, man?"

I take a deep breath, pump up the incline and the speed on the treadmill, and mutter, "No," before I take off.

SHE FINDS ME in the library on Tuesday right after my meeting with the private tutor the team set up for me. I'm packing up my stuff when I recognize the familiar odd positioning of her feet next to mine.

I look up at her, and then around at the library.

Everyone is watching. Even the librarian.

She touches my forearm, and I slide back out of her reach.

"Can we talk?"

"Are you sure you wanna do that?" I ask.

A couple of smaller sports blogs have already picked up the story, and even though everyone involved refused to talk to them, it didn't stop them from speculating.

It wasn't exactly smart for us to be seen together.

"Please, Carson. Just for a sec?"

I nod, and follow her back to the same obscure stacks containing books about copyright law that we spoke in a few weeks ago.

As soon as we're away from prying eyes, she drops her bag and throws her arms around me. "I'm so sorry. This is all my fault. I was so stupid."

By the time I slough off the stiffness in my shoulders enough to hug her back, she's already stepping away from me.

"You okay?" I ask. That's all that really matters to me. Everything else I can deal with.

"Humiliated, mostly. And very, very sorry."

"You don't have anything to be sorry about."

She widens her eyes and nods. "Yes, I do. None of this would have happened if I hadn't freaked out in Silas's room."

"You're okay?" I ask again, hoping she knows that I'm referring to that night in particular because I don't really have the words to voice it.

"Yeah, I am. I just heard this rumor, and—"

"The bet," I say.

She jolts back a step. "Yeah, how did you know?"

"Coach asked me about it."

"Oh God. I swear I didn't tell him that. I just told him that I heard a rumor. He must have gotten it from someone else on the team."

"But that's what you thought? That that's what I was doing?"

"No!" Her voice is too loud, and a couple heads peek around the corner to look at us. She lowers her volume and starts again. "No. I didn't think that. I questioned it for a few moments when I saw you being all buddy-buddy with Silas, but decided you wouldn't do something like that. What followed wasn't about the bet so much as it was about some other issues that I've been dealing with for years now. That was me trying to hit my self-destruct button, and using you to do it. And I'm sorry."

"What other issues?" I ask, wondering what could possibly be so bad that she would have crumbled so completely.

"Issues we can talk about when there's not someone eavesdropping the next aisle over." She glares at someone through the gap between the top of a row of books and the shelf above it, and they scamper away.

"You moved back home?"

"Temporarily. Dad got a little worked up about everything, and I decided it was easier for everyone involved if I let him feel like he was in control for a little while."

"That's probably a good idea."

She looks shocked that I agree with her, like she expected me to put up a fight.

"You think so?"

"I do. I think we both took things a little faster than we should have, and we let it all spin a little out of control."

She pauses for a few seconds, and then nods slowly.

"Yeah. Yeah, I guess we did."

I step a fraction of an inch closer, and then stop myself. "I'm glad you're okay, Dallas. I was worried."

Then, for both of us, I turn and walk away.

Chapter 28

Dallas

They say misery loves company, and I'm fairly certain I occupy all of her time the next few days. I'm so pathetic, even she is probably sick of me. I go to class, while people whisper behind my back. I eat lunch with Stella, while people whisper behind my back. I gradually descend into madness, while people whisper behind my back.

I go to work, and I complete my homework, and I crawl home, where I spend most of my time alone . . . continuing to be miserable. Because even despite all that, things must keep moving. I have a plan, after all. Work. Save up money. Audition to transfer to a real dance program. And do what I have to do . . . no matter what Dad says. And now . . . that plan is kind of all I have left.

I take Annaiss up on her offer to talk. She asks me about the picture, and I tell her the same thing that I tell everyone who asks.

It's not what it looks like. Carson would never hurt me.

At least not intentionally . . . not like that.

But I don't want to talk about any of that. It's still too raw and close to the surface. So, instead, we talk about dance. I tell her about Dad and my frustrations with his inability to see dance as a career. We talk about school and programs and summer intensives, and I concentrate on the things I can control.

Thursday morning, Dad asks if I'll go with him to some dinner that a board member is hosting for a few faculty members and important alumni who are in town for homecoming.

I tell him no.

I am maxed out on pretending, and I just don't have the energy or inclination to perform for a group like that.

So instead, I spend my Thursday curled up with the most depressing book I can find, one that will give me an excuse to feel sad without feeling pitiful also. I feel plenty sad when it's over, but plenty pitiful, too.

I'm curled up on my bed, swaddled in blankets when there's a knock on my door and Dad steps inside.

"You hungry?" he asks. "I brought Tucker's home."

I sit up, still strangled by blankets. "I thought you had that dinner tonight."

He's wearing dress pants and a tie that he struggles to loosen as he looks at me.

"I did. I went there, made my appearances, and then I came home to have dinner with my daughter."

God, even *Dad* thinks I'm pathetic. I must be in terrible shape.

"Yeah. Give me a second. I'll be right out."

He closes my door, and I hear him walk down the hallway. I throw off the covers, and look down at the pajamas I changed into as soon as I got home. *Eh. They'll do.*

I pad down the hallway, pause, go back and grab the smaller blanket off the foot of my bed, wrap it around my shoulders, and then go to join Dad.

When he says he brought Tucker's . . . he means he brought *all* of Tucker's. I swear there's enough food to feed the Weasley family for only the two of us.

"I wasn't sure what you wanted, so I just got a few of your favorites. Figure we can warm up whatever we don't eat later."

"Thanks Dad."

He nods, and starts piling various barbecued and fried meats onto his plate. I'm not all that hungry, but I do the same because I know he's trying. He's still Dad, though, so even with the thoughtful meal, we sit down on the couch in front of his giant television, and he turns on game film.

He's nervous about Homecoming. We're 3–1, and this game could set the tone for the rest of the season. It could decide whether the team bounces back from the drama with Levi (and the drama I caused with Carson), or whether it will crumble under the weight of it all. This one game could dictate the rest of Dad's career in college football, or potentially ruin it. Rusk only signed him on a one-year contract, and even though nothing that's happened has been his fault, they could easily refuse to renew his contract if they want to.

And then there's no telling what would happen to us, to me.

If he moved to some other university, would he make me go with him? Would he trust me enough to let me stay at Rusk? Not that I actually *want* to stay at Rusk, but it's a better option than a lot of the universities he could end up at.

He needs the win. *Carson* needs the win.

Hell, I think I need it, too.

After dad has rewound one portion of the film three times to watch it again and again, I finally cut in and say, "It's gonna be okay, Dad. The team is ready. Carson is ready. It will all work out."

He finishes chewing the brisket he'd just scooped into his mouth and surveys me. "Isn't it supposed to be my job to say everything's gonna be okay?"

I shrug. "That's one job with plenty of work to go around. Besides . . . you know what you're doing. You're wasting energy second-guessing yourself."

"Some days I think I'd be better off sticking my head in the sand and rolling the dice. That's how much I know what I'm doing."

I shoot him a half smile. "Interesting visual. I'd like to see that."

He shakes his head, shoveling another helping of brisket into his mouth.

"I'm sorry," he says. "I know you don't like football. Never have."

"Not never, Dad. There were moments when I really loved it, actually."

"Coulda fooled me."

"It's not easy coming second to a sport, Dad. You'll have to forgive me if I handled it badly sometimes."

He sets down the remote that he was holding in his left hand so he could stop and manipulate the film as needed.

"Is that what you think? That football was more important to me than you?"

I consider his question for a moment. Yes, a big part of me thought that, but that was the side of me that tended toward dramatics.

"It's not that I think you saw football as more important, but more that you connected better to football than you ever did to me. You understood the game, and it understood you back. And I was left on the sideline, confused and on the outside of both."

He whistles softly through his teeth. "I really screwed up this whole parenting thing, didn't I? You go years thinking you did all right, never realizing just how much damage you caused."

"You did the best you could, Dad. I had a roof and a bed and food and necessities . . . that's more than a lot of people can say. Besides, I didn't turn out *that* bad."

"You turned out just fine, but I don't know how much of it was my doing." He considers me for a moment and adds, "You look so much like your mother. Just like her, except for the height. You'd tower over her."

I could count on one hand the number of times he'd mentioned Mom in front of me.

Careful to keep my gaze directed down toward my food, I ask, "Do you miss her?"

He blows out a breath, his eyes similarly fixed on the game on the TV. "I don't know. It's been a long time since I gave myself the option of missing her. I've been wondering, though, if she would have handled this all better. If she would have known what to do."

Good to know the whole clueless thing doesn't go away with age.

"Don't beat yourself up over stuff like that, Dad. She didn't stick around. You did. It's crazy to let yourself lose to a memory."

"When did you get to be so smart?"

"Mistakes can be awfully good teachers."

He hums, pondering that for a moment, and then goes back to his meal.

In the silence, I gather up the courage to say something that I've been thinking about for a few days.

"Dad?"

"Hmm?"

"In February, I'm going to Dallas to audition for a summer dance intensive with the San Francisco Conservatory of Dance."

He sets down the remote again. "You are?"

"Yes," I reply firmly. "I know you're not comfortable with me going to college in another state. But I'm not comfortable doing nothing when I know positively that dancing is what I want to do with my life. As I see it, this is a compromise. If I'm accepted, it's a six-week program with the added opportunity to do a chore-ography residency where I'd get to create a piece of my own to be danced by the workshop dancers. It can be a trial run. A stepping-stone. And if things go okay, maybe you'll see that I can handle going to school out of state."

He stares at me for several long moments, and I can tell he's trying to be reasonable. We've just had possibly the longest, most civil conversation of our lives, and he doesn't want to ruin it.

"Is this about McClain?" he asks. "Are you doing this because you're mad at me?"

I smile and choke down a sad laugh. "No, Dad. It's not about that. It's about me. I need to learn how not to walk away, how to fight for what I want, because if I don't learn soon, I'll have nothing left to fight for. This is about me learning how to take after the parent that stuck around instead of the one who gave up."

He looks away from me, clears his throat, and when he looks back, the skin around his eyes has gone pink.

"You know, when your mom left I remember wondering how I was going to manage alone. Eighteen years seemed like such a long time to be responsible for another person, and now it feels like the clock ran out in no time. I guess I just thought I'd have more time before you grew up and stopped needing me."

"I don't think that's something I'll ever grow out of, Dad. Whether I live here or a thousand miles away."

He swallows, nodding his head a few times, and says, "February, then?"

"Yeah. And then end of May is when I'll go if I'm accepted."

His head keeps bobbing, processing, and I wonder if he's just humoring me because I'm sad. I think he surprises us both when he decides. "After the season is over, we'll take a look together, then, maybe talk to your dance teachers. Make sure you've got the best possible chance of getting in."

I can feel the tears welling again, always so close to the surface these days, and he must see them too, because he clears his throat and turns toward the safety of the television again.

I stay for another hour or two, watching the film with Dad. After he's had his fill watching film of the other team, he switches and watches his own team, trying to pinpoint any weaknesses he might have missed standing on the sidelines. I watch for a little while, but when all my eyes do is follow Carson, I decide to leave him to it.

I'M FEELING A little better on Friday, which is why I'm still wearing normal clothes instead of pajamas when Stella knocks on the window that looks in my bedroom from the side of the house.

I pull back the curtains, and when I see her, I pull up the glass to let her in.

"What happened to knocking on the door like a normal person?"

She pops through the small opening with perfect agility and says, "When I spoke to your dad yesterday, he led me to believe that you're barely leaving your bed. So I thought this would be easier."

I open my arms wide and gesture around the room, specifically toward the desk in the corner, where I'd been camped out reading.

"I'm fine, as you can see."

"Bullshit. You've done nothing but study and work and dance all week."

"That's a fairly accurate depiction of how I've spent the last several years of my life, so I'm not sure exactly what you're worried about."

"I'm *worried* about dragging you along to the homecoming bonfire and pep rally with me tonight, so I don't have to go alone like a complete loser."

"*Really?* That's the last thing I want to do tonight."

"Too bad. I'm calling in another stamp."

"You wouldn't."

She crosses her arms over her chest. "*Stamp of approval.* I know for a fact that you don't have work or dance tonight, and it's time you got out of this house and got back to being a normal college student."

"Normal college students frequently take naps and eat junk food and watch movies and don't leave their house all weekend. That was my plan. Don't mess with my plan!"

"Too late. The stamp has already been issued, and *you* can't say no."

"You are the worst." I throw myself onto my bed, wishing I'd changed into pajamas after all.

"You mean best."

"No, I mean worst. You suck."

"I don't suck. I . . . I don't know what the opposite of suck is, but I'm that."

"Awesome?"

"Yes. Awesome. That's what I am, and you will thank me for this."

"Unlikely." I crawl up my bed and bury my face in my pillow while Stella starts ransacking my closet and throwing clothes on top of me as if I'm not even there.

Chapter 29

Carson

The team is as loud and excited as I've ever seen them. As we file onto the makeshift stage they've set up not far from the bonfire, they're chanting, "Bleed red," and jumping around, slapping each other on the shoulders. I jump when everyone around me does, so that I don't stick out, but I'm too tired to chant.

I ran myself ragged this week, not just because it's an important game, but because it was the only way I could find any semblance of quiet. Torres starts up an "impromptu" rap that I heard him practicing in the locker room a few days ago, but we all humor him, responding when he calls for it and cheering him on. When I get to the middle of the stage, I squeeze in next to Silas, who stands silent, smiling, but not getting caught up in the hype.

"Ready, QB?"

I nod, and he leaves me alone, thankfully.

The gathered crowd is huge, and we wave while they scream. Well, I wave while most everyone else shows off.

Coach looks amused, and he nods when our eyes catch. When all the players have filed onto the stage, he steps up to the microphone.

"Good evening, Wildcats!"

Hands raise up in the crowd like a rolling wave, curved into claws and shaking as the people yell.

Coach lifts his hands, and the crowd settles down.

"I'm not one for speeches."

A few feet behind me Torres calls out, "Riiiiight."

The crowd laughs and Coach whirls around like he's searching for the culprit. Torres is the picture of innocence, and I sigh and shake my head when he grins at me.

"Fine. I'm not one for speeches that don't involve yelling."

I crack a smile.

"Last night, as I was watching game film, my daughter told me that mistakes make good teachers." My chest tightens, and the cool fall air burns even sharper in my lungs. "We've had our fair share of mistakes this season, but these young men behind me have learned a lesson from every single one of them." He smiles. "I can't promise you that we won't have more mistakes in the future. They happen, in life and in football. But a strong team, and a strong man, learns how to grow. Anybody who has watched this team from their first game can tell how much growing they've done. And I can guarantee you that the Hawks know it, too." He raises up his hand in the Wildcat claw, and the crowd follows, screaming. Over them, he yells into the mic, "Tomorrow is our time to take the lessons we've learned and do some teaching of our own! Now, go wild!"

The crowd roars, and the band starts up the fight song. The cheerleaders and the dance team are down below us, dancing to music, and in the center of the crowd, people begin backing up as they prepare to light the tower of stacked wood.

I don't know if my eyes are just trained to spot her or if I'm going mad and seeing her everywhere, but I catch sight of Dallas in the first row of the crowd. Stella is beside her, so maybe I'm not going crazy, but before I decide for sure, flames tear through the wood, and she disappears behind the fire and smoke.

As the team begins making their way off the stage, Coach claps me on the shoulder. "Get some rest tonight, McClain. You look tired."

I dip my chin once. "Yes, sir."

I think that's it, so I turn to go, but he stops me one more time.

"Dallas is here tonight with her friend Stella." I stiffen, wondering if he'll order me to keep my distance. "I still want you in bed by a decent time, but if you happen to run across her, I think she'd be glad to see you." He pats me one more time on the shoulder, and then strolls past me, leaving me to follow behind.

I'm not positive, but I think that *might* just count as permission.

It takes me a while to get past the crowd. Everyone is trying to talk to the players or catch their attention, and I seem to be the only one moving against the flow. By the time I get to where I thought I saw Dallas, there's not a tall redhead in sight. I stand there for several long minutes searching. The wind has shifted, sending the smoke from the blaze into my watery eyes—probably why they moved, too. In all the thousands of people here, I know I don't stand a chance of finding her.

Instead, I find Ryan still standing near the stage where I last saw him talking to Torres and Brookes and ask, "Hey, do you have Stella's number?"

He lifts an eyebrow. "I do. Why?"

"Can I have it?"

He looks like he wants to argue about me answering a question with another question, but he doesn't. He hands over his phone without a fight, and I steal the number before going off to search for a quiet place to call.

Brookes calls out, "Go get 'em tiger!" as I leave.

Torres does a mock cheer, complete with a red and black pom-pom he must have charmed off a cheerleader. I smile, flipping them both off as I walk away.

TWO HOURS LATER when I'm supposed to be resting (Coach's orders), I'm making potentially the worst or best decision of my life. I check my watch again. Stella promised she'd have Dallas home by eleven, and she told me which window is hers.

The lights are all off, and I just pray to God that Coach is a heavy sleeper. I don't even want to think about what he'd do if he found me. I'd most likely be going home missing a body part or two.

I duck under the peach tree outside her window, step over the shrubbery that lines the house, and knock quietly on the glass. I don't hear anything, so after about thirty seconds, I knock again.

"Oh my God, Stella. What did I tell you about using the—"
She tears open the curtain and her jaw drops before she finishes.
"—door."

"What are you . . ."

"Can I come in?" I whisper.

Please, please don't let Coach be a light sleeper.

She shakes off her surprise and heaves up the glass partition of
her window. I grip the brick exterior of the house and push one leg
through. I nearly endanger my ability to have children a few times
as I try to squeeze my too-long limbs through the opening. Dallas
has to keep a hold on me to make sure I don't fall and wake the
entire neighborhood, but after a mortifying minute or two, I'm in
and she closes the window behind me.

She wears a pair of Rusk sweatpants in black slung low on her
hips. They're paired with a strappy white tank top, which I can't
see much of because she's got her arms clamped over her chest.
Doesn't matter, though. With her creamy skin and soft hair and
striking eyes, there's plenty else for me to look at.

"What are you *doing* here?"

"You didn't have a balcony for me to climb, but I figured this
was the next best thing."

She covers her mouth with her hand and blinks at me a few
times before glancing at her closed bedroom door.

"You have got to be out of your mind."

I grin. "A little bit." Or at least it's felt that way this week.

"If he catches you—"

I step closer and lay my hands on the curves of her shoulders.

"He'll kill me and use my body as a Halloween decoration. I know."

"I'm serious, Carson. You're lucky that he's taken all this so well, and it hasn't affected your spot on the team. I don't know if you'll get that lucky again."

I run a hand up from her shoulder to the hollow of her neck. Goose bumps break out over her skin, and she closes her eyes.

"Lucky was hearing you scream at that frat party. Lucky was you falling quite literally into my lap. I've had a lot of luck the last few months, Daredevil. And I'm just here hoping that it hasn't run out. Besides . . . I think your dad actually gave me permission."

"To sneak in my bedroom window, *really*?"

"Not for that. But he told me I should find you at the bonfire. It's not my fault that there were an ass-ton of people there."

"Ass-ton? *Ass-ton?* Really romantic . . ."

I slide my hand up from her neck to tangle in her hair and tip her head back to look at her. "You can make fun of how I talk another time. Right now, I just need you to tell me if I've screwed this up too badly for you to forgive me."

She licks her lips, and I almost forget what answer I'm waiting for.

"And what exactly did you do to screw this up?"

"I let you walk away from me without a fight. I thought I was doing what was best for both of us."

"I wasn't going to walk away, you know. I was going to make you sneak around with me until things with Dad settled down, but I had no intention of giving you up until you all but pushed me away."

My heart twists in its cage.

"This is why you are the smart one."

She smiles, but she still looks almost sad.

"That thing your dad mentioned tonight about learning from mistakes. Was I that mistake?"

I resist the urge to tighten my hold on her in case I am, in case I'm too late.

"The only mistake I made was not being honest with you about what I was feeling, so let me fix that now."

She steps into my embrace, dropping the shield of her arms and wrapping them around my waist.

"Carson McClain, you scare me like nothing has ever scared me before. You drive me crazy and make me laugh and push my buttons on purpose. You make me feel safe and smart and pretty. Sometimes I think I might actually melt when you wrap your arms around me, and right now I feel a little bit like I might die if you don't kiss me."

I have a thousand things I want to say in response, but I'm not about to keep her waiting for another second.

I swoop down to lay my lips against hers, and her fingers dig into my lower back as soon as our mouths touch. I cup her head, burying both my hands in the long hair that has driven me wild since the first night I saw her.

I kiss her harder, exploring her mouth like it's the first time, and I swear she's even sweeter than I remember.

She takes a step back, pulling me with her toward her bed. I can feel her frenzied breaths against my mouth and I whisper, "I've missed you."

The back of her knees hit the mattress, and she pulls until we crash back on the bed, my body pressing down into hers. I lift myself up on my elbows while she inches her way farther up the bed. I stalk after her, caging her in with my arms and legs on either side of her.

I lean down, nipping at the skin of her jaw, and she squirms below me, stretching her arms up above her head. I continue down, teasing her neck with my tongue and growl, "I've missed how you taste *right here.*"

Her legs fall open, her knees bumping against mine, and I shift until I'm kneeling between her thighs.

I run a hand down over the curve of her breast, her nipples hard through the thin fabric of her tank top. I lean down, capturing one in my mouth while I settle my hips against hers.

"Oh God."

I flick the tightened nub with my tongue through the fabric, and she shifts her hips up into mine, rubbing against me. I smooth a hand up her thigh, loving the curve of lean muscle as it leads up to her ass. I cup her, pulling her hips up while I press down, and she moans.

I lean back up to take her mouth. "I've missed hearing that noise, and I want to hear it again and again. And I will when we're not in your father's house."

She shivers beneath me, and pulls her legs up tightly around my waist.

I slide my hands up to tangle with hers where they still rest above her head. I let more of my weight fall against her, until it feels like my chest is melded against hers. With our foreheads pressed together, I look into her heavy-lidded eyes, and for perhaps the first time ever, she doesn't look wary or scared.

"I've missed everything about you." I place a gentle, lingering kiss on her mouth before pulling back. I roll off her, tugging her with me so that we're facing each other on our sides. "I don't want to spend one second more than I have to away from you, but for now, for tonight, I need to go."

"Wait!" She squeezes my hands tight and brings them closer to rest between us on her chest. "Can you stay? Just for a little while longer?"

I resist the urge to look at her door, to worry about how close her father is right now. Instead, I nod, and she snuggles in close, wrapping her arms around my middle.

"We'll figure it all out, Dallas . . . how to make things work with your dad, and how to get past the things that scare you."

She grips the back of my T-shirt, pulling me in even closer.

"The things that scare me . . . *It might take some time.*"

"We've got plenty of that. Why don't you make a list?" I grin. "We can just check off one thing at a time."

"A list, huh?"

"Mmhmm."

"I do like lists."

"That's something that we have in common."

She pulls her head back from my chest, and I tip my face down to meet her eyes. She says, "Honesty?"

I nod back. "Always."

"Honestly . . . I want you more than I ever thought possible, and sometimes that makes me want to run because I don't know how I would survive losing you. Sometimes I hold people at arm's length, so that it's harder for them to hurt me."

"I'm not at arm's length now," I say.

"No." She cracks a small smile. "No, from the very beginning I couldn't resist letting you in. That's why you terrify me so much."

"Listen to me, Daredevil." I smooth a hand over her cheek, then across her forehead, wanting to wipe away the worried lines there. "You asked me once what fixes me the way dance fixes you. I'm still not sure I've found that thing that pulls me together, but I've found *who* pulls me together. You're the only thing that makes me feel better when I'm tired or frustrated. You're the thing that quiets all my worries and doubts and fears. You're it for me. So run if you'd like, but I'll follow. You can try to hold me at arm's length, but I'll never stop trying to pull you close. Be scared if you must, but you're not going to lose me. Not unless your dad comes in and finds me here, then neither of us will have a choice."

She laughs and leans up to press her cheek against mine.

"You've got me awfully close to saying those three big words that we're probably not ready for."

"Is that so?"

"Just warning you, so when I slip up you'll know I tried."

She's parroting my own words back at me from the night we met. I kiss her again before pulling myself out of her arms and back to the window. Before I make my exit and head home to rest for the night, I whisper across the room, "I look forward to that slipup."

Chapter 30

Dallas

I can't sleep after Carson leaves. I've got this stupid grin on my face, and for the first time I feel the sting of being trapped back in my childhood home. If I were still living in the dorm, I could have gone with him . . . spent the night wrapped in his arms.

I hug one of my pillows close, but it's not the same. I add another, trying to make a more Carson-sized lump, but there's no replicating his warmth or the hardness of his muscles.

Also . . . I feel massively pathetic.

That doesn't stop me from reaching for my phone on my bedside table and dialing him.

He answers on the second ring, his voice low and gruff and oh so perfect.

"Dallas? Are you okay?"

"Did I wake you?" I ask.

"No. I just laid down. Is something the matter?"

"Yes. I can't get my pillows to be Carson-shaped enough. It's a problem."

He chuckles, and I wish I were there to hear it rumble through his broad chest. "Good. I would hate to find myself one day replaced by pillows."

I don't have anything else to say, and I'm just over here smiling, but he can't see that. And now I feel like an idiot for having called him.

"Does the team have to be at the parade in the morning?"

I hear rustling, and imagine him shifting in his bed.

"No. That's more of a fraternity and sorority thing. And it's too early on a game day to convince any of the players to be there."

"Oh."

I'd already told Stella I would go. I'm meeting her on campus at 7:30 A.M. so we get a decent spot. I was shocked Stella was actually willing to roll out of bed before nine, but she's pretty adamant about getting the full college experience. Now that I know he won't be there, I'm much less excited.

Floats schmoats.

"I know one player who might be convinced to attend, if you were going."

"Oh really? Is he cute? Is he a receiver? I've always kind of had a thing for receivers. Torres seems fun."

He actually growls on the other end. "Don't make me come back over there, Cole."

If only.

"Did I say receiver? I meant quarterback. Silly me, I get all those positions mixed up. Football is just so confusing."

"Riiiight."

"Yep. I definitely meant quarterback. There's this one . . . tall and kinda gorgeous—"

"Kinda?"

I roll my eyes. "Someone is needy tonight."

"Who tried to make a pillow version of me?"

"Anyway, so, tall and gorgeous quarterback. Is he by chance the one who might make a parade appearance?"

"If he did, where might he find one tall and gorgeous redhead?"

"The brick wall around the quad, on the Fifth Street side, at seven thirty."

He groans. "So early. You're lucky I love you."

The line goes silent. I squeeze my eyes shut, and I'm unsure whether this is the best or worst thing that's ever happened. I'm unsure whether he means it or if it was just an accident.

He says, "Huh. Guess it was me who slipped up."

Neither of us speaks for several long moments. With my eyes still tightly closed, I say, "I do feel pretty lucky. I'll see you in the morning?"

"Yeah. I'll be there. Good night, Daredevil."

"Carson?"

"Hmm?" He sounds tired, and I feel a little bad for keeping him up, for making him wake up early, especially when I know how hard he works himself.

"I think you're pretty lucky, too."

"Oh, I've never doubted that."

I smile, and my constrained heart feels fit to burst.

We say good night again, and then after a bit more pillow arranging, I manage to fall asleep.

I SHOW UP at the dorm thirty minutes early, and Stella is still drooling on her pillow when I open the door.

I flip on the light, and she groans.

"Turn it off."

"You've only got half an hour until we're supposed to be down at the quad."

"Mornings have got to be the love child of Satan and . . . something else really bad that I'm too tired to think of. Leave me alone."

"Oh no, missy." I walk over and pull back her covers. "This parade was your idea."

She whines and makes a grab for the covers. "And I'm known for my *terrible* ideas. You know this."

Pulling her pillow over her head, she flops over so that she's facing away from me.

"Don't make me do it, Stella."

Muffled by her pillow, she calls back, "Do *what?*"

"I'm calling in a stamp."

Her pillow goes flying, and I only barely manage to duck. Even so, it skims the top of my head.

"You're using a stamp on *this?*"

"Yep," I say, popping the *p*, and crossing my arms over my chest. "You've got to learn to follow through on your commitments."

"Hello!" She draws a circle around her face. "Commitment-phobe. You know this, too."

I look at my cell phone. "Twenty-six minutes now. And we need to leave at least five minutes early."

Scowling, she throws her legs over the edge of the bed, wincing when her toes touch the cold tile floor. "Mornings are the love child of Satan and *you*."

"Love you back."

Despite her grumbling, we manage to leave a couple minutes before seven thirty. With her short hair, she can get ready incredibly fast, unlike me and my monstrous mane.

When we stroll up the sidewalk toward the quad, I spot Carson already there waiting for us.

Stella shoots me a sly grin. "Now I get why you used the stamp. So I take it you had a pleasant surprise at your window last night?"

"That was you?"

She shrugs. "I was merely a facilitator."

Carson is dressed in jeans and his familiar scuffed boots. He's wearing his team sweatshirt, and he gives me this sleepy, sweet smile that makes my heart throb. I can see people watching him. By now everyone knows who he is, and they're wondering why the starting quarterback is standing all alone on the sidewalk. I don't spare a single care for any of the people watching when I walk up to him and throw my arms around his neck.

He pulls me close, his hands slipping beneath my jacket to press into the small of my back.

"Good morning," he murmurs into my ear, his stubble tickling my cheek.

Then, because I am done caring about gossip, and I actually

want everyone to know he's mine, I kiss him right there on the sidewalk with at least twenty people watching.

The kiss lasts for several long seconds, neither of us willing to be the one who steps back. But when I hear a few whistles and Stella pretending to gag behind my back, I pull back smiling.

"Good morning," I say.

"Yes, it is."

"Seriously," Stella says. "I'm going to need Benadryl to hold off the hives if you guys keep doing that."

Carson gives me another short kiss, and Stella throws up her hands. "I think I liked it better when you two were incognito. There was much less nausea."

With one arm wrapped around my shoulder, he smiles at her. "Thanks for the help last night, Stella."

She waves him off and starts walking away. I think she's actually bolting until she uses the nearby stairs up to the quad to help her climb up on top of the brick wall. She walks back toward us, and then plops down on the brick that's just below my shoulders.

Carson helps me jump up beside her, and then he settles in between my knees, leaving me just a couple inches above him. He leans against the brick and wraps his arms around my waist.

Stella says, "This whole third-wheel thing is going to be happening a lot, isn't it?"

"We could always get you a fourth wheel," I say.

"It's like you're actually *trying* to make me gag."

We talk for a while longer, and when we hear the first strains of music from the band around the corner signaling the start of the parade, Carson turns around to face the street. He leans back against me, propping his elbows up on my thighs, and I wrap my arms around him.

The band comes by first, hundreds of them dressed in full uniform and filling the early morning air with the fight song, and "Smoke on the Water," and all the other songs I'll forever associate with football.

Then come the floats. The fraternities and sororities work for months and put ridiculous amounts of money into them, and they're crazy good because of it. Not all of them make sense with football—there's a *Wizard of Oz* one with a yellow brick road, and a house on a witch, and even a tornado. They've got students dressed up as characters waving and throwing out candy to the families and students that have filled the sidewalk in front of us. There's a pirate one too, and one with Thor crushing what appears to be a hawk (the opposing team's mascot) with his massive hammer.

There's a giant floating wildcat, maneuvered by students with strings. The homecoming-queen nominees come by in a fancy car, claws up in lieu of the pageant-style waves.

A student organization walks by with individual signs made for each player, and at the very front is a sign for Carson with his number and a painted football that says, "McClain's domain."

Stella and I cheer loudly, and Carson just shakes his head, laughing.

Pointing at me, Stella yells, "Here's some more of McClain's domain, right here!"

I roll my eyes and shove her, and she pretends like she's going to topple back off the wall. I let her have her fun, and then I lean down close to Carson's ear.

"You're looking awfully smug."

He leans to the side, looking up at me over his shoulder.

"What? I'm not allowed to enjoy the idea of you being mine?"

I smile, enjoying the thought myself.

"Fine. Enjoy away."

"Oh, I plan to."

Stella cuts in. "Can you please do that enjoying at his place?"

We promise to do just that, and when the parade is over, we walk Stella back to the dorm, and then head to his apartment.

Despite Stella's teasing, we're both yawning by the time we make it up the stairs and through his door. We kick off our shoes and shed our winter layers. Carson lies down on the couch, and I grab his blanket and settle down beside him. With my head on his chest and his arms around me, I feel certain that I've never been more comfortable.

"Carson?"

Sleepily, he kisses my forehead and replies, "Hmm?"

"I kinda love you, too."

He takes a deep breath, his chest rising steeply below my cheek.

"Kinda?"

"Still so needy," I tease. "Fine. I love you."

He tips my head up, and looks down at me. His eyes are clear and vivid blue, and his smile would take me to my knees if I weren't already laying down.

"I'll always need you, Daredevil."

Chapter 31

Carson

C oach Cole has to shout in the locker room to be heard over the roar from the stadium above us before the game. The bands are already playing, and the people are screaming, and their energy bleeds through the walls until we're all buzzing with it.

I bounce my knees, trying to stay warm. Silas is doing the same, and we nod at each other. The tension is high tonight. We've got our biggest crowd of the season so far, and there are a lot of eyes out there expecting a show.

The coaches are lined up around the room, almost as on edge as the players. Ryan is there with them, and he too gives me a nod.

It's the only thing to do, really, when you meet someone else's eyes. We're all trying to stay quiet and focused.

Coach finishes with all his little reminders about the other team's weaknesses that we've discussed throughout the week, along with our own that we need to be aware of. He steps away from the whiteboard that's covered in plays and notes and takes his time looking around the room, meeting each of our eyes.

"Tonight is our night, gentlemen. They may call it homecoming for the alumni and the tradition and the festivities, but for us today that grass is your home. It's yours to protect, yours to control. Today is the day where we put that number three behind us, and bring home win number four. Today we let go of the past, and move on to our future. Today, I expect you to leave absolutely everything you have on that field. If we have to drag each other back into this locker room, bloody and exhausted and in pain, that's okay. Because we'll be dragging that win in with us."

He steps over toward the exit, and I notice a tarp hanging over the door that wasn't there before. We all remain where we are while Coach reaches up and tugs the thing down.

In clean black letters just above the door, it reads:

"No Easy Days."

"Today, we start a new tradition, gentlemen. It's time we let go of the old Rusk. We're no longer one of the weakest teams in the conference. We've been put through the fire, and we've come out stronger for it. Now who's ready to prove it?"

We surge to our feet with a roar, and I let myself be carried away by the energy of the group. Our bodies crash into one another as we raise our hands up and scream.

As we line up and file out the door, each player reaches up and slaps a hand on the phrase above the door.

And I know as I stare at those words that it's the hard days that end up being the most important in the end.

Four fifteen-minute quarters. That's all we've got.

I can lay it all out there for sixty minutes, and I trust that my team will do the same.

We gather in the blow-up tunnel that leads from our locker room out onto the field. They've got the fog machines going, so that it's hard to see anything that isn't right in front of us.

The crowd is deafening outside, and I make my way up to the front of the team, and Silas is there waiting for me. I'm still a little unsure how to feel about the guy, but he's undeniably the other leader of this team.

We're nothing alike. Where I'm all about discipline and focus, Moore is pure heart. I wouldn't trust him with a thing off this field, but on it, I know he'll always have my back, and he'll give it everything he's got.

When everyone is inside the tunnel, huddled close, I shout, "Are we ready?"

The team roars back.

Silas shouts, "Will today be easy?"

The returned "No" drowns out even the crowd.

I yell, "How many wins are we leaving with today?"

"Four!"

Silas and I turn to face the end of the tunnel, and the team howls behind us.

When we burst out of the tunnel and out onto the field, my ears ring from the noise, even through my helmet.

I don't let myself look at the stands, knowing I wouldn't be able to find Dallas in the masses even if I did.

Coach catches me before we head out for the coin flip. He places his hand on my helmet. He does this before every game. Usually he looks past my face guard, into my eyes, and asks, "You got this?"

It's become our routine.

Today, though, it's different. He looks at me for a few long seconds, and then in lieu of his normal question he nods and makes a statement instead.

"You've got this."

From the start, luck is on our side, and we win the coin flip.

We receive, and Brookes catches the opening kick and tears up the field. Moore sticks with him, blocking as they run. Brookes goes down just past the fifty, and then it's my turn.

The stadium is loud right up until the moment I take the field, and then it all just disappears. There's no nerves, no fear, no nothing. Instead it feels exactly like Coach said . . . like I've come home.

I've spent hours and days and years preparing for this, so now I can just turn off everything else and do what I know how to do. I run, and I pass, and I hand off, interspersed with hits and misses.

But I just get back up. I keep going. We're a team, and the more we play, the more we begin to click together, each person doing their part to move the overall machine.

When I'm not on the field, I walk the sidelines, checking in with the other players. I talk them up when they need it, listen when they tell me what's working and what's not.

One quarter passes, then another.

Halftime is a blur of coaches and plays and analyzing what's happened so far.

When the final buzzer sounds, and we've won by six, it almost doesn't feel real. Not even with the team surrounding me, screaming. Not even when Coach is in front of me, his hand back on my helmet, reminding me that I can take it off now. I pull it off, and all the noise rushes back in.

It takes me a few seconds to tune in to what Coach is saying. I miss all of it but the end.

"You did good, son."

The field is flooding with students decked out in red, and the team is making their escape back into the locker room. I follow, a smile tugging at my face as it all starts to settle in.

Win number four.

I don't know what's coming next. Our hardest games of the season are still ahead of us, and I don't know if we're good enough yet, but I know we're better than we've ever been.

I know *I'm* better than I've ever been.

And when my eyes land on Dallas waiting for me near the entrance to the locker room, wearing one of my workout shirts with my number and name written across the back . . .

Well, things just keep getting better.

She throws her arms over my shoulders, lifts up onto her tiptoes, and kisses me. And once again, all the other noise disappears.

There is only her body, her lips, the smell of her hair, and the tug of her fingers through my damp hair. Her lips move harder over mine, and I hate the pads that keep her from getting closer to me.

I don't hear the cleared throat behind me. Dallas waves Stella off when she thumps her shoulder, and I know that everything else has disappeared for her, too.

It takes a hand on my shoulder before I even pull back enough to breathe. Dallas's eyes are soft and so green, and they widen when they catch sight of the hand on my shoulder.

I look, and then wish I hadn't.

Coach Cole is at my back, his lips in a firm line, and my arms are still around his daughter's waist.

He clears his throat again and says to Dallas instead of me, "I need my quarterback, Dallas. I'll send him back to you when we're done."

She unwinds her arms from me to hug him instead, and when I take my first steps toward the locker room, Coach's eyes are closed, and he's hugging her back.

Dallas

I love the silence before the music starts.

There's potential in the quiet, an opening for something new and beautiful to enter the world. I close my eyes, relaxing my muscles, and think back to that moment at the beginning of the year when I'd been so sure that this place would only hold misery for me.

I remember the way it had felt when I saw Carson at Dad's practice. Even then, I think a part of me knew how perfect we would be together. That's why it hurt so badly.

It's easy to tap back into that feeling now as the music starts, and I begin the dance I choreographed that night as I sat in my car trying not to cry.

It's still angry and raw, but there's softness in it now, too. The happiness I've found has crept in, and rather than just being about pain and loss, it's a story about what can grow out of that.

I'll always be the girl who grew up without a mom. I'll never forget what it was like to grow up sharing my dad with football. I'll remember forever how I almost let my bitterness and my fear keep me from moving on.

Those things will always be in me, but they no longer feel like separate pieces or different versions of myself. Somewhere along the way those things were stitched together, and I no longer need to hold myself together by holding other people at bay.

It wasn't the prettiest journey.

Sometimes I was stupid, and I let my anger get the better of me too often. But if there's anything I've learned from creating this dance, it's that sometimes mistakes bloom into the most colorful moments. They're unexpected and different, and that's where the character of the dance lives.

I relive the last year through my movements, and I know that every single moment was worth it.

It got me into the summer program in San Francisco, and on the choreography track, too.

And more important, it got me to a point where I'm at peace with the past and a little less scared of the future.

Dance fixed me. As it always does.

I'm the last performance of the end-of-the-year recital, and when the music ends, and I look out at the applauding crowd, I find Dad and Carson standing together, clapping.

Carson winks at me, and Dad's clapping so hard, you'd think I'd just brought home the Heisman. The season didn't end up exactly how they both wanted. There were too many other tough teams in the conference, but a solid 6–6 record was still a vast improvement over the years before. But Carson got his scholarship, and Dad's contract was renewed.

And as Dad told Carson at the end of the season, "We're just getting started."

I feel that way, too . . . like my life has just really begun.

I exit the stage, in a hurry to change out of my costume and go meet them. I don't bother messing with the hair that's twisted into a tight chignon at the back of my head. Nor do I bother removing the dark eye makeup; I'm too impatient.

I pull on a skirt, a tank top, and some flip-flops, and find Carson waiting for me in the hallway that connects the dressing rooms to the auditorium.

I throw myself into his arms, and he catches me, swinging me around once before letting my toes rest on the floor again.

"You are amazing," he breathes into my ear. "I love you. So much."

I'm still breathing heavy from the dance and my mad dash to get changed, but that doesn't stop me from pulling him down for a kiss.

He cups my neck, kissing me slowly until my breathing settles and it's my heart's turn to race out of control.

"Your dad will want to see you," Carson mumbles against my mouth.

"He can wait. I'm not quite done here."

He laughs. "We've got plenty of time tonight."

"Shut up and kiss me, quarterback."

"Yes, ma'am."

It's another five minutes before I'm willing to part with Carson and our isolated hallway to join the other dancers and the lingering crowd out in the auditorium.

The rumor about Carson's ill treatment of me hadn't lasted more than a week or two after we made our relationship public at homecoming. He was too sweet for anybody to believe it for long, and now we've traded out that nasty gossip for the unending attention of being the school's golden couple.

Maybe it's because most of the athletes don't stick with one girl long enough for people to know they're a couple. Or maybe it's because the quarterback and the coach's daughter just make a good story. Either way, I cherish every second of alone time we can get before we're back under the watchful eye of the gossip mongers . . . and my father.

Though when we enter the auditorium, he's not waiting for me like I expected. I scan the room, waiting for him to come striding out of the crowds, but I don't see him. I'm just about to tell Carson that maybe I shouldn't have made him wait *quite* so long, when I catch sight of his familiar hulking back.

It's not until Carson and I walk up the aisle next to him that I realize who has him deep in conversation.

Annaiss. My dance professor. The one who first mentioned the San Francisco program to me.

She's dressed in a pretty purple dress, and her dark hair is silky and shiny. She's smiling, and when dad says something, she laughs and puts a hand on his forearm.

I raise an eyebrow at Carson and he smirks. "Way to go, Coach."

I flick his shoulder. "Ew. He is my *dad*. Not Ryan or Silas or Torres. And she's my *teacher*."

He rolls his eyes, and when I go to flick him again, he catches my hand and laces our fingers together. "Come on, Daredevil. Let's go say hello." I let him drag me forward and he adds, "Be nice."

Annaiss spots me first, and she inches back just a hair. "Dallas, I think that might be the best I've ever seen you do that routine. You're going to grow leaps and bounds in San Francisco."

Carson squeezes my hand, and I smile. "Thanks, Annaiss. I'm looking forward to it."

I leave in less than a month, right after final exams, and I'm at that point where I'm both wishing for time to speed up so I can leave already, and hoping it will slow down so I can spend a little more time with Carson before I have to leave him for six weeks.

I stand in front of Dad, and we're both still feeling out how this new supportive version of him works. He's never going to be the supernice and encouraging kind of father. He shows his support through yelling and making people do sprints and push-ups. I'm a little afraid that one day he's going to learn enough about dance to actually put me through my paces, and then I'll *definitely* be in trouble.

He wraps one arm around my shoulder, and pulls me in for our usual awkward side-hug.

"You were the best one up there, kiddo."

"It's not really a competition, but thanks, Dad."

He gives me a look and I know he's probably thinking, *Everything is a competition.*

"You two have big plans tonight?"

I barely restrain my blush, because *yeah* . . . we've definitely got big plans.

"We do," I say. "Carson's cooking for me."

He laughs. "I'm trying to anyway."

Dad claps Carson on the shoulder. "Good luck. It can't be any worse than the food she grew up on."

"That's for sure," I mumble.

"Hey, now," Dad says, and Annaiss laughs, low and throaty, and oh my God, I have to get out of here or I'm going to be sick. I finally understand how Stella feels when she gets all awkward around Carson and me.

"We're going to go," I say. "But thanks for coming, Dad. It means a lot."

He places his usual kiss on my head, which would hurt if I hadn't inherited his hard head.

I say goodbye, and leave him to do whatever it is that he's going to do, which I refuse to contemplate for my own sanity.

Even so, I spend the ride to Carson's complaining.

"She has to be like eight or nine years younger than him. That's weird, right? I mean . . . *weird.*"

Carson won't even reply. He just laughs harder the more worked up I get.

"I mean, that's the equivalent of me dating some pimply pre-teen."

I think Carson might actually be in danger of a collapsed lung from laughter.

"Or that would be like me dating someone in his late twenties. Like Coach Oz."

Carson pushes his truck into park a second too soon, and the whole thing jerks, sending me into my seat belt.

"Let's not joke about you dating one of my coaches, hmm?"

Stella always goes on and on about how hot Coach Oz is, and it drives Carson crazy. He slides out of the truck and rounds the front to come open my door.

I unbuckle my seat belt and say, "It's the same thing, though! Imagine how pissed Dad would be."

"Yeah, I'm having no issue imagining that kind of anger."

"I mean, Coach Oz—"

I don't even manage to finish my sentence before Carson hauls me out of the truck and over his shoulder. He stalks over to the stairs to his apartment, and starts up them with me still in his arms.

"Man, you really don't like it when I mention Coach—"

Something firm whacks at my backside, and I gasp.

"Carson McClain, did you just *spank* me?"

He just does it again in response before pushing his front door open and carrying me inside.

"Jeez! It's not like I'm actually *interested* in—"

He pulls me back over his shoulder, depositing my feet on the floor, and presses me back against his closed door. He hovers above me, his eyes dark and his chest brushing mine with every breath.

With his arms braced on either side of me, he asks, "Are you done teasing me?"

I smile coyly. "That depends . . ."

"On?"

I duck out from the cage he's formed around me and take a few steps toward the hallway leading to his bedroom.

"On whether you can wait a little while longer for dinner."

I don't actually wait for him to answer before I turn around, peeling off my tank top on the way to his bedroom.

I hear him groan and a thunk that's most likely his head hitting the door. His quick footsteps follow, and I've just pushed open his bedroom door when he overtakes me.

He pulls me up, cradling me in his arms as he steps through the doorway. I squeal in response, and I don't manage to hook my arms around his neck before he deposits me on the edge of his bed. His room is pristine and smells like vanilla from a candle on his bedside table. His bed is perfectly made, and a bundle of tulips rests against the pillows.

I swallow and turn to face him, but I think I might have pushed him a little beyond his control. He's kneeling in front of me, and his eyes are fixed on the bare skin of my waist and the strapless blue bra I've worn for the occasion.

He removes my flip-flops and tosses them over his shoulder before running hands up the backs of my calves.

I lean back, bracing my hands on the bed, and he follows me

forward, placing a hot kiss just above the button on my skirt. My arms shake, and now I'm the one being teased.

"You know," he says, his voice raspy and deep. "I was actually hungry."

"You can go start dinner if you want. I'll wait here." I reach back and unhook my bra, tossing it over his shoulder like he did my shoes.

He growls low in his throat, standing to lean over me until I lay all the way back. "You're playing with fire, Daredevil."

I hook my fingers around his belt buckle and use it to pull him closer.

"Is that why it's so hot in here?"

I drag my nails lightly down his abdomen until I can slip them just beneath the band of his jeans.

He swallows and closes his eyes, and I can see his arms shaking on either side of my head.

"Still hungry?" I ask.

"Yes."

He crushes his lips to mine, and then his body follows, pressing down into mine.

His kisses are so hard and fast and desperate that I'm breathing heavy just trying to keep up. I slip my hands up the back of his shirt, digging my fingers into his lower back in the way I know drives him crazy. When I can't keep up with the punishing pace, he leaves my mouth to drop kisses down my neck and chest. I've got his shirt pulled all the way up to his shoulders when he sucks the tip of my breast into his mouth, and I buck beneath him.

He uses his teeth just enough that I break out in goose bumps, and I swear if I could tear his shirt off him I would.

"Off," I beg, tugging on it, but he ignores me in favor of switching to my other breast.

I let go of his shirt to grip his hair, and I'm gulping in air as fast as I can.

He flicks me with his tongue, and I cry out. Desperate, I reach for his shirt again and say, "Please."

He lifts up, sliding back until he's kneeling in front of me again.

"It's my turn to tease, love."

And tease he does, the heat of his breath chasing over the sensitive skin of my thighs as he reaches beneath my skirt to tug at the blue panties that soon join their counterpart in being tossed across the room.

In the half a year that we've been dating, we've taken our time learning each other's bodies, building up to this night, and when his tongue touches my center, I moan, gripping the comforter and undoing the pristine way he made his bed.

He's so good at this—dipping and swirling and flicking his tongue in all the right places. His stubble brushes my sensitive skin, and my hips buck up toward him. He alternates among breathing and kissing and sucking, and brings me close to the edge in record time.

Then he pulls back, dragging his lips down my thigh.

I groan in disappointment, and he laughs darkly.

"See? It's not nice to tease."

He pulls my skirt down over my hips, leaving me naked and him fully clothed.

"You're cruel," I whisper.

He leans down, planting a soft kiss on my lips, and says, "No, I just love you."

"And I'd love it if I weren't the only naked one here."

He hums against my lips and then murmurs, "Soon."

I groan and then try to bargain. "The shirt, at least. Please?"

He knows how much I like his upper body. It really is cruel and unusual punishment to keep it from me.

He relents, slipping it up and over his head, and then tossing it to join my clothes on the floor.

His lips return to my neck to tease me some more, but when I get to slide my hands over his skin, I don't mind.

He might think he's in charge just because he's on top, but I know enough about him to give a little torture back. I run my fingers softly down his side, and his mouth on my collarbone presses harder. I lean my head up, placing a kiss on his shoulder before dragging my teeth over the same spot. His breath catches, and I use his hesitation to wrap my legs around him and pull until our hips are crushed together.

I roll my hips up into his and sigh. I love everything we do together, but there's an ache between my legs that's beyond need.

"Dallas," he warns.

I do it again, moaning this time because I know he doesn't like me silent.

"Damn it."

"Carson, please."

I'm not even really teasing him with my breathy plea. I can feel him against me, and I am wound so tightly that I can barely think straight. I keep pushing up into him, wanting to be closer, but taking whatever friction I can get.

I don't even realize that my nails are digging into his shoulders, until Carson pulls my hands away, pinning my wrists above my head.

"You don't play fair," he growls.

I drag my heavy lids up and meet his electric gaze. "I'm not playing anymore. I just need you."

His mouth slams down on mine again, and I do my best to fight his hold as he kisses me. When I can't get my hands free, I settle for pulling him as close as I can with my legs, arching my body up into his.

When my bare chest brushes his, the tight buds of my nipples dragging over his bare skin, he shudders and pulls away, releasing my hands and unwinding my legs from his waist.

Apparently done teasing, he undoes his belt with quick hands and pushes off his remaining clothes until he matches me. He pauses to grab protection from his bedside table, and then he's back with me, his face hovering over mine, and his body still not close enough.

"You're sure?" he asks.

I pause from drinking him in to look up into his eyes, and I know positively that I love him.

"Now that you mention it, I'm a little hungry. Maybe we should break for dinner."

He kisses me again and lowers his body to cover my own.

"No more jokes for you," he says.

I don't even have a reply, too caught up in the feeling of having absolutely nothing between us. He's like silk and steel against me, and the tip of him brushes the bundle of nerves at my center, tearing another moan from me. I close my eyes, and I want him so badly that I feel weak with it.

Another thrust, the length of him sliding through my folds driving me absolutely mad. He sinks inside me, and even though it's not my first time, it feels like it is. Because this . . . this is in a whole other world from every other physical experience I've ever had.

It burns just a little as he stretches me, but that all disappears behind the myriad of other sensations. A small part of me didn't believe that things could get better than they already were between us, but I was so *very* wrong. I can feel him everywhere, and each slow drag of his body against mine has me gasping.

I love you.

I think it over and over again as our bodies come together. He thrusts a little harder, bringing him as deep as he can go. One hand curls possessively around my breast as he grinds down into me. Fire is burning up my spine, and when he plucks at my nipple, I nearly scream.

As usual, I have no filter, so when he moves harder, faster, I cry out, "Oh, yes, that. Like that."

His lips take mine in a hungry kiss, and he gives me what I want, his muscled body colliding deliciously with mine.

God, I love you, I think again.

Or maybe I say it out loud, because his lips brush over mine, and he replies, "I love you, too."

And out of all the plans I've made for my life, falling in love was the one thing I didn't envision, the only thing you can't really plan for.

I don't know what's next, not for me or him.

All I know is that Carson McClain came into my life and disrupted absolutely everything, but I wouldn't have it any other way.

Acknowledgments

Oh my. Where to begin? There are so many people to thank for this book. I have to mention my dad again. Everything I know about football came from you. And just about everything in this book that I *didn't* know about football came from you, too. And Mom, you're my anchor. I don't know what I would do without you. Amy and Jenn, thanks for for also being coach's daughters, and providing me with insight beyond my own into that life. Amy, thank you for reading this in its early days and loving it so much. You kept me going.

Kendall Foote, the one and only KDI. Thank you for letting me pick your brain about college sports. Your insight was absolutely invaluable. I adore you. Lindsay, thanks for being my first reader, as always. It never fails . . . I give you my terrible first drafts, and you actually read them and stay my friend. It's kind of miraculous. Patrick and Shelly, thank you for all that you do that allows me to focus and write. And Shelly and Bethany, thanks for helping me brainstorm cover ideas and look at cover models. It was a real hardship, I know.

And thank you to my amazing editor, Amanda. This book almost certainly would not exist without you. Not only because of the way you helped shape the story and characters, but because this was a story you wanted and were drawn to from the moment I mentioned it in passing at BEA. Suzie, Kathleen, Pouya, Joanna, Danielle, and all the other New Leaf lovelies— thank you for being my champions and for working so incredibly hard. You're the best! Jessie, Kelly, and Molly—thank you for being so excited about this series. You've all done so much planning and brainstorming and work, I owe so much to you. And thank you to the rest of the Harper team that pieced this book together—from copyedits to cover to awesome behind-the-scenes trailer—you're all incredible.

And to my super awesome fans and the beautiful and brilliant book bloggers who make this all possible—you have all of my thanks! I am constantly amazed at your support. Shout-out to a few of the awesome people I've met in the last year: Alana Lee Rock, you're a super fan and I will always have to say your full name. Elbie, an awkward dragon brought us together, but I think you're all-around awesome. (Can't wait to meet you at RT!) Judy and Jordan from Vegas and Richmond, you are amazing. It was great to see you again. Ursula from Miami, not only do you share a name with my favorite Disney villain, you've also got some pretty cool tats. I'm so excited to see where this new series will lead, and I know I'll continue to meet and get to know some awesome fans! Thank you!

Behind the Book

I grew up in a small Texas town as a coach's daughter. It's hard to put into words the role that football and sports played in my childhood. All I can say is that my memories of Friday nights are more vivid than anything else. When I think about my childhood, I remember the smell of the field, the bright lights, the concession stands, and the plague of crickets. Football wasn't just a sport . . . it was a social setting, a way of life. I remember tumbling down the bleachers when I was little and hanging out beneath them when I got old enough to run around on my own. I remember being devastated when I didn't snag one of the plastic footballs that the cheerleaders threw. I remember the tailgate parties, the away games, and the way a win or a loss could uplift or tear down an entire town.

Then, as I got older, I remember when football became more connected to boys. In middle school, going to the game was about as close as you could get to a "date." I also distinctly remember my first middle school dance and how, out of nowhere, older boys I'd never met were asking me to dance. It didn't take long to figure out they were sucking up to the coach's daughter. On the flip side, the boys my age were still petrified of my father. Then there was the time my dad made a rule in practice that my current boyfriend had to do push-ups every time the whistle blew (thanks, Dad).

Texas football is a unique world in and of itself, but being the coach's daughter became part of who I was, as inseparable from my identity as my freckled skin and super loud voice. Sometimes I loved football and a lot of times I hated it, but it's the only childhood I know. So when I tell stories (as I so often do), an inordinate number of them are about my life growing up in Texas. It was one such story that led to the creation of this book. At a conference in New York, I was chatting with my editor, agent, and a few other authors and bloggers, and we got to talking about how Texas in many ways feels like a foreign country. There are things that are completely normal in Texas that the rest of the world finds absolutely bizarre. This particular story was about Texas homecoming mums, the massive fake flower and ribbon monstrosities that are a rite of passage for any Texas girl. If you don't know what they are, google them. It will baffle you. It wasn't until a few months later that my editor brought up the idea of writing a series about the Texas football life that I knew so well.

I told her, *absolutely! I can definitely do that*. After all, who better to write a story about a coach's daughter than someone who'd lived it? Never could I have anticipated how simultaneously difficult and easy this book would be to write. It was easy because as they say, you should write what you know. But writing what I knew also required me to delve back into those years as the coach's daughter, which don't feel like that long ago. The relationship between Dallas and her dad is scarily similar to the one

I had with my own father. We're both insanely stubborn and too much alike, and when I decided I wanted to do theater, it caused a rift in our relationship that exploded into arguments at every turn. Unlike Dallas, I did manage to cut myself off from football as soon as I graduated high school. And as soon as I could, I left Texas for the Northeast, desperate to get away from that small-town Texas life that had driven me crazy even as it shaped me into the person I am.

Writing those scenes with Dallas and the coach required me to take a long, honest look at my past. All the while, my dad was graciously answering questions about different positions and types of defense and offense and practice drills. I think we talked more about football within a few weeks than we talked about it the entire rest of my life combined. In fact, it was the most we'd talked about anything *period* in a long time. Writing Dallas's story was a bit like a do-over for me. Whereas I held onto my bitterness and resentment for many years, I got to free Dallas of it. And in doing so I freed myself, too. This book taught me to love Texas again in a way that I'd forgotten, and it helped me understand a father that I spent too long pushing away.

So, this is my tribute to Texas and to coaches' daughters and to the coaches themselves. It wasn't the simplest life, but I also wouldn't trade it for anything.

Cora Carmack and Rusk University return with . . .
ALL BROKE DOWN

Dylan fights for lost causes. Probably because she used to be one.

Environmental issues, civil rights, corrupt corporations and politicians—you name it, she's probably been involved in a protest. When her latest cause lands her in jail overnight, she meets Silas Moore. He's in for a different kind of fighting. And though he's arrogant and infuriating, she can't help being fascinated with him. Yet another lost cause.

Football and trouble are the only things that have ever come naturally to Silas. And it's trouble that lands him in a cell next to do-gooder Dylan. He's met girls like her before—*fixers*, he calls them, desperate to heal the damage and make him into their ideal boyfriend. But he doesn't think he's broken, and he definitely doesn't need a girlfriend trying to change him. Until, that is, his anger issues and rash decisions threaten the only thing he really cares about: his spot on the Rusk University football team. Dylan might just be the perfect girl to help.

Because Silas Moore needs some fixing after all.

Coming Fall 2014

GET BETWEEN THE COVERS
WITH NEW BOOKS FROM YOUR
FAVORITE NEW ADULT AUTHORS

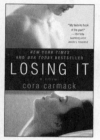

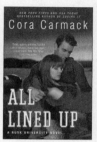